LONG WEEKEND

A Novelization by
BRETT MCBEAN
Based on the screenplay by Everett De Roche

Encyclopocalypse Publications
www.encyclopocalypse.com

FOREWORD

BY JAMIE BLANKS - DIRECTOR OF LONG WEEKEND
(2008)

I started at Haileybury College in Melbourne, Australia in 1983 when I was 12 years old. I had already decided, following a 16mm screening of John Carpenter's THE FOG, that I would become a film director and composer. A TV screening of HALLOWEEN weeks later solidified that thinking. Both films had terrified me to the bone, and I had loved it.

I was too young to go see new movies on my own but I loved looking at the newspaper ads every day and seeing what new movies were being shown. Back in the early '80s, there was a new horror movie or two playing every week. I could read books however and I recall reading Robert Bloch's PSYCHO long before I saw Hitchcock's movie.

One day I saw an ad for a new movie, PSYCHO II. I soon learned that the film's director, Richard Franklin, was not only an Australian, but had attended the exact same high school I was at. That knowledge was thrilling, knowing that it was possible to get from Australia to the United States and work in Hollywood. Years later I met Richard after writing him a letter. He agreed to attend the screening of my film school graduating short SILENT NUMBER in 1993. We became friends and I got to work with him on several commercials when I started work at

The Film House, a production company owned by Australian producer and director Fred Schepisi.

I'd sought out Richard's early Australian films PATRICK and ROADGAMES while still in high school after my parents bought a VHS machine and two terrific video stores opened close to my home. It was through these movies I became familiar with the work of Everett DeRoche, who wrote not only Richard's movie but many of the Australian genre films of the '70s and '80s. Years later I would go on to co-edit a documentary celebrating the careers of Richard and Everett, and many other unsung heroes of Australian genre cinema.

I would also get the chance to work with Everett twice. First on the film adaptation of a screenplay he'd written in the '70s and had remained unproduced until my 2006 film version, STORM WARNING.

Everett and I became close friends, and he would be present every single day during the film's production. He was always at my side, watching the various takes be completed and having input on creative decisions with me, including what notes we would sometimes give to the actors and cinematographer. He was a wonderful, inspiring and good natured collaborator and we became fast friends quickly.

We got to work a second time on the script that would bookend Everett's career. It was the first scripts of his to be produced and my remake of it in 2008 was the last movie Everett saw go before the cameras before his death in 2014. As we did on STORM WARNING, Everett was present for the entire production. He joined us on location at Wilsons Promontory in November and December of 2007 for the entire shoot.

We both felt it was time again to tell this story, a tale of two people toxic to the environment and to each other. We remained very faithful to the story Everett had penned back in the '70s and even brought the original film's cinematographer, Vincent Monton, back to direct and shoot 2nd unit for me.

When the idea of a novelisation was put to me I immediately thought of the incredibly talented Australian writer Brett McBean to turn Everett's story into a book. I was overjoyed that Brett accepted the assignment and you hold the result of his hard work in your hands right now.

I think Everett would have been delighted with how Brett has interpreted his screenplay into a finely written novel. We are able to explore the interior lives of the characters so much more richly in a book than it was possible to do on film. I think Brett has done Everett proud with this excellent adaptation of the screenplay and in how he expands on the ideas Everett was exploring in the story.

Thank you for supporting Encylopocalypse by purchasing this book. They are doing wonderful things with novelisations for movies that never received one upon release. I think LONG WEEKEND is a highly deserving candidate for this treatment and I hope it gives greater depth for those who have seen the movie and a riveting experience for those who are having this story told to them for the first time.

My deepest thanks to Brett for taking on the formidable challenge of adapting the work of Australia's most highly regarded and inspirational genre screenwriter. I miss Everett all the time and I remain deeply grateful to have had the experience of working with him twice. I will never forget him and will always remember how much fun we had working together. It was truly a pleasure and a privilege to work with the great man.

Jamie Blanks
   Melbourne, Australia
   October 23rd, 2023

ACKNOWLEDGMENTS

The original *Long Weekend* has been a favourite of mine ever since I first watched the movie, alone, on a tiny black & white portable TV, when I was around fourteen years old. So it's with immense honour (along with a giddy sense of the unreal) that, thirty years later, I was asked to turn this seminal work of Australian cinematic horror into a novel. For that, I have numerous people to thank.

First I owe an enormous debt of gratitude to Jamie Blanks, for putting my name forward for this project, and for putting up with my many phone calls during the writing process. I want to thank the De Roche family for allowing me to be part of the *Long Weekend* legacy. Thanks to the Encyclopocalypse crew for making this project happen. Thanks to Richard Brennan for giving the go ahead for the use of the awesome original artwork. Most of all, I want to thank Everett De Roche, for penning such a brilliant screenplay, and for helping to create a landmark in Aussie cinema. I hope I did you proud.

1

SHE TURNED OFF THE TAP, killing the sound of the miniature waterfall, stood back, and looked down at her garden, at the small collection of potted plants bobbing in the partially filled bathtub. A great wash of shame flooded through her. She had been a bad caretaker, a terrible mother, to her plants. What had apparently been un-killable she had courted to death's door.

Like the maidenhair fern. It looked desperately sick, its delicate leaves pale and appearing singed. She feared it was beyond help. Most weren't as bad as the fern. Hopefully, they were still salvageable, but they were teetering on the edge. None looked especially healthy: the Swiss Cheese looked past its used by date; the Boston fern sad and droopy; the Ficus was turning yellow; the snake plant spotted, with some tips shrivelled, like cancer was eating away at its pretty patterned leaves. And the Devil's ivy looked withered, its tendrils clawing at her as if pleading for help. Only the spider plant appeared strong, healthy; although a closer inspection revealed it, too, was wilting.

They had all been green and lush, once. Thriving. But, over time, they started growing tired and sick. Desperate for some love and attention. The colour faded; their vitality drained.

Christ, why does everything I touch turn to shit? Why can't I make things work?

It was going to be an unusually hot weekend. Three days in an oppressive environment, the early autumn heat sucking the plants dry of life and burning the foliage, with no one to water them, to help strip away the heat, would surely kill them, including the hardy spider. In a vain effort to keep her plants from dying, she had moved them from their familiar spots around the house into the bathroom—the coolest room in the two-storey—and sat them in a bed of cold water where they could drink their fill and, hopefully, hold on until she got back from the long weekend.

At the thought of the trip, she took a draw from her cigarette and sighed. A cloud of smoke washed over the garden and hovered for a few moments before dissipating. She stood in the bathroom and thought about what was to come, about all that had happened. Her free hand absently found its way to her stomach, touching the emptiness that matched her heart.

Behind her, the radio droned. The evening traffic report: heavy, of course, it being peak hour, but worse than usual, the workers eager to get home to begin the Easter weekend holiday. When the newscaster mentioned Punt Road—'congested', the tinny voice said; 'long delays'—Marcia's body clenched, and her head throbbed.

Shit, she thought. Peter was going to be in an even worse mood than usual. He had planned on leaving work early, wanted an early start, be up at the beach by midnight. If he got stuck on Punt Road, he wouldn't be home till seven, maybe later.

Looking down, she saw her hand resting on her belly. Frowning, she jerked it away. With the early evening sun shining through the bathroom window in striking rays, she shut the curtains, coating the room in dusky darkness. The telephone rang.

Christ, I hope that's not Peter, calling to tell me he's just leaving work now.

She left the bathroom and moved into the kitchen, smoke trailing after her. As she passed the radio ('forecast for the upcoming Easter long weekend is unsettled, humid but cloudy with a strong chance of thunderstorms...') she switched it off and snatched up the phone. "Hello?"

"You haven't left yet?"

She eased out a breath. "No, still here. Waiting on His Highness to arrive back at his castle."

Marcia ground the spent cigarette into the closest tray. Then, super multi-tasker housewife that she was, she moved over to the fridge to finish packing for the trip. The phone cord extended like a curled rope, almost knocking the box sitting on the counter.

"You two still fighting?"

"When aren't we? We're barely talking at the moment, and when we do, we argue."

"So, no movement from his end?"

Marcia grabbed the frozen chicken from the freezer. It was icy, slippery. As she attempted to pick it up with one hand, the chicken slipped from her grasp and fell to the floor.

Cricket, curled in the doorway, flinched, and looked up.

"Shit."

"What, love?"

"Dropped the chicken."

"Is that some euphemism...?"

Marcia almost smiled. "No, I literally dropped the chicken. Last of the packing. I promised Sir Peter I'd have everything ready by the time he got home. No delays," Marcia said, deepening her voice in an imitation of her husband. "As soon as I get home, we're off. I want everything ready."

Marcia bent down and, with the receiver wedged in the nook between her head and shoulder, scooped the chicken off the floor. Cricket eyed the chook, licking her lips.

"Not for you, fatso," she muttered, and the overweight chocolate Labrador whined, and then slumped her head back down.

"What did you call me?"

"What? Oh, sorry, talking to the dog. So anyway, you're still going, aren't you?"

"Leaving at the crack of dawn. I just wanted to call and make sure you guys weren't coming. Thought, maybe, I could convince you to change your mind."

"I want to, Carol. I really do. I'm going to miss spending time with you and Mark."

At the mention of Mark, she felt a hot tingling below, like a fire had been lit in her pants.

"But... after everything... Peter's still dealing with it all, and he has his heart set on going to this damned beach. And you know what he's like when he digs in. He can be a real shit."

"Sorry, love. It's all my fault. I feel terrible..."

"Don't. You did nothing wrong."

"You don't hate me?"

"Of course not."

"But Pete does."

"No. He hates me. He's just mad at you, but that'll pass."

"Portsea will be lonely without you. But camping is right up your alley..."

Marcia dropped the chicken into the icebox, along with the milk and butter and the beers. She grinned, but there was no humour in her eyes. "Oh yes, darling, you know how much I love camping."

"And it's... where again?"

"Some beach up on the north coast. It's like five hours away."

"Doesn't he know there are beaches in Victoria?"

"Yes, but this one holds a special meaning, apparently. His dad used to take him there when he was a kid. He hasn't been there since the fifties. It'll be the first time since his dad died.

Christ, we'll probably get there and find it's gone, turned into private beach houses or mined to within an inch of its life."

"And won't you be sorry?"

"Devastated. We'd have to stay at the local hotel and then I can spend the time making him see sense, and tomorrow we can drive down and spend the weekend with you and Mark."

With Mark... The tingling sensation grew, but guilt turned her cheeks hot. She was on the line with Carol, for Christ's sake, her best friend...

At the sound of a car door thumping shut outside, Marcia flinched, the tingling faded.

With surprising speed, Cricket jumped up and disappeared, no doubt fleeing towards the front door.

"He's home. Gotta go."

"I'd say have fun, but..."

"At least you guys will. If I don't see you tomorrow, catch up sometime next week?"

"Sure thing."

"Bye, darl."

"Later, love."

The cord retreated as Marcia hung up the phone. From the cupboard, she grabbed a handful of dog food cans, opened them up, and dumped the sloppy chunks of meat into Cricket's bowl. The sweet, salty smell of cheap meat and gravy turned her stomach. When the bowl was full, she threw the empty cans into the bin, wiped her hands on the tea towel, and then moved through the dim house.

Cricket was whining and pawing at the front door. Marcia opened the door and Cricket bounded out just as Peter was pulling a parcel from the backseat of the Jaguar.

"Hey, girl!"

Peter shut the car door, reached down and scratched Cricket behind the ears. Then he walked over to the 4X4, the dog following, and opened the back doors of the Nissan Patrol.

"What ya got there?"

Without turning to greet her, or even face her, Peter answered, "Spear gun. Picked it up in town today."

Marcia stopped on the path halfway between the front door and the Nissan, folded her arms across her chest. "Thought you might get stuck in traffic."

"Said I would leave early, and I did. The roads weren't pretty, let me tell you. Seems half of Melbourne had the same idea to leave work early, but I think I missed the worst of it."

Cricket jumped up into the back of the Patrol, somehow managing the feat even with her excess blubber. She did a few turns, finding space among the sleeping bags, camping gear, and boxes of groceries, and then plopped down and looked out at her master, eyes pleading, hopeful.

"Not this time, girl," Peter said. Then, softer, but still loud enough for Marcia to hear, "The boss says you have to stay home, that you're a nuisance. Come on, down you get."

The Lab sighed, and then, reluctantly, jumped back down.

Peter propped the long parcel against the back of the truck, turned and finally looked at his wife. "How's it coming? All packed?"

"Nearly. Just the icebox and your toiletries. Everything else is in the truck as requested."

Peter stepped over to her. He leaned in close, pecked her on the cheek.

Marcia felt the urge to turn away, but fought against it.

"Good girl."

Good girl? Christ, does she get a treat, too?

"Don't be too impressed. I had nothing else to do all day except clean and pack. Really, a dog could do it. You could train Cricket to pack your bags and carry them out to the truck."

Peter grinned with one side of his mouth. His green eyes bristled with contempt; he usually hid his derision well beneath his smooth, boyishly handsome face. "Well, you smell better. Do I have time for a quick shower?"

Peter's work clothes were crinkled, and she noticed pit

stains on the blue shirt. He smelled stale and could certainly do with a wash.

"I thought you wanted to get away as soon as possible? You're the one who wants to set up camp in the dead of night."

"Fine, I won't shower."

Peter moved away, back over to the Nissan. He reached up to the roof racks, checking the surfboard was secured.

"I filled Cricket's bowl with food. Water bowl's filled up, too."

Finished checking the surfboard, Peter frowned at her across the driveway. "I thought you were going to ask Mrs Dunlane to feed Cricket?"

Marcia looked back at the fence that divided their two-storey from the more modest single-storey next door. Speaking quietly, she said, "We hardly know her, Pete. I didn't feel right asking her to baby-sit *your* dog."

Peter looked down at Cricket. The dog sat on the concrete in the shadow of the 4X4, staring at the open doors of the truck as if still hoping for an invitation.

"Marcia, it's not that big of a deal. I just thought... ah, forget it."

"What's the problem? There are three whole cans of food in the bowl. She won't starve. She's too fat as it is."

Peter sighed. "Mars, you can't just plop down a pile of dog food and expect the dog to ration its feed... especially a Lab... she'll likely eat it all in one go and then..."

"Yes, it's a miracle the canine species survived millions of years without..."

Peter waved a hand as a kind of truce. "Okay... yes, sorry, you're right. I'm sure Cricket will be fine. She's a smart dog. We good?"

Marcia shrugged.

"Just wait till we get to Moondah Beach; fresh air, sunshine, a chance to unwind, to start over, to forget about... things."

Marcia craved none of those things. Well, maybe she wanted

to forget, but she had grown up in the suburbs and rarely spent time in the country or down at the beach. She was a city girl. She liked the concrete, the hustle and bustle, hell, even the smog. Too much fresh air made her queasy. Sun baked her fair skin. Potted plants were about as much nature as she cared for. So, the thought of spending three days at some desolate beach didn't exactly fill her with delight. It did the opposite; it filled her with unease.

"Sure. Whatever. I'll finish packing."

Peter picked up the long parcel. The bag rustled as he started slipping the spear gun out. At the sight of the barrel, Marcia turned away.

"Just make it snappy. It'll be a shit-fight on the roads out of Melbourne, and I don't want to get too caught up in it."

Marcia started back towards the house. A tight, scorching knot had formed in her gut. As she moved inside, the knot travelled up to her chest and, as the sound of paper rustling fell away, the fiery sensation moved up into her throat and lodged there. For a moment, she felt like she was suffocating. Hot pinpricks danced across her skin and down her windpipe.

She contemplated turning around, but something (fear?) stopped her.

Instead, she continued forward, into the shrouded house, and soon the burning went away, as did the suffocating feeling, but not the unease.

———

As the windscreen wipers slashed against the torrent outside, Peter kept a steady pace on the highway, wedged between a soft top convertible behind and a white camper in front. He looked over at the woman who appeared to be sleeping in the passenger seat.

His wife, but in name only. She may as well have been a stranger. They may be married, but they hadn't been husband

and wife for years. Theirs was not a partnership, but a union between two individuals. She looked the same on the outside as the woman he had married eight years ago. A tad fuller in the face, perhaps. And lines were creeping in that indicated her twenties were almost behind her, that youth was in the rear-view mirror. Not too far behind, Marcia was only twenty-eight, not fifty-eight, but the glow and freshness of even five years ago had given way to harder edges that only come with the piling on of years; the look of a life lived and not always with happiness.

She was still attractive, no doubt about that. Still had the same long, blonde hair (though it was shorter now than when they first met, and it had lost some of its luminance), same trim yet curvy figure (maybe slightly pudgy in certain areas; Mars didn't exercise as much as she used to, and she ate too much chocolate and biscuits, probably other things while he was at work), and her face, though not stunning, was perfectly pretty in that typical Aussie way. She looked like a beach bunny, even though she had never lived near the beach and didn't like it in any meaningful way.

No, it was the inside that had changed.

The fun, carefree Mars he had fallen for had, over time, become colder, more distant. She smiled rarely. Her attitude snippier. Maybe he was partly to blame for her change in personality. Hell, not maybe. He *was* partly to blame. He knew he was far from perfect. Long hours spent at work, the extras hours schmoozing with clients, the nights boozing it up with mates (not to mention his indiscretions); they had surely contributed to Marcia's increasingly frosty personality. But Christ, he had to make a living. She enjoyed living in a big house in Caulfield? Liked buying expensive clothes, shoes, jewellery? Liked going to nice restaurants? That all cost money, honey, and, as his dad had been fond of drilling into him, that stuff doesn't grow on trees. If it did, the world would be a barren, airless place. So yes, he worked too hard and partied too much and maybe didn't give her enough attention, but she wasn't Miss Perfect. She had a snake's tongue. She could spit acid when she wanted to—and she had hellishly good aim. She wasn't frigid, but he couldn't remember the last time she had come and offered herself to him. He wasn't proud he had cheated, but could she really blame him? He had needs. And really, compared to her wrongs, his fucking around with Freda wasn't so bad. It had all been a bit of fun. Nobody got hurt. Not really. But what she had done... that amounted to some kind of sin. And to not tell him about it... not talk it over and make such an important decision together? That was just cruel.

There was so much animosity between them. What did he think this weekend would solve?

A weekend at the beach and *Voila*! Their marriage would miraculously be healed? They'd leave Moondah happily married again, and everything that had happened would be wiped away, like some giant sponge cleaning away dirt?

Did he even still love her?

Yes. Maybe. Probably.

But he couldn't forget so easily.

He suddenly felt stuffy, overheated. The weather had turned to shit, as predicted, but the heat had only been tempered. It hadn't dissipated. If anything, it was worse with the arrival of the rain. The night was sticky, and he hated humidity.

He itched to wind down the window, but he didn't fancy getting water in the car.

Even though they got away relatively early, the traffic on the highway heading north was still heavy. Not crawling at a snail's pace heavy, but they hadn't yet got near the speed limit. The road was just a sea of vehicles, a spread of lights that cut through the darkness, though in the rain the headlights looked like yellow smears of paint, the brake lights splotches of blood.

Damn this traffic. He felt cooped up. He wanted to be sailing down the highway at high speeds, no cars behind or in front, just the open road and Moondah Beach up ahead. He wanted to be surrounded by freedom.

Damn the Clark account. He would have left work even earlier if not for them and their picky ways. They hadn't liked the print ad he and his team had spent a week preparing. Too hard, not family friendly enough. Christ, it was an advertisement for soup. What's family friendly about soup? Fuck soup. It wasn't thirst quenching, and it wasn't a full meal —it was nothing. Nothing but a pain in his arse, a meeting that went almost two hours longer than scheduled, resulting in him getting home later than planned and being stuck in an endless parade of other Easter weekenders leaving the harsh, stressful environs of the city for the open space and unspoiled vistas of the country, the beach.

Well, so far, it had been pretty bloody stressful. And still another three hours to go.

Three hours cooped up in the truck together. He hoped Marcia continued to sleep.

Over the beating of the rain, the radio crackled as they left the big smoke behind. Some talk show. He usually didn't care for talkback, but Marcia liked it. He had wanted to listen to music, but she had asked for it to be on. Marcia was asleep now, so he had free rein, and he craved music.

Before he cut ties with civilisation, he gave an ear to the conversation. Whoever was talking was talking about wildlife and disease.

'... while it's uncommon for wildlife diseases to lead directly to population extinction in the absence of other severe threats, the Tasmanian devil facial cancer is a new and unusual disease and there is no hard evidence for population or individual resistance or recovery. Furthermore, there is also a concern that if the population is diminished, it may be difficult for them to ever recover...'

"Boring," he muttered, and switched it off.

"I was listening to that."

Marcia's voice gave Peter a start. "Thought you were asleep."

"Sorry."

"Losing the signal. Was going to put on some music."

"Whatever."

Marcia sounded bored, not tired. She was slumped against the passenger door, like she planned on sleeping, but her body wouldn't let her get there. She was as far from him as possible within the confines of the cab. He was surprised she hadn't climbed into the back, so she could really put some distance between them.

Despite being closest to the glove box, Marcia didn't offer to sift through the tapes, so Peter reached over, opened the door of the glove box and, taking his eyes momentarily off the view in front, dove in and started pawing at the cassettes.

The first he picked was one of Marcia's, Olivia Newton-John, so he dropped that and tried again. He had just snagged another cassette when Marcia yelped.

"Peter!"

He looked up in time to see the white camper coming up fast.

He snapped upright and stepped on the brake. The Patrol came to a jolted halt no more than half a metre in front of the camper. Its red brake lights glared at him through the rain.

"Hell, Peter. You almost ran into it."

"But I didn't. I saw 'em."

But it was close. His heart thumped; his hands were shaking.

A girl of about eight peered out at them from the back of the camper. She was a thin, petite thing, with long, wavy, golden hair and round eyes that were sad. She wasn't smiling. Just staring.

Marcia shifted in her seat. "What's going on? Why isn't the traffic moving?"

Peter reached back down towards the open glove box.

Somehow, the contents hadn't spilled out when he abruptly stopped the car.

A hand grabbed his wrist.

"You just concentrate on driving."

Peter leaned upright. Marcia sifted through the tapes.

The wipers continued to beat a steady rhythm like a bass guitar, the rain pattered the car like a snare drum. The girl continued to watch from the back window.

Peter swallowed.

Finally, the camper's red eyes blinked off, and the vehicle eased forward. The little girl faded from view and Peter sighed. He continued driving.

Music came on. Rock music, his kind of music, though Marcia turned the volume down, and not wanting to start (or was that continue?) a fight, he let it slide.

Marcia settled back into her defensive position, hugging herself on the other side of the cab like she was cold.

"Want the heater on?"

"Heater? It must be close to thirty degrees, and with the rain, it's humid."

"I know. I thought... you look cold."

"Well, I'm not."

"Okay."

He waited a few minutes, the music not enough to cover the heavy silence between them. "You speak to Carol?"

"Yes."

"So, she knows we can't make it?"

"Yes."

"It's just this year, Mars. I couldn't handle it this year. I needed time by myself. *We* needed time, just the two of us. Maybe next year we'll do the couple thing again."

No response.

"I'm sure they'll get along just fine without us this weekend."

More icy silence.

"They're still heading down to Portsea, right?"

"Yes."

Peter thumped the wheel. "Come on, Marcia. We're still fighting?"

"Who's fighting? I'm just answering your questions."

"Cut the crap. Look, I know you're angry with me about the change in plans. I just thought we should back off for a while... with what happened and all. We need time away from them. I know Carol's your best friend. Hell, Mark's a good friend of mine. But it's been strained between us since I found out. And how I found out. Not from you, but from Mark..."

"I know what happened, Peter."

"I just thought it'd be a good time to head up to Moondah Beach. I haven't been there since I was a boy. It's a special place. I have a lot of fond memories. I thought it'd be good for you to just lie on the beach and recuperate..."

"Recuperate?" Marcia huffed. "Like I'm recovering from some disease? I don't have cancer, Peter..."

"It's me, too, love. I need a break, some time to think, to get in some surfing while..."

"While I'm stuck on the beach bored shitless? Sorry, I mean recuperating."

"Jesus, Marcia. Okay, I get it. You don't like camping, but we're not exactly roughing it."

"Two thousand dollars' worth of camping gear, I should hope not. For that price, we could have spent the weekend in the VIP suite at the Southern Cross. Or are you bored with hotel rooms? God knows you've spent enough time in them..."

"Get fucked," Peter spat. He'd had enough. He tried being civil, but clearly that wasn't going to work.

He turned up the music.

This time Marcia didn't bother lowering the volume. She just huffed and slammed her body against the passenger door, turning her head to stare out at the darkness.

Finally, the highway split into two lanes. Peter pulled out

from behind the white camper. As they passed the van, Peter glanced across the car, past Marcia, past the rain, and looked through the driver's side window of the camper. A burly man about ten years older than Peter sat in the driver's seat. His face was a creased, angry mask. He looked to be shouting. Above the rain, Peter could hear his deep voice, muffled by the weather, the vehicles. He glanced briefly as he drove past and saw a woman in the passenger seat. Like the girl in the back, she had wavy blonde hair. Her mouth was moving, but Peter couldn't hear her voice. She moved her arms about, pointing to the man, to the back. Just before Peter sped up, he saw her wipe her eyes.

"Another happy couple," Marcia muttered.

Peter ignored her. Once he was past the van, he pulled back into the left lane. The traffic having dispersed, he took the truck up to the speed limit, pushed a little past it, glad to finally be travelling free, away from the congestion, the road dark and empty ahead.

———

Peter yawned. He had been on the road for close to four hours without a break. The Patrol's fuel was holding up, but he wanted to fill up the spare petrol container. He had passed a sign a little way back that warned: LAST FUEL BEFORE TATHRA. He'd take a much-needed break when they reached the town.

He stretched the muscles in his face, blinked hard. He wanted to roll down the window, get some fresh air blowing in, but the rain still pelted down, so he had to suffer the stuffy confines inside the car.

At least Marcia was asleep. Finally. She fell into dreamland about an hour back, so he'd had a good chunk of peace. Just him, his music and the rain.

Traffic had gradually thinned out, so now, about fifty

kilometres north of the border, theirs was the only vehicle on the road. Occasionally headlights burned through the night, throwing watery light his way as the vehicle passed by, but there was no one ahead of him, no one behind. He had the road all to himself and he was glad for that.

He was beginning to get a tingly sensation the closer he got to the beach. He had been looking forward to this holiday for weeks, ever since he got the idea. Actually, the idea hadn't occurred to him so much as dropped on him, literally. He had been cleaning out the closet in the spare room, something he hadn't done since... well, he doubted he had ever sorted through that closet. He left those kinds of jobs for Marcia. But he had been drinking. The rawness from what he had learned about Marcia was still a festering wound. He had been one glass of whisky away from total drunkenness, but he wasn't quite there yet, so, heavily tipsy, he had staggered into the spare bedroom downstairs, a room he rarely went in. He had no need to; it was mostly a place where junk was kept. It also served as Marcia's sewing room, but there was a bed in there and he figured, since they were fighting and he didn't much want to see Marcia, let alone sleep in the same room as her, he wanted to see if he could hole up in there for the night. It was either that, or the sofa. Again. And he was already well acquainted with the sofa. She was comfy but narrow, and it being low, Cricket tended to wake him by licking his face and he was tired of doggy drool.

The ceiling light was too bright. He had turned on the freestanding lamp, switched off the overhead light and then looked around. The room was a bit musty, crammed with too many boxes and unwanted junk, but the bed was made up and, though it was only a single, it was both wider and higher than the sofa, so it was automatically a better option.

He was about to leave to refill his tumbler when he glanced at the cupboard. He stopped. Felt something faint, like a scratching at the back of his brain. Something about the cupboard, or, more specifically, something inside. Stuffed inside a box, pushed to the back, long forgotten.

He set his empty tumbler down, opened the cupboard door, and reached to the top shelf. He didn't know how he knew, but somehow, he knew exactly where to look. He didn't even know what he was looking for, just knew it was in a box, at the back of the cupboard, on the top shelf.

It was almost like something was whispering to him, guiding him. He couldn't make out any words, or if the voice was even speaking in English, but there was a whispering, along with the scratching; almost like a breeze, the sound of a branch creaking, of twigs scraping at the air.

He pushed aside boxes and dragged the one he was looking for forward. He reached inside, pawed at the contents, not sure what had been placed in the box, hoping he wouldn't encounter an unfriendly huntsman. When that didn't work, he grabbed the box with both hands, intending to bring the box down to the floor. But, with hands feeling numb and airy from too much Scotch, he fumbled, the box tipped towards him, and various crap fell out, striking him in the face.

He lost his balance, crashed down, falling onto his backside, but it didn't hurt, not in his state. Instead, he giggled, sitting there like a kid waiting for roll call in primary school.

Dolls from when his grandparents went to England back in the fifties, other items from holidays more local, trinkets such as little statues of the Sydney Opera House, a stuffed koala, lay scattered around him.

He looked down. His laughter stopped when he saw what was in his lap.

Tears sprang to his eyes.

He picked up the slingshot. Held the wooden paddle, tested the rubber straps; still intact, still durable. It was his old Wham-O slingshot, a genuine Sportsman that he got for his tenth birthday. The first year his dad had taken him camping, where he had spent most of the time firing pellets and small rocks at bottles, birds, even sea creatures. He had loved the slingshot, had even slept with it when curled up at nights in his sleeping bag.

He had forgotten it even existed. He was amazed he'd still kept it and that it was still in good working order, with the original strap and everything.

That first summer, camping with Dad at the beach, had been the best one of all. It was before he got sick. When everything still felt good and possible.

Christ, where was that? he wondered as he pushed up to his feet. He wobbled. The room started spinning. Clutching his Wham-O, he sat on the bed. *What was the name of that beach?*

Like it had been shot at him by the Wham-O, the name came to him: Moondah Beach.

Sitting there that night three weeks ago, heart and soul broken and thinking he was beyond repair, Peter had thought about the upcoming Easter long weekend holiday. They usually spent it with Mark and Carol at Portsea. He didn't want to go to Portsea, and not with them. Not this year.

Still too raw. Still too much to process.

That's when he decided they would drive up to the New South Wales coast and spend the weekend at Moondah Beach. Clutching the slingshot tight, eyes red and filled with tears, he smiled a genuine smile for the first time in a long while. Yes, that's where they'd go.

The whispering, the scratching, stopped the moment he decided.

There was only calm.

He wanted to recapture that calm, wanted to recapture some semblance of what he'd felt as a kid, that first year up at Moondah Beach, the year he'd turned ten and got the slingshot for his birthday.

He hoped this weekend would bring him what he so desperately needed.

He looked over at Marcia, curled up in the passenger seat.

Sometimes, like now, he felt some of the old feelings; a longing for her, to be around her. But then he remembered, and coldness blew through him, anger boiled in his gut, and he wanted to... well, he didn't know. He wasn't a violent man, but sometimes he dreamed of doing harm to her, as bitter a taste as that left in him.

Christ, he thought, turning back to the road.

Look at what he had become. Look at what *they* had become. More like enemies than loving husband and wife.

I'm stupid if I think a mere trip to the beach will help solve all our problems.

With the rain streaming down, the wipers constant and getting on his nerves, he plucked the packet of cigarettes from his top pocket and with well-practiced precision, flipped open the lid, tapped out a cigarette and caught the end between his teeth and withdrew the stick. He dropped the packet back in his pocket, pulled out the lighter, went to flick it on, but fumbled and the lighter fell to his lap.

He looked down, saw the small Bic resting on his groin. He picked it up, tried again. This time he got a flame. He looked up, was about to touch the flame to the tip of the cigarette, but instead froze at the sight of the kangaroo.

The animal stood upright in the middle of the road, also frozen, its black eyes staring and surprised.

Peter dropped the lighter, started to swerve, but it was too late. He was going too fast; the roo was too close. With a sickening thud, the front of the Patrol slammed into the kangaroo. He winced as it travelled beneath the truck, felt the creature bouncing against the underside and the road, until mercifully the banging went away. For a few terrible moments, he feared losing control of the truck. He weaved over the road but managed to bring the Patrol back in line. Once he was driving straight and steady, he looked up in the rear-view mirror; saw the large marsupial tumbling along the road.

"Shit," he muttered.

He glanced at Marcia. She mumbled under her breath, shifted a little, but remained asleep.

He considered stopping. Maybe the beast was injured, not dead.

He continued driving.

Surely the animal had been killed on impact. He'd hit it at a hundred kilometres an hour; there was no way the roo would still be alive.

Besides, it was already late, and there was still a way to go before they reached Moondah Beach.

Peter shook his head. "Fucking kangaroos."

He retrieved his lighter, lit the cigarette without incident, and took some much-needed puffs as he sped on through the watery darkness.

Once the fuel container was close to filled, Peter took out the nozzle, drizzling petrol onto the ground, placed the pump back onto the bowser and screwed the lid on his can. He carried the jerrycan to the back of the truck and slotted the container in among the camping gear.

He wandered around to the open driver's side, leaned in. "Gonna head over to the pub and grab some booze."

Marcia, rather than her usual scowling expression, looked distracted, uneasy. To Peter's bleary eyes, she almost looked scared. "What's wrong?"

"Nothing. What could be wrong?"

Her gaze flicked to the back of the car, before quickly turning to stare out the front windscreen.

Frowning, Peter looked into the back and surveyed the small area. Seeing nothing out of the ordinary, he shook his head. "Be right back."

He turned and looked out at the waterfall that awaited him. The pub sat across the road, not far away, but the rain still poured down and he knew he'd get soaked making the quick journey. He was mostly dry parked beneath the canopy of the fuel station. He didn't want to leave the shelter, but he wanted something stronger than beer; needed some fortitude if he was going to survive the weekend, and he hadn't had time to stop off and grab something earlier, so it was now or never.

"Here we go," he muttered, and started forward.

The rain beat down as he stepped out from under the canopy. The cold drops felt like bullets as they sprayed down. The rain was so dense and unremitting it was as if the world was trying to drown him. He hardly slowed to cross the road, just enough to make sure there were no vehicles bearing down on him. All was dark in either direction, so he fled across the road to the small, rural public house.

He crashed into the pub. Stern, blankly curious faces snapped in his direction at the intrusion. He stood there dripping water on the floor. His shirt clung to him like a second skin. His pants, though not as wet, still felt damp, and mildly uncomfortable. He hated the feeling of being wet while clothed.

There were four men inside the pub, including the barman. An ancient fellow with a thin, white beard barely concealing a sallow, drawn face sat on a stool at the counter; a bloke around Peter's age stood nearby, one elbow firmly planted on the bar. He wore stubbies, a singlet, a cap, and had a mean countenance. The last bloke, around fifty and sporting a big belly and a smooth, round face, sat farthest away, lonesome at a back table. He looked dejected, like he'd recently been slapped with some bad news.

All three patrons nursed beers and cigarettes. There was an aura of melancholy in the modest pub; it hung heavy, as heavy as the smell of alcohol and smoke.

Peter, already feeling out of place, especially as wet as he was, moved over to the bar. He nodded to the two men by the counter, then offered a brief, pleasant smile to the barman.

"Sorry about your floor."

The barman stepped away, into a back room. He came out with a towel. Tossed it over the counter. Peter just managed to grab it. He looked at the pale green towel that was old and slightly greasy and patterned with stains. He was unsure what the barman expected him to do with it. Wipe the floor, maybe? That wasn't his job. Wasn't his fault it was bucketing down outside.

The other men in the pub were dry. Peter figured they had been here a while.

"Well?" the barman said.

The barman was short and thin, but his forearms looked moulded from leather and stuffed with iron rods.

Peter hesitated.

"You gonna stand there dripping on my floor or you gonna dry yourself?"

Peter laughed, nervously, and started rubbing the towel over his hair, his face (the towel smelled of old beer and something else, something astringent), and his shirt.

"Why didn't ya park closer?"

Peter looked at the man in the cap. His voice matched his appearance: gruff, harsh, like chiselled steel.

"I..." Peter realised he didn't have a good answer. Why didn't he drive the short distance from the fuel station to the pub? "I don't know. Silly, you're right."

"If ya sheila had any sense, she'd drive over and park it outside, so you wouldn't have to go through the shit again."

"Or bring you an umbrella," the old man said, voice weak, raspy.

"Yeah, an umbrella," the younger man said, still leaning against the bar, still sneering. "Or maybe she don't like ya too much? My missus, she'd know better than to let me get drenched."

"Well," Peter said, swallowing. "She was asleep, and I didn't want to wake her."

The man in the cap, whose chest filled out the singlet like his torso was a tree trunk, which made his arms thick, hairy branches, huffed, and then straightened slowly. He brought the mug to his craggy face and took a long drink.

"What'll you have?"

Peter turned to the barman. He handed back the damp towel. The barman took it, slung it over a shoulder.

"Can I get a couple of bottles of Bundy to go?"

The barman moved away.

A sudden noise, like a gunshot, startled Peter. He looked sideways, saw that the big man with the cap had slammed his empty mug on the counter. Glaring at Peter, he burped, then announced to the room, "Goin' for a piss. I'll have another, Danny."

With deliberate movements, the man, who Peter pegged for a truckie—he had briefly caught sight of a big rig outside and Peter wondered if it belonged to him—moved away from the bar and, like he owned the place, strolled down towards the back to where the toilets were.

While he waited for his drinks, Peter looked over at the man sitting at the table. He was a big bloke. Not just tall, but his body stretched his plaid shirt, and his chair was pushed back from the table to accommodate his considerable girth. Sweat beaded his plump, oily face and dripped from his double chin. His light-coloured hair, washed out like it had once been sunny blond but was now bleached, was combed back in an old-fashioned way, a pompadour style, just how Peter's father used to comb his hair. But it wasn't just the hair that reminded Peter of his father. This man was heavier than Ivan, but Ivan was always clean-shaven, just like the bloke at the table, and Ivan also had haunted eyes, much like the stranger. Especially towards the end, when the cancer had spread and Dad could see the darkness coming up fast. His eyes held a look of a man not yet wanting to make that final journey, but knowing he had no choice. A man filled with too much regret, too much pain. The eyes of a man unhappy with himself.

The stranger at the table held his gaze on nothing as he clutched his beer. There was even a hint of tears, but that might have been perspiration. All the same, Peter felt uncomfortable watching him, like he was intruding in the man's private pain, so he looked away. His eyes fell on the old-timer, a wasted shell of a man, but at least he didn't possess a haunted look. The opposite: he had a kind face, kind eyes.

Peter cleared his throat. When he spoke, his voice sounded croaky, a touch jittery. "Kinda quiet for a long weekend, eh?"

The old man, taken by surprise, blinked up at Peter.

"What? Oh, well, it's too far from anywhere. All we get is the lost and the locals."

"Well, I'm not a local, so I guess that makes me one of the lost."

Peter meant for it to sound light-hearted, but in here, it sounded odd and... true.

But it wasn't true. He knew where he was headed.

The barman returned with a bag. He placed the bag on the counter, the bottles inside clanged.

"Thirty bucks."

Peter fished around for his wallet, which was damp when he pulled it out. He hoped the money wasn't wet. Luckily, the notes were dry.

"Where you from, the city?" the barman asked as he took the money.

"Melbourne."

"Where you headed?"

"Moondah Beach."

The barman stared at him.

"Know it?"

"Nope."

Peter felt like frowning but refrained. He looked down at the old man. "You know it?"

"Know what?"

"Moondah Beach."

"Never heard of it."

Now the frown came. There was no stopping it. "It's not far from here. Local surf break... one of the best surf beaches on the south coast. At least, it used to be."

The barman opened the till, the till crashed open, he slipped in the money, then sent the register crashing back.

"That so?"

The barman grabbed a clean mug and poured a fresh beer, set it on the counter beside the drained one, collected the empty.

"I used to camp there with my old man a long time ago. We'd fish, he'd surf, we'd make a fire."

"I've fished every patch of sand between here and Merimbula," the old man said. "Never heard of a... what did you say it's called?"

"Moon... dah. The turn off was just past an abattoir."

"I know the abattoir. Don't know the beach."

At the sound of heavy steps on the floor, Peter glanced over his shoulder and saw the man in the cap stroll back up to the bar. He took hold of the full mug of beer, downed a mouthful.

"Maybe it's known by another name," Peter said, facing the bar.

"Maybe," the barman said. "You said it's close by?"

"About twenty minutes north."

The barman shook his head.

"Lots of tracks up that way," the old man said. "No one goes up there anymore, not since the sand mining finished in, what... sixty-three?"

"Four," the man behind the bar said, and then he once again disappeared into the back room.

"Maybe it doesn't exist," the man with the cap said, returning to his position of elbow down, glass up.

"It did, once."

"Strange we don't know it," the old man said.

Peter glanced over at the man at the table. He considered

asking him if he knew about Moondah. But he didn't feel right interrupting him. Besides, it didn't matter. Just because these guys had never heard of the beach, didn't mean it wasn't there. He knew it was, he remembered from when he was young. And he had looked it up on a map before setting out, and it was there, printed on the page. Okay, so it was an older map, nearly ten years out of date, but Christ, beaches didn't just up and disappear. It was there. It had to be.

The barman came out of the back room, pushing a mop and bucket. He stepped out from behind the bar, the wheels of the bucket squeaking as he rolled it towards the entrance.

"It's really coming down out there," the barman said. He took out the mop and started wiping up the wetness. "Why do you wanna set up camp tonight in this weather? At this beach that doesn't exist? It'd be impossible, all the rain. Best stay at a motel and wait for the sky to clear up. There's one a few minutes up the road."

"Don't think so. I came here to camp, and camping is what I plan on doing."

Peter snatched the blue bag from off the counter. He glanced at the two gents by the bar. "Well... see ya."

The old timer, sucking on his smoke (looked like a hand rolled, no filter), lowered his cigarette, huffed out smoke, raised his glass and said, "May you have fair winds and following seas."

The man in the cap just glared at Peter, his black eyes boring into Peter's soul.

The gent at the table finally broke out of his reverie and looked over. Peter caught the man's eyes, but he had to look away. The similarity to his dad's eyes was too unnerving. But he noticed that the man's eyes were red, watery, like he had been crying. And his face bled pain. In the brief time their eyes were locked, Peter thought he saw not just sadness there, but a pleading; a pleading for Peter not to leave.

Ridiculous, Peter knew, and he shook the thought away,

figuring he was just exhausted from the five-hour drive, the fighting with Marcia, the inclement weather. He had never met the man before. Hell, he hadn't even spoken to the guy. What he thought he saw, the odd knowing glint, was surely all in his head.

Peter started for the door, the bottles of rum knocking together as he walked.

The barman was still mopping up the water, though the worst of it was gone. The floor was slick but free from puddles.

Peter stopped by the door. The rain was still coming down, but, and perhaps it was just hope muddying his perception, it looked to be lessening.

He looked through the glass to the Patrol parked across the road, looking like a metal beast in the dirty night. He couldn't tell if Marcia was awake. Probably. She knew how to drive the truck. Why hadn't she moved the car closer to the pub, so he didn't get drenched on his return?

He was dwelling on this, and gearing himself up for another rainy onslaught, when the rain faded to a drizzle, and then petered out. Just like someone had turned off a giant tap in the sky.

"Well, wouldn't ya know," Peter said, smiling. He glanced across at the barman, who had stopped mopping and had come up beside Peter to look outside. "Look at that. Must be a sign."

The barman nodded. "Well, good luck."

"Thanks."

Peter pushed open the door. The air had a clean smell, with a hint of sulphur. As he trudged towards the road, he glanced at the truck parked outside the pub. Some kind of cattle transporter, though he could see, between the side slats, that it was empty.

He practically skipped across the road. Back at his car, he saw the driver's side door was closed. He pulled on the handle, but it wouldn't budge. Looking in, he saw Marcia sitting there, arms folded. She was staring ahead, eyes locked on nothing he could see. But they looked fearful.

He knocked on the driver's side window.

Marcia jumped.

She turned and when she saw him, she paused, before reaching over and unlocking the door.

He hopped in, put the bag in the back. "What's going on? Why did you lock the door?"

"Safety."

Peter chuckled. "From what?"

"I dunno," Marcia snapped back. "I heard..."

Peter closed the door. "Heard what?"

Marcia started biting her nails. "Nothing, I guess. It's just... out here, makes me nervous. It's so dark and... open."

Peter sparked up the engine. "We're almost there. Only another fifteen, twenty minutes. And the rain's stopped. That's good."

Marcia didn't respond.

As Peter pulled out of the fuel station, he looked over at the pub. A face stared out through the window. The man with the cap.

He remained by the window and watched them drive away, and though there was no way Peter could tell from such a distance, he was sure the man was grinning.

———

Fifteen minutes after leaving the pub, Peter started looking for the turnoff. The world was dark out here. There were no other vehicles, no buildings, no streetlights. No civilisation. Just nature. It was dry, too, as if the rain had bypassed the area.

"Keep a lookout," Peter mumbled around his cigarette.

"What am I looking for?"

"I told you; I remember a sign for an abattoir just before the track to Moondah. I remember because I asked Dad what the word meant the first time we came up here."

"What did he say?"

Peter took out the cigarette. He puffed out smoke. "Told me it's where they kill animals for the food we eat."

"That was honest."

"That was my dad. Hell, it's the truth. Why sugar-coat it? Although I felt like crying when he told me that. And I felt sick for a week afterwards every time I ate a pork chop or meatloaf."

Peter wound down the window. Clean country air washed in, cooling his face. The smell of earth and sweet eucalypt drifted into the car. A nice smell. Familiar, even though he had spent the past twenty years mostly cooped up among steel and concrete, surrounded by petrol fumes and industry. He felt oddly at home out here. The city felt a million miles away, like some distant alien planet.

The country air was welcoming, but what he really craved was the briny ocean spray, the smell of hot sand.

"Where are you?" he muttered, driving slowly, eyes locked on the road ahead.

He sucked the last of the smoke, then casually tossed the butt out the window. He breathed out, mist momentarily obscuring the view. When the smoke cleared, he saw a large sign up ahead. The sign was old, the red lettering faded, but it was unmistakable: TARONGA ABATTOIR 5ks.

"This is it," Peter said.

He felt a rush. He had been worried the sign would be long gone, worried he'd miss the turnoff and never make it to Moondah Beach. But, for once, the world was being kind to him.

About twenty metres past the sign, Peter saw the opening in the bush. The space was narrow, a lot more overgrown than he remembered, and would be easily missed if you weren't looking out for it.

He made the left turn, off the sealed road and onto the sandy track.

Almost immediately, the truck started jostling. No flat, smooth road, this, but a rough track full of dips and pits.

"Did you see that?" Marcia said shortly after they started down the track.

"See what?"

"A sign. It was falling down, looked old, but I thought I saw something about private property."

Peter, hunched at the wheel, eyes boring at the view ahead, a hint of a smile on his face, huffed. "I don't think so, Mars. This is a public beach. You must have misread."

"I don't think so. Are you sure this is the place? That we're on the right path?"

"I'm positive."

The Patrol rattled as he drove. Soon he came to a fork. Some unnamed track cut through the forest of tea-trees to the left. Peter slowed, enough to decide to keep to the right-hand track. The left seemed to wind back towards the highway.

Soon the trees closed in, and the way the trunks curved, white and almost aglow in the headlights, they looked like bones. The track narrowed, and when the spindly ends of the branches started scraping against the sides of the truck, reminding him of the scratching he'd heard that night in the spare bedroom, he felt a coldness sweep through him.

The track continued to splinter off the deeper he drove; not a clear, single road as expected, but a maze of narrow, sandy tracks that disorientated him and made his head dizzy.

The thick forest of bone-like trees cut off any light from the night sky, leaving just the car's headlights to illuminate the darkness. Marcia's hands were clamped on the dashboard in front as she was jostled about like some ride at Luna Park.

Funny, but Peter didn't recall the drive to the beach being this long, this wild. He also didn't remember so many offshoots. He was a kid back then, and hadn't bothered to concentrate on the drive, but still, it looked a lot different than what was stored in his memory.

Nerves started seeping in. This had to be the right place, he told himself. The turnoff just past the abattoir sign. Just like he remembered.

He shook the feelings away.

He felt it, deep down. This was the right place.

But the track kept going. Sand kicked up behind them, looking like a light fog in the mirror. The dark road ahead, with the trees acting as a canopy, resembled a mouth swallowing them.

"Do you know where we are?" Marcia, voice rattling, sounded worried.

"Yeah, I'm sure the ocean's just over there." He nodded to the right. "We just have to find our way through."

"We shouldn't have to find our way through, Peter. It should be a clear path. If we're meant to be here. Which I'm not sure we are."

The track started angling to the left, away from where Peter thought the beach was located. But, with no forks leading to other tracks ahead, he had no choice but to remain on the path. The gloomy scrub was endless, the track seemingly curving to nowhere.

Finally, the track split in two. Peter felt relief swarm through him, especially when he saw a gum tree, standing proudly among the smaller bushes and tea trees, an arrow carved into its trunk. The arrow pointed down the right-hand track, and figuring this a good sign, surely it meant the beach was only a short distance away, he turned onto the new track.

However, this track proved even wilder, bumpier, than the one they were just on. But it was heading in the right direction. At least Peter was confident it was the right direction. He turned his head towards the open window. Breathed in. Beneath the dry, woody aromas of the bush, he detected the wonderful saltiness of the ocean.

"We're heading in the right direction," he said without looking at his wife. "Smell that? The ocean."

"All I smell is exhaust fumes."

Peter powered on, heedless of the dips in the track. He was close to Moondah, he was certain.

"Peter, slow down."

Peter gripped the wheel. He pushed through the maw of beach scrub.

"Peter, slow down!"

"Almost there."

Tea trees whipped by, their claws scratching. Wind howled through the window.

Another sound, almost a growl.

"You hear that?" Marcia gasped.

Peter did, or at least he thought he did. But he put it down to the wind, or the sound of the gears grumbling as he shifted. "What?"

"Sounded like an animal. I heard it earlier, while you were busy with the petrol and again when you were inside the pub."

Marcia turned and looked into the back of the truck.

"You're hearing things, Mars."

"Maybe you'd better stop."

"Stop? We're almost there."

Yet, the track kept going. Not opening up to soft sand, high rolling dunes, and the vast expanse of the Tasman Sea, but just the dirty sand-dusted track and more scrub.

Marcia turned back. "Are we lost?"

Peter didn't answer. Instead, he concentrated on ploughing ahead, the smell of the beach, the ocean, now just a whisper.

When Peter saw it, he pushed hard on the brakes. The Patrol jerked to a stop. Marcia jolted forward.

"Jesus, Peter. What the hell?"

The car sat there, engine rumbling, the headlights casting an unholy glow over the bony trees.

"I didn't mean for you to stop so suddenly."

Peter stared with disbelief at the tree.

When Marcia saw it, she let out a whimper. "That's... is that the same tree?"

Peter snapped open the door, stepped out. Marcia remained in the truck. He walked over to the tree and stared at the towering gum with the arrow carved into its trunk. The arrow pointed down the track, the right of the two that lay before them; the long, dark track that looked like a snake with its mouth open.

Surely not the same one they had taken only a short while ago.

Peter reached out and fingered the rough bark, as if maybe it was some figment. No. The trunk was real. The arrow dug into the old tree sometime in the past, also real.

Peter shivered. The air had grown cool. Clothes still damp, he felt dressed in ice.

It wasn't possible. The track couldn't have circled around. He had driven in a straight line.

Head hurting, he started back towards the car. Passing the front of the Patrol, he noticed something that wasn't usually there. He stepped closer. Crouched in front of the bullbar, moths fluttering around him by the twin eyes of the headlights, he saw something stuck to the metal bars, something hairy. The hair, light brown, looked like some deformed caterpillar. Red smeared the bullbar. He reached out, touched the substance. Sticky, like red glue.

The kangaroo, he thought, and a sour taste filled his mouth.

He straightened, wiped his soiled fingers on his pants.

"What's the matter?"

Marcia was leaning out the passenger window, looking down at him.

"I, ah... hit a kangaroo earlier."

Marcia frowned. "Okay."

"There's some blood and hair stuck to the front of the truck."

Bypassing this bit of news, Marcia said, "So, is it the tree we passed earlier?"

Peter shrugged.

"It is, isn't it? Shit, we've been going around in circles."

"How can it be the same tree? We've been on the same track for... I mean, how the hell could we have gone in...?"

Peter shook his head, unable to finish the sentence. He stepped back up into the driver's seat, reached over, and picked up the bag containing the bottles of rum. He took one bottle out, placed it back with the camping gear, nestling it with the sleeping bags, then stepped down. He pulled the second bottle of Bundy out, and with force, tossed the blue plastic bag away. It was carried by the wind, before landing on a Banksia.

Through the brisk night air, something wailed. It sounded to Peter a cross between a cow lowing and the pained cry of a newborn. Goosebumps prickled on his arms.

"Did you hear *that*?" Marcia said, voice soft.

Peter unscrewed the bottle cap, took a good helping. The rum helped to burn away the foul taste in his mouth. Heat spread through his chilled body. "Yeah, I heard it." He took another drink, then raised the bottle. "Want a belt?"

"Where the fuck are we, Peter?"

Peter was about to answer, even though he had no idea what he was going to tell her, when a noise sounded from the back of the car. This time, Peter couldn't ignore it. Like the distant wailing, he couldn't put it down to the wind or the gears or his imagination.

"Peter...!" Marcia's eyes were knitted with fear.

"Yeah, yeah."

He took another swill of rum as he stalked towards the back of the truck. Already he was beginning to feel the effects of the alcohol. The cold no longer bothered him. His head felt light, his limbs tingly. He set the bottle down, took a breath, and then pulled open the doors.

From within, he saw two eyes glowing.

If he had been stone sober, he might have shut the doors and high-tailed it back to the front, told Marcia to get out of the car, and with the car shut up, taken off down the track, circles be damned.

But he didn't. And when he saw the creature the eyes belonged to, he smiled.

"Cricket!"

The dog, body mostly buried among the packed tent and suitcases, gave a whine. Unsure if she was in trouble, she remained wedged in her hiding spot, until Peter reached in and gave her head a scratch, her coat a ruffle. "Hey, girl. What are you doing back here, huh? Hey, Mars, we've got a stowaway."

"You're not serious?" Marcia, still seated up front, swiftly swapped fear for anger. "You knew, didn't you?"

"Huh?"

"When I wasn't looking. You put her in the back, didn't tell me. Figured by the time I found out, we'd be too far from home to do anything about it."

"You don't think much of me, Mars. I don't keep secrets."

He regretted saying it the moment the words left his mouth.

Marcia shrieked a cold, callous laugh. "You don't keep secrets? Please."

He gave Cricket one last pat and then closed the doors. He picked up the rum, climbed back into the driver's seat. Then he sat there, sucking on the bottle like a baby at the breast.

The eerie wailing sounded again, mournful, echoing through the night like God Himself was weeping.

"We don't belong here," Marcia said, almost too soft to hear.

He looked across at Marcia. Sitting there in the passenger seat, she looked small, like a scared child.

"Can I make a suggestion?" she said. "Let's head back and spend the night at the motel. Wasn't that far back."

Peter gazed through the windscreen at the two tracks, at the scrub, at the arrow carved into the tree. He was sure they were close to Moondah, but he was exhausted and starting to get extra sleepy from the rum, so resting was looking more appealing than driving.

"Things will be better in the morning," Marcia continued. "I'm sure we'll find the beach when it's daylight."

Peter sighed. "It's too late to make camp, anyway."

Through the thicket, whips of lightning momentarily lit up the black night. A few seconds later, the heavens grumbled.

From the back, Cricket whined.

"It's okay, girl," Peter called.

The dog had always hated storms.

"That scares me," Marcia said.

"It's far away. It won't hit us."

"But it might," Marcia said. "It could rain again. All the more reason to head to the motel."

Peter thought about the time spent driving through the maze of tracks. It had been hard enough reaching this point. He didn't want to do that again, not when they were so close to Moondah. He didn't want to leave.

He turned off the lights, followed by the engine. "We'll sleep here."

"What, in the car?"

"Beach can't be far off. I can sense it. We'll find it first light."

"Great, let's spend the night in the fucking car instead of in a nice, warm, cosy motel room."

"It's too late to check in. Not that long till dawn."

"You never take on board any of my suggestions. Whatever King Peter wants, King Peter gets, never mind what I want."

"You're perfectly capable of making your own decisions without consulting me. That's been more than established."

Marcia glared at him with ice.

"I'm staying here, and that's that. You don't like it, fine, then walk. Just make sure to take a jacket. It's getting nippy out there."

"I hate you."

"Right back at ya."

Peter settled down in his seat. Sipped some more rum, but only a little. The alcohol had done its job.

With a huff, Marcia climbed into the back and started rummaging around. Peter was drifting off when Marcia sat back in her seat, rocking the truck. He opened one eye and looked over at her. She slipped on a jumper, a beanie, and then took out her sleeping bag. She started unzipping it, which proved difficult in such a confined space. She muttered and cursed under her breath. Peter grinned lazily. Once she had the sleeping bag opened, she draped it over her like a blanket.

"This is so uncomfortable," she said.

"Why don't you spread out in the back?"

"It's too full back there. I'd have to unload the bags and tent and stuff. Besides, Cricket's back there."

Peter whistled. Cricket came scurrying across the back, up to the front. She made herself at home beside Peter. "There, now you have it all to yourself."

Marcia remained up front.

She wrapped herself up like the sleeping bag was a cocoon and then fell silent.

Peter, with his last surge of energy, reached back, found a blanket, and draped it over himself. "Night, girl," he said to Cricket, gave her a final scratch, and then he took a last nip of rum, put the cap back on, nestled the bottle by his side, and fell asleep almost immediately, the sound of the wind like whispers through the night.

2

WHAT WOKE Marcia wasn't the sun streaming through the windscreen, rays magnified as they pierced the window. It wasn't the clammy heat circulating inside the Patrol, like she had fallen asleep in an oven. It wasn't the sharp squawking of birds, cacophonous in their morning song, or even her desperate thirst giving her a dry mouth, tacky lips, and the beginning of a headache. No, it was the sound of something being struck.

The noise—repetitive, sudden, thudding—baffled Marcia at first. It was as if the pounding inside her head was being amplified for all the world to hear.

As the sound continued, Marcia rose to a sitting position. The sleeping bag, only half covering her, slithered away, and she winced as a sharp stinging shot through her neck. Her back felt made of wood. Moving slowly, she eased up and looked out the driver's side window. Squinting against the bright morning light, she wondered if she was still sleeping, because the sight that greeted her seemed too unreal to believe. To the right of the truck lay a large clearing, which was at odds with the canopy of trees she remembered surrounding the track last night. The tent was up, sitting at the edge of the wide, green space. A fire burned nicely in the middle of the clearing; the flames contained by a circle of rocks. Nearby, the folding table was up and bookended by two chairs, with some of the groceries already unpacked. Cricket sat near the table, watching her master, who was by a tree with an axe, and was chopping into the trunk like a thin, boyish woodsman.

She had been tired last night, sure, but so much she had slept through Peter emptying out half the truck, putting up the tent, the chairs and table, and building a fire?

It was early, just past seven; Peter must have been up before dawn.

Marcia kicked off the sleeping bag. She was clad only in her bra and underpants. She had woken sometime in the pre-dawn hours, hot and sweating. The inside of the car had been sauna-like. Barely cogent, she had stripped down to her underwear, rolled down her window half-way, and kept the sleeping bag loosely wrapped. It seemed like a dream now, but she remembered the feel of the breeze drifting in through the passenger window—fresh and warm, but still cooler than the air inside the truck. She remembered giving a quick eye to Peter, snoring in his seat. She remembered Cricket being awake and how her dark eyes looked unsettled, even wary. She certainly remembered hearing the horrible wailing noise. She had just settled back, was almost asleep, when the noise that sounded like a baby crying echoed through the still, balmy morning. To her ears, the creature sounded in great anguish, and Marcia wanted to block out the sound. Peter didn't stir, but Cricket had whined softly.

Her eyes had started tearing as the sound dug into her heart and tore at her soul. Just some ocean creature, she told herself. Probably a mating call. But it sounded sadder than that.

As far as Marcia knew, she fell asleep with the creature still keening.

Her eyes were crusted with dry tears, her cheeks gritty with salt. She badly needed a shower. She also needed to cover up.

She felt too exposed, but the morning was already heating up, so she picked up her shirt from off the floor, put it on, and then hopped out of the truck.

The grass was soft underfoot, springy. The smell of smoke was pervasive. But there was a sour tinge to it. She saw, sizzling in the pan, what looked like strips of bacon.

Peter stopped his axe work—he hadn't gotten far, had barely made a dint in the trunk—and faced Marcia. He looked ridiculous standing there. The way he was dressed—light blue t-shirt and white shorts—and coupled with his smooth, youthful face and gangly body, he looked more like a boy scout than a rugged man of nature.

"Morning." He swiped an arm across his dripping forehead and then rested the axe over a shoulder.

"What are you doing to that tree?"

"What do you think? Chopping it down."

"Why?"

Peter shrugged. "Why not?" Then he added, almost as an afterthought, "Firewood, I guess."

Marcia didn't know much about the outdoors, but she didn't think it looked like a good tree for burning. From what she could see from the broken bark, the wood looked green, and she knew green wood didn't burn well.

"Did you move the car or something?"

"No."

"Then where are we?"

"We were close last night. I was right. Another fifty metres or so and we'd have made it to the beach."

"So, we stopped... here?"

Peter smiled. He waved his free arm across the clearing. "That's right. We're here. The sun's shining, the birds are chirping..."

"And the bacon's burning."

Peter looked over at the fire. His smile dropped, then he dropped the axe. "Fuck," he spat, and hurried over. Using a tea towel, he took the frying pan off the flames and set it on one of the rocks. "Well, that's ruined. Sorry, Mars. Wanted to surprise you with a nice breakfast of bacon and eggs."

Marcia stepped closer and looked down at the bacon, which resembled charred bits of wood.

"It'll have to be toast and eggs, no bacon." Peter straightened.

Spotting the orange juice, Marcia moved over to the table, poured herself a full paper cup of juice, drank it down in a few greedy gulps. Her eyes wandered, surveying the area: a thick tangle of scrub beyond the clearing, lots of bushes, gum trees...

Marcia frowned at the sight of the tree near the front of the truck. A hot, prickly sensation swirled in her tummy.

"Peter..."

"Huh?"

"That tree, the one with the arrow, it's just over there." She pointed to the gum with the arrow carved into its trunk.

Peter picked up the burnt bacon and tossed it over to Cricket. The dog got up, sniffed the meat, decided burnt was better than nothing, and gobbled it down.

"Yeah. If we'd driven just a little..."

"No, look. The track ends here. If it ends here by the marked tree, how could we have gone in circles?"

Peter huffed. Wiped his hands on his shorts. "Obviously we didn't."

"But..."

"Christ, Mars. I don't know what happened. It was late, dark. I was dead tired. Probably a different tree we passed, pointing the way to this one. Anyway, what does it matter? We're here now."

Marcia glanced again at the tree. It sure looked like the one they passed last night, twice. The uneasy feeling remained.

"That's all you care about, the damned tree. I mean, all the work I did this morning. Gee, Peter, thanks, you did a great job setting up the campsite."

He sounded like a pouty child. Looked like it, too. Her immediate response was to not enable his immature behaviour, to go in the opposite direction of what he wanted. Either ignore him or call him out.

But it was a new day. As much as she didn't want to be here, she had to admit, the sunny morning, the crisp autumn air, the quiet, the smell of the fire, it was all nice. It had a calming effect, and maybe they could try not arguing today. At least, not so early. And not before breakfast. So she smiled. She moved closer to him. "Thank you, Peter. You did a great job setting up the campsite."

Peter bridged the gap further. "You're making fun of me."

"No, I'm not. I appreciate it, really."

Peter leaned forward, pecked her on the forehead. "I guess that'll do. Come on, I want to show you something."

He took her by the hand and led her across the clearing to a sandy path. Cricket jumped up and bounded forward to join them. They walked a short distance down the track and soon came to a bluff. Peter stopped and Marcia stopped beside him. They were overlooking a beach. Its sand was like snow. Beyond, the gentle surf broke against the shore, and farther out the ocean was like blue glass, the sun blinding where it struck the water. Low hills, some covered in dense scrubland that looked like moss, others bare rock that looked like giant turtle shells, formed a horseshoe that cupped a portion of the ocean. The large, curved bay reminded Marcia of a giant teacup full to the brim. Except this cup had a gap where the water flowed out and the overflow was so enormous her brain couldn't grasp its true size.

Cricket gave a bark, a happy sound, and then trotted off to explore the scrub.

"What do you think?"

Objectively speaking, it was a lovely sight. Pristine, isolated, there wasn't another living thing in sight, aside from the birds floating in the sky. Marcia knew she should have been wowed, been in awe of nature in all her beauty. To most people, it represented relaxation, a chance to unwind, soak up the sun, and frolic in the waters. To her, it was an oppressive sight. It represented everything she wasn't. She was out of her comfort zone, and she didn't like being in that place. All she could think of was sand getting everywhere, the salty ocean water drying and making her skin itch; falling asleep and getting burnt; no television, no restaurants, no meeting up with friends for a few drinks.

"There aren't any toilets, are there?"

Peter sighed. "I bring you here and show you paradise, and all you can think about is where to take a crap?"

"I'm not the outdoors type, Peter. You know that."

"Yeah, I know. But just try, okay? So you dig a hole and squat over that for a few days. Won't kill you."

Marcia knew she had to make a decision. Fight Peter on this trip, act snarky at every turn, remind him of where she really wanted to go this weekend, and that she hated camping and nature... or try to make the best of things. Swallow her pride and try to get along.

"No, I guess not."

She figured, if she was going to make the effort to be polite, she might as well go the extra step. "Look, about last night. What I said. I was tired, scared. I didn't mean what I said. About... you know, hating you."

"Know what?"

Peter turned her around. He put his arms around her. He smelled of sweat and smoke.

"What?"

"I think I still love you."

Peter, whose face was stubbornly hanging on to its vestiges of boyish youth, despite age starting to creep in, especially around the eyes, smiled.

"Do you?"

"Even though you can be a grumpy old sourpuss."

Marcia playfully thumped him on the shoulder. "Who you calling old?"

"Know what else?"

"What?"

"There's something in your hair!"

Marcia frantically bat at her hair. "What? Where?"

She hated critters more than camping. Spiders were the worst. "A spider? Is it a spider?"

She saw Peter crack a smile. Then he started laughing.

"No, it's a... a Bunyip."

Marcia stopped pawing at her head and when she hit him next, she made sure he felt it. "You prick!"

He grabbed her. Whether deliberately or through loss of balance, she found herself tumbling down the sandy bank. Peter tumbled down after her. She cried out in initial surprise, but the cry soon turned to laughter. She came to a stop at the base of the bluff. With all the commotion, Cricket, yapping, came bounding down and, standing close by, continued to bark and jump.

Suddenly, Peter was on top of her, showering her with sand, blocking out the worst of the sun. Both laughing like children. Peter pinned her arms down in the soft, white sand.

Through the laughter, the panting, Peter said, "What did you call me?"

Marcia couldn't help but smile, though she tried her hardest to push it away. "A prick."

"That's what I thought."

He remained straddling her. He gripped her arms harder, probably just a playful response to her name-calling. Probably.

"If you want, later, I'll show you a prick."

Marcia squirmed. Peter was getting too heavy, his grip too tight. "You'd better get off or else I'll piss myself."

It was true, she did need to go to the toilet. But she wanted him off, regardless.

There was a moment when Peter, staring into her eyes,

looked like he wasn't going to move. But he let go and rolled off.

"That was mean, tricking me like that."

Peter rose up on his elbows and squinted at her. "But kinda funny."

Marcia stood up. Brushed sand off her body, shook her hair. Looked both ways down the beach.

"You can go anywhere, Mars. No one around to see you. Except me."

"I know, it just... feels funny going out in the open."

"It's just nature. We're only animals, after all."

Marcia started walking left down the beach. Her bare feet made squelching noises in the sand.

"Love me?" Peter called out.

Marcia stopped, turned around.

She licked her lips. Tasted salt. "Maybe."

While Peter sat in the truck listening to the radio, Marcia's hands were plunged in soapy water. She was almost done with the breakfast dishes. The pan was the last, but it was proving stubborn, the burnt grease difficult to shift.

Damn Peter, she thought, scrubbing hard at the pan, *can't even cook bacon without ruining it. Typical of King Peter; messes up and then expects me to clean up afterwards.*

The muscles in her arm strained, her hand started cramping, yet still she scrubbed.

Finally, with the water black and the suds flecked with what looked like soot, she drew the pan out of the tub and saw it was clean.

She stood there, panting, feeling like she had finished a rigorous workout.

Once she got her breath back, she dried the pan with a wad of paper towelling, put the pan in the second tub with all the clean and dry dishes, and then took the tub filled with dirty water and walked out of the clearing into the outlying scrub. She dumped the water onto the ground. As she watched the dark, oily water splash over the grass, the earth, she thought about her sudden burst of anger directed at Peter. Maybe it shouldn't have, but the rush of anger surprised her. Peter had done a lot this morning, setting up the whole campsite, and was trying to do a nice thing by having bacon ready when she woke up. So, he overcooked the food. Wasn't like he burnt the bacon on purpose. Still, the anger that had shot to the surface so easily, so quickly, was frightening.

She was mad at him for many reasons, reasons that ran deep and stretched back years. Simply burning some rashers wasn't that big of a deal, not in the grand scheme of things. The morning had been nice, as nice as could be expected. They hadn't been at each other's throats, and she almost felt something resembling attraction to him, which hadn't happened in a long while. So why she should get so riled up over something so trivial baffled her.

She carried the empty tub back to the camp.

Peter had decamped from the truck and was playing around with the spear gun. Without the drone of the radio, the world was quiet.

"Weather's supposed to turn shitty later in the afternoon," Peter said. "Maybe I should get in a surf this morning."

As Marcia set down the tub, she saw a flood of ants on the ground around the table. At present, they seemed more interested in the scraps of food that had fallen or been tossed down—bits of bread, some scrambled egg, globs of strawberry jam; they were even swarming over the tea bag. A bin bag for all the scraps would be smart, but that could wait. She needed to take care of the ants before they started moving up the table and got to the food on top. A few outliers were already scurrying up and down the legs; only a matter of time before they realised there was a feast above their tiny heads.

"Where's the insecticide?"

"Huh? Oh, it's in the tent."

Marcia hurried into the tent, which, even with the flap open, was starting to heat up. She found the insect spray, and back outside, unleashed a deadly torrent. The insecticide rained down on the carpet of tiny black ants, coating them with the white spray. She made sure to get to the ones crawling up the table legs. When the smell started clouding around her, burning her nostrils, she straightened, took a few steps back and continued spraying the ground around the table.

"I think that's more than enough, Mars. You're drowning the little buggers."

The area around the table looked like the surf as it broke, all white and foamy. It bubbled as it got to work, suffocating the insects. Soon, the spray started fading, falling away into the earth, and leaving behind a carpet of dead, soggy ants.

"There, that should do it."

Marcia turned around. Peter was staring down at the ants with a strange look: distant, face crumpled, as if thinking about a bad memory.

"You didn't have to use half the can, Mars."

"I didn't. Anyway, what's the big deal? We don't want ants all over our food."

"Wouldn't be any ants if you kept the camp clean."

Marcia opened her mouth to shoot back, but she stopped, reminding herself she was going to try to play nice. "What are you planning on doing with that?" She nodded to the spear gun Peter was still clutching.

"Dunno. Shoot fish."

"Just be careful, okay? You know how I hate guns."

"It's not a gun, Mars."

"It's a type of gun. It shoots, doesn't it?"

"Spears, not bullets."

Peter turned away from the sea of dead ants and set the

spear gun across the arms of a folding chair. He disappeared into the tent.

Marcia moved over to the truck, to the small fridge in the cargo area. Sometime during the morning, Peter had plugged in the fridge and transferred all the items from the icebox to the portable refrigerator. She opened the door and peered in. Not much choice for dinner, just chicken or beef, but then they were only planning on staying two nights, so two proteins were all they needed.

She turned at the sound of Peter coming back out of the tent. He was carrying a backpack and was stuffing in binoculars and something she hadn't seen before, something that looked like a toy.

"What's that?"

"What, this?"

He held up the strange object: a wooden fork with a big rubber band attached. "It's my slingshot."

"Your... what? Where'd you get it?"

"Found it in a box in the spare room. I got it as a kid, from my dad."

"It's that old?"

"Still works."

He put the slingshot into his bag, then walked over. He gently pushed her aside, reached into the fridge, and grabbed two bottles of beer.

"You going somewhere?"

"Thought I might check out the area, do a little exploring."

Marcia waited for an invite. She didn't necessarily care about exploring the dunes, the scrub—it was all the same, so why bother—and she wanted to shower, get cleaned up, but she wanted Peter to *want* her to come. When the invite didn't come, she felt herself deflate. Still, it wasn't unexpected.

"Well, I'm going to stay and get the shower up and running," she told him. "Maybe clean up the camp, because, you know, that's my job. It's why I'm here, right?"

Peter ignored her.

Once his beers were packed, he zipped up the bag.

"What do you want for dinner tonight?" Marcia said, flatly. "Steak or chicken?"

"How about some fish?"

"We didn't bring any."

"I know. But I'll catch some and we'll have fresh fish for dinner."

She wasn't particularly fond of fish. And the thought of eating something freshly killed, so she had to see it whole, beady black eyes and all, didn't sit well in her gut. "I'll defrost something just in case." She took the chicken from the fridge and started towards the table.

"You don't need to," Peter called. "I'll catch some fish. I know how to, you know."

"Right, of course you do. With your gun."

"It's not a gun, Marcia! And yes, I do know how."

Marcia had just placed the frozen chicken on the table, was in the process of turning around to appease her husband, when she heard a snapping sound, and something flew by her face. She felt air whip her skin, accompanied by a whooshing sound, and then the object sank into a nearby trunk with a dull *thwack*. Marcia stood there, shock pulsing through her body.

"Jesus!" Peter cried.

He dropped his backpack and rushed over. He took hold of her by her arms. "Are you okay?"

Marcia turned and looked at the tree. Peter's tree, the one he had been chopping at with the axe. Just above the broken bark, a long metal shaft protruded from the trunk.

Marcia took a deep, quivering breath and then closed her eyes. "Fuck," she muttered.

Behind her eyes, as if her mind was a projector replaying the scene, she could see the spear shooting past her, only this time, the spear hits her in the side of the head, the tip pierces her brain, blood shoots out and she is knocked to the ground, dead.

She flung open her eyes and swallowed.

"You sure you're okay?"

Marcia nodded. "Close call, though."

Frowning, Peter let go and went over to the spear gun, still spread across the chair. He picked it up. "Odd. Safety's still on. It shouldn't have fired with the safety on. Damned thing must be faulty."

He set the gun down and wandered over to the shaft stuck in the tree. Still shaken, Marcia watched as he gripped the shaft with his dominant hand and pulled. The spear didn't come out. He gripped the shaft with both hands and tugged harder. He grunted. Still, the shaft held on tight. He tried again. Strained, pulled, but eventually gave up.

He wandered back. "I'm sorry, Mars. Christ, I almost... you could have been hurt."

"But I wasn't."

"No. You weren't."

Peter attempted a smile, but it faltered. He moved away, snatched up his bag, called for Cricket, and then took off out of the clearing.

Marcia watched the man and his dog disappear. Once they were gone, she fell to her knees, put her hands up to her face and wept.

———

The beach resembled a crescent moon: so white and so bright it almost glowed. The sand was powder-soft, and, aside from where he and Marcia had tumbled and where she had walked to do her business, untouched. He knew it wasn't true, but being here, without any other human contact, he could pretend he and Mars were the first people to set foot on this terrain. This was uncharted territory. He was the first man to explore these pristine beaches, this wild, scrubby bushland. Thinking this gave him a rise, a surge of power, and as he wandered up the beach, he hadn't felt so alive, not in years.

He had felt a pull to this beach, beyond even the desire to re-connect to an especially fond time of his childhood, almost like this patch of nature was calling to him. Silly, but that's how he felt. He was glad he came. Glad he forced Marcia to come despite her reluctance, instead of travelling once again to boring old Portsea. He felt like he belonged here. This was his territory; here, he was the master.

He remembered a time when his father had been the one in charge. Back then, his dad had seemed like a giant of a man, Robinson Crusoe, Allan Quatermain, and James Bond, all rolled into one. Of course, Peter knew his dad was just a man, flawed like all humans, just stronger and more capable than most. He knew how to build a fire without the need for matches; knew how to catch fish with just a spear. He was a marvel at using his hands to build things, even though he wasn't a builder by trade. The first time they camped at Moondah, Dad had built Peter a treehouse up in an old gum tree near the campsite. A simple construction, really just a few planks of wood for the floor, some low walls made out of wooden limbs. But to him, it was the best thing ever built. Using the ladder his dad had nailed to the trunk of the tree (plank off-cuts) he could climb up to his house and sit there and look out over the bay, or just lie there and look up at the bush canopy, at the sky beyond. He could pretend he was shipwrecked and hiding from pirates. Up in that treehouse was where he stored his collection of seashells, dead starfish and anything else he found washed up on the beach that was odd or interesting—including a rusty knife blade, sans handle. That had been a great treasure and featured in most of his adventures involving marauding pirates.

Peter had looked for the treehouse when he woke up this morning. Before unloading the truck, before putting up the tent, the first thing he did when he realised where they were was to look for the treehouse. He searched the bushland surrounding the clearing but could find no trace of it. Not even a lonely plank nailed to a trunk. Not finding any remnants of the treehouse was disappointing. It felt like a part of him, his dad, was gone, lost to the ravages of time.

Seeing the campsite and the nearby beach after so many years had also been a small letdown. Not that it wasn't beautiful and just what he wanted for this weekend; just that it hadn't matched what he held in his memories for so long. If not for the turnoff being where he remembered, he might have thought he had gone to the wrong place. The site had been smaller than he remembered, the earth rockier. As a boy, he remembered a great sea of green; a huge clearing that could accommodate five tents if need be. The clearing of today would be lucky to house two. The beach had been as soft and white as he remembered, but the bay felt narrower, like the surrounding land had been squeezed together. When he was young, the bay had felt massive. Still a contained place, a private place that only he and Dad knew about, but big enough for Peter to spend all day exploring. Then, the trees and bushes had seemed a jungle; now, it was just scrubby bushland. He supposed that was the difference between young eyes and the eyes of an older person. Things seemed bigger, wilder, and held more promise of adventure when you were young. Now, all he saw was the reality. Still pretty, still rustic, but not quite as majestic.

But he was here. Even if it wasn't quite the same as he remembered, he would make the most of it. With his dad no longer around, Peter was the one in charge. This was his domain now. And whatever mixed feelings he had, he still felt like he belonged here.

He looked around for Cricket. Saw her up the beach, near the water, making a mess of the sand. She looked happy, too. Like she also belonged here. She was free, unbounded by the restrictions of a house, the dangerous streets, the steel and concrete of the suburbs. He hated the thought of Cricket stuck at home, with nothing but a pile of canned dog food and a still, dark house as company. She would have been miserable cooped up in there. Much better she was here.

Cricket came bounding back, a stick clamped between her jaws.

"What ya got there, girl?"

Cricket, tail slapping the air vigorously, dropped the stick by Peter's feet. He picked it up. The stick, about thirty centimetres long and damp from the sea, was tapered at one end and reminded him of a spear. He thought about what had happened at the campsite.

Close. Too bloody close. He still couldn't understand how it had happened. He hadn't seen it, just heard the snap as the shaft was shot from the gun, the whistle as the long metal spear sailed through the air. Marcia's gasp. The sound of the arrow striking wood.

Christ, what would have happened if...

But it didn't.

Still, the thought crossed his mind, unbidden, and he looked out at the seemingly endless ocean, the water gently undulating. There were plenty of big rocks around. He had rope...

Christ! No, what the hell was he thinking?

If something like that happened, he'd go for help. Of course he would.

Cricket barking shocked him from his thoughts. He looked down at the retriever, tongue hanging out, eyes expectant.

"Sorry, girl." He tossed the stick. Cricket took off after it as the wooden stake sailed through the air.

He continued walking, enjoying the feel of the fresh ocean breeze on his face. Enjoying the freedom.

Finished showering (if you could call standing naked in the middle of the scrub beneath a canvas bag tied to a branch as water dribbled over you a shower—she called it primitive), and finished brushing her teeth, Marcia felt vaguely human again. She still felt gritty sand on her body, in crevices, in her hair, but she guessed such was the glamorous life of a camper—never feeling fully clean, never totally free of sand. So much better than staying at a nice motel in civilised Portsea, where showers were indoors and actually had some force.

She unwrapped the towel from around her head, letting her sandy-coloured hair fall down in damp strands. She slipped a cheesecloth cover-up over her bikini top and bottom. She was clean, dressed, and ready.

Ready for what? There was nothing to do here. Peter was off exploring. She had no house to clean, no errands to run.

She could go down to the beach and swim. But she wasn't a fan of the water. She wasn't a strong swimmer. She could read. She had a hefty tome she had only recently started and more than enough time to make a sizeable dent in it.

So few choices... so much time.

Marcia sighed to the wind, which didn't much care for her middle-class predicament. It persisted regardless, warm and slight and tinged with salt air. Her eyes fell on the long spear embedded in the trunk of the tree. She shivered as she thought of how close it had come to striking her. Just a little more to the right, or if she had taken a small step forward...

Her chest tightened, like the air had been sucked out of her body. Her palms grew clammy.

Peter claimed it was a freak accident, but it had to have been his fault. He mustn't have set it correctly, forgotten to put the safety on, or something. Spear guns didn't just fire without an intervening force, not unless someone did something incorrect. So, it hadn't been an accident so much as carelessness on Peter's part. He hadn't meant for it to happen... at least, she was fairly confident he hadn't.

Marcia walked over to the shaft. She took hold of it with her right hand. The metal felt warm, basking in the full sunshine.

She pulled on it, but it remained stuck. She gripped it with both hands. Propped one foot against the base of the tree and, using all her strength, pulled again. She held her breath as she pulled at the shaft; her arms started hurting, sweat beaded and then dripped down her face. The spear wouldn't budge.

"Stupid thing," she said and kicked the tree.

She looked around. Spotted the axe. Retrieved it and with purpose, strode back over to the tree. She raised the axe. The axe was heavy and as she started swinging, she found it hard to keep her balance. She struck at the trunk, attempting to hit the area where the point of the spear was embedded. She sometimes hit close to the spear. More often than not, she struck too wide. She chopped at the tree over and over, attempting to dislodge the spear. All she did was wear herself out. She barely made a mark in the tree and the spear remained lodged.

With anger replacing fear, she continued chopping at the tree.

Something dropped from the sky.

Surprised, Marcia jumped back. Looking down, she saw a large egg. She lowered the axe, swiped an arm across her forehead, and gazed up. Amid the foliage, she thought she saw a nest, high up. She couldn't see a bird.

She propped the axe against the tree. She had managed to cut away some more bark, managed to expose a trifle more of the metal rod. Though when she tried jiggling the spear free, it still held firm.

"Damn you," she muttered, glowering at the spear. "I hate you."

Admitting defeat, she turned her attention to the egg. She scooped it up. Amazingly, it hadn't cracked in the fall. The egg, pale yellow and speckled with brown, about the size of a baseball but shaped like a football, was heavy and felt solid.

Holding the egg, a strange chill coursed through her.

She was holding life in her hand, yet she felt very little. Was that odd for a woman? Shouldn't she feel something? Awe at holding something living? At the very least, bad for the mother bird who would come back to the nest to find her soon-to-be-baby missing? She knew she should feel some emotion, but all she felt was empty. Not sad, or regretful, or hell, even jealous. Just flat, no different from if she was holding a pretty stone.

Was I right to do what I did? Marcia wondered, the thought striking her like a lightning bolt. It felt right at the time.

The way she felt now with the egg—or the lack of feeling—only confirmed that yes, she had made the right choice.

Still, she recalled what she was like in the weeks afterwards. Confused, guilty. Crying often and easily. She had been sure at the time she didn't want to bring a new life into her existing, broken one; was sure she had done the right thing, but that hadn't stopped the barrel of emotions. Now, here in the hot, white light of Moondah Beach, she felt none of those strong, conflicting emotions. She felt almost numb, as if the life before coming here was someone else's, someone she only felt thinly connected to.

Or maybe she was just tired. Numb from a terribly uncomfortable and disrupted sleep, from the constant bickering with Peter, from being made to come here when it was the last place in the world she felt like spending the long weekend.

Yes, that was surely it.

She considered leaving the egg on the ground for when the mummy bird returned. After all, she had no real use for it. But weren't birds supposed to reject their unborn babies if an egg had been touched by human hands? If that were true, then it would be better to keep it than just to leave it untended. Besides, it was pretty in an ordinary way. And it was hers, now. To do as she pleased. Peter had his spear gun; she had her egg.

She left the tree with the spear still entrenched in its body and took her new toy into the tent.

———

The late morning sun was a fireball and as he stood in the shallows, gulping the beer, he imagined the sun melting everything, like in that famous painting by Picasso. The sand turned to white glue, the water blue crayon, the trees and bushes green wax. He pictured himself and Cricket turning into puddles of goo, and he chuckled.

He swallowed the last drop of beer, looked over at his dog. Cricket was sniffing around the beach, tail up, on a scavenger hunt. "What do you think of that, girl?" he called out. "A doggy puddle."

Cricket looked up, wagged her tail, and then resumed her hunting.

Peter tossed the bottle. It landed with a small splash in the surf and remained bobbing on top of the water. He slipped the backpack off his shoulder, zipped it open, and took out his Wham-O. He tossed the bag onto the sand, then waded through the water, bending over to look for suitable ammo. He found lots of pebbles, but most were flat. Finally, he found a small, round stone. Straightening up, he settled the pebble into the pouch and then looked for the empty beer bottle.

"Where are you?" he muttered, scanning the brilliant ocean. When he spotted the bottle about fifteen metres away, riding the waves, heading towards shore, he planted himself firmly in the warm shallows and held the stock in his right hand. He closed his right eye, pulled back the band. Sighted his target.

"Prepare to meet your maker, dirtbag," he drawled.

With a quick, yet gentle release of his fingers, the rubber band flicked forward, the pebble shot out and an instant later the bottle shattered like miniature fireworks, only instead of flares, glass exploded.

"Bingo! First go." He watched the broken bottle disappear beneath the waves. He smiled. "Still got it."

He had always been a better-than-average shot as a boy. His slingshot abilities had impressed even his dad.

He waded out of the surf, collected his bag, put back his

slingshot. He looked around for Cricket. Saw her up the beach. She was stopped, head down. He powered towards her. "See that, girl? Hit the target on the first go."

Cricket wasn't impressed. She was more interested in something on the sand. Peter approached. "What did you find, girl?"

Rather than picking it up in her mouth or playfully toying with it, Cricket seemed more suspicious. She sniffed it but left it alone. Peter picked it up. Odd, the items you found washed up on the shore. It was a plastic doll, the old-fashioned kind. It was naked and had one arm missing. Its head, with its long, ratty, blonde hair, was turned around.

"You've seen better days, Mars," he said with a curled smile.

He had said it without thought, but now that he looked closer, the doll did share a vague resemblance to Marcia. The discarded doll had been on the beach awhile; it was dirty with a slimy, blue-green substance. The doll smelled like something dead. Whatever coated the plastic, probably some kind of mould, was rotten and Peter dropped the doll. His fingers were smeared with the slimy fungus, so he washed them in the ocean and once they were clean, he brought his fingers to his nose. Still a faint smell.

Cricket remained close to the doll, curious but wary.

Gazing down at the doll, Peter wondered about the owner: who was the girl who once owned this doll? Did she live in the area or far away? Did she leave it on the beach during a family holiday, or was it lost at sea during a cruise? Did it happen a long time ago, or more recently? How upset was she when she discovered her doll was missing?

With these thoughts rolling around in his head, intense feelings of sadness and loss pulsed through him. He didn't know why: it was just some stupid doll. He didn't know the girl who had lost it. Still, seeing the toy lying there on the sand, alone and broken, he couldn't help but feel a little sad. How did the doll lose its arm, get its head twisted around?

Who cares? Peter told himself. *I'm being stupid. Christ, what's wrong with me?*

Cricket whined and started backing away from the mouldy, foul-smelling doll.

"Yeah, I know."

He scanned the beach for any other items that might have once belonged to a young girl. He saw nothing except white sand, some saltbush, the occasional clump of seaweed.

"Want to continue exploring, girl?"

Cricket barked once.

"Yeah, you're right. Promised I would catch some fish for dinner. Let's give it a go. But we need to find a better spot, away from that putrid thing."

He moved away from the doll. Even when he was far away and the doll was no longer in sight, the odd sense of loss remained.

He didn't know how he was going to catch fish without his spear gun. All he had was the stick Cricket had found. But then a whittled stick was all his dad had used. Whether ocean or freshwater body, his dad would manage to spear enough fish to last the entire holiday. Peter had always preferred the taste of marine fish: red snapper, mulloway, tailor. Those were the fishes he remembered best from his time camping on the New South Wales coast with his father. But he also remembered catching those fish was more difficult than catching the inland freshwater varieties. The times Dad had fished in the ocean waters had more to do with the warmth of the sun, the fresh ocean air, the Zen of the activity, rather than the abundance of fish he caught. For that, he turned away from the ocean and headed inland. Still, Peter figured he'd give it a go. If his dad had been able to spear fish in the ocean, then surely he could, too.

When he spied a sandbank about twenty metres off the shore, he stopped. "Here's a good spot," he said down to Cricket. He had vague memories of Dad mentioning sandbanks being a good place to snag some snapper, especially if the water was flat, docile. Something about the water washing over the sandbar creating a disturbance, dredging up the shellfish to the surface, which in turn enticed the fish.

"Good thing I kept this," Peter said as he slid the tapered stick from a sleeve of his backpack. "It's no spear gun, but it'll have to do. Wish me luck."

Cricket, panting, looked up at him with a blank expression.

"This is for you, too. I catch a big snapper and you'll be eating like a king tonight."

With stick in hand, Peter waded out into the ocean. The water by the shore was warm and lovely. In a short time the cold gripped him as he continued out farther, towards the sandbar that was just visible above the water. The water reached to his waist before it started to dip and soon, he was up on the long, narrow bank of sand, dripping saltwater from his shorts, the bottom of his shirt. Out here, the water had a muddy taint as the ocean gently washed over the bank. Although he could still see through the murkiness, enough to see if a large snapper swam by. He got into position with the spear angled towards the water. He stilled his body. Then started moving slowly, in circles, looking on either side of the bank for big, red fish.

———

Marcia lay on top of her sleeping bag and tried to read. But her mind kept wandering.

She put the book down when she realised she had read the same paragraph three times and still didn't know what was written. It was useless. Maybe she'd try again later when her mind wasn't so preoccupied.

It wasn't that she hated the book. She was enjoying *The Adventurers*; it was as engrossing—and naughty—as everyone said. She just found it hard to concentrate. The cicadas outside were loud and insistent, but the noise didn't bother her. It was hot inside the tent, but she had taken off her cover and was down to her bikini, and with the tent flap open, the breeze, gentle though it was, still cooled her down as it washed over her skin. The problem was, she couldn't stop thinking. Her mind ticked over about a multitude of things, but mostly she thought about Mark.

He was her best friend's husband. She knew he was off limits, and yet she couldn't stop thinking about him.

Nothing wrong with thinking, she told herself. *Peter's done a hell of a lot worse.*

All the same, she felt guilty. More so because she felt like she was betraying Carol. Peter's feelings be damned.

Mark was tall, muscular. He had shaggy dark hair, a full, healthy moustache. He was a suit and tie man like Peter, and was about the same age, but he was older somehow, more mature. He was more of a *man*. He fixed things around his house. Peter could screw in a light bulb, but beyond that, he was useless. Mark could build a deck, mend a fence, the roof. Many times, she had been over at Carol's when Mark was in fix-it mode, and she would furtively admire his strong, tanned back, his muscular chest shaded with just the right amount of hair. Even his sweat was sexy.

Her eyes fell on the egg. The big speckled egg sat on the floor of the tent by her side of the bed. Just sat there, doing nothing except incubating, supporting, a life.

She moved her right hand onto her flat stomach. Left it there, the skin hot, a little sweaty. She concentrated on the movement as she breathed; up, down, like the lapping of the surf.

It had been a few weeks since she had the life taken out of her. It hadn't hurt as much as she feared, but it hadn't been a pleasant experience, either. The pain had been mild and dull. Afterwards, some spotting, some aching, but no worse than the average period pain. She had felt flat with bouts of crying.

Sometimes regretful, especially when the wine flowed, but mostly she was relieved. She wanted to be a mother someday, but not now, not the way their relationship was so fractured and strained. She wasn't even sure she wanted the father to be Peter.

Peter the Cheater.

Peter the Distant.

Peter, who most of the time treated her like a maid, a second-class citizen, in her own house. Peter, who would rather drink with his mates or slink off to cheap motel rooms with Freda the secretary, or some other bimbo he picked up at the pub, than spend time with her. Peter with the often-fiery temper.

She couldn't bring a child into such a world; one starved of unconditional love and respect. She had to do it. Had to make the choice.

Now Mark, he'd make a good father. He was a good provider and treated Carol with respect. He was devoted to Carol and had never once cheated.

At least, not that Marcia was aware. Carol had never spoken of any affairs, or even suspicions of one. And Carol told her everything.

Would Mark make an exception with me? she wondered, as her body flushed with heat.

She had caught him looking at her on more than one occasion. Looks that suggested he saw her as more than just a friend. She was sure he was attracted to her. If she wanted to, she could have him.

Give Peter back a taste of his own medicine. See how he liked it.

Still gazing at the egg, Marcia's hand snaked down her stomach towards her groin. She slipped her hand under the bathers, continued over her mound, stopping when she touched flesh.

She drew in a breath.

The large speckled egg faded and then disappeared entirely

as she closed her eyes and thought of Mark. Strong, handsome Mark.

———

The day was really starting to heat up. Peter had chugged the second of the beers he had packed, but he was still thirsty, still teeming with sweat. Cricket was panting, her shiny, brown coat looking leathery under the sun.

"I think we should find some shade, find a pond or something," Peter said as he trudged through the sand. Cricket padded alongside, looking in desperate need of a drink. Maybe he'd have better luck spearfishing in the streams and lakes inland. He hadn't caught anything out in the ocean. He saw plenty of fish, looked like snapper, big ones, but whenever he stabbed at them with the stick he missed, was too slow, and the fish sped away. He remained out there on the sandbank for a good twenty minutes before the sun grew too hot, and the frustration grew too potent. The failure stung like the sweat that continually dripped into his eyes.

They needed to get out of the blaring sun, and maybe, just maybe, he'd spear something in one of the freshwater bodies.

From his days camping with Dad, he remembered numerous freshwater bodies scattered throughout the bush. Often Dad would take him inland, away from the ocean, and at a lake or stream, spear in hand, he'd catch Estuary Perch or Bass, even yabbies, although Dad usually left the latter to Peter. Peter, not nearly as proficient a fisher as Dad, mostly spent his time dangling meat from a string tied to a stick and sitting by the banks of a dam, would usually snag a yabby or two during the week-long holiday.

Peter smiled at the memories of fishing with his dad. But the smile soon fell away as he remembered his failure, the embarrassment like a slap to the face, stinging his pride all over again.

Surely, he'd be able to snag something. Even if it was just some yabbies. Regardless of his fishing success, he wanted to head back soon. He was aching to head out on the surfboard, especially now the day was warm and beginning to get blowy, the surf starting to come up. Have something to drink, eat. See what the missus was up to. No doubt she had more complaining to do. After lunch, he'd go for a surf.

The beach curved. As they rounded the bend, Cricket began barking. Peter was looking out at the ocean, at the waves swelling and then breaking, the foamy water coating the wet sand before being sucked back in. "What is it?" he asked, absently.

He noticed that Cricket had stalled. Alert, standing on all fours, she was looking inland. The bluffs were becoming higher, the vegetation dense. Peter halted. "What?" Cricket yapped once more. He looked up and saw smoke drifting from the tops of the trees about a hundred metres away. The smoke rose up into the sky in a thin trail of grey, sullying the otherwise perfect sheet of blue.

"What the hell?"

Peter felt a sudden rush of anger. He pulled the binoculars from his bag and aimed them towards the patch of woods in which the smoke was emanating. He saw nothing, just trees and shrubs. He lowered the binoculars, turned, and spat to the sand.

"Looks like we're not the only inhabitants," he said down to Cricket.

He felt cheated. This was his beach, his slice of paradise. He didn't want to share it with anyone else.

"Come on, girl. Let's go check it out."

Looping the binoculars around his neck, he snatched up his bag. Rifled through his backpack until he found both shoes. With an unwarranted amount of animosity, he pulled on his blue Adidas sneakers and, as he stalked across the beach towards the bluff, he wished he had brought along his spear gun. Be good having a weapon, just in case. Something better than a mangy stick. Never knew who you might meet out here. Not everyone who craved the privacy and isolation of Moondah was as friendly as he was.

———

Marcia's mind conjured up all kinds of images. Mostly they were of Mark. Sometimes Peter appeared, but always in a submissive role. In those, she humiliated him by making him watch her and Mark. Or she made him do stuff to her that he never would do in real life. Peter was strictly a missionary guy. Very occasionally from behind. He liked it when she pleasured him, but he never went down and gave her any pleasure. In her mind, Mark did. Oh yes, Mark most certainly pleasured her.

She panted and moaned. Her skin, flushed, was slick with perspiration. She kept her pants and top on, and while her right hand was busy below, she slipped her left under the bikini top and fondled her breasts.

The whirring of the cicadas barely registered. If the birds squawked, she didn't hear them. She was lost in her fantasy.

She imagined Mark coming to her house when Peter was at work, unannounced, not invited. He grabbed her the moment she answered the door. Like a brute, some primitive force, he picked her up and carried her up to her bedroom. The same bedroom she shared with Peter. He threw her down, not too forcefully, but with passion, and then, without talking, he pulled off her pants, her underwear, and put his face down there.

Once he had done that, he stripped off, pushed her legs up, and entered her.

The intensity grew, spreading through her like a fireball.

Close. So damned close.

Marcia whimpered. Her body shivered even though it felt pulsating with fire.

Breaking through the fantasy, drowning out her heavy

breathing, came the mournful wailing. For a disorientating moment, Marcia thought the sound had come from her own mouth, but she hadn't quite reached that point. When she realised the sound had come from beyond, she stopped, withdrew her hand from her groin, took her hand away from her breast, and sat up. Too fast, evidently, as her head started to spin, and she sat there, still panting, waiting for the dizziness to pass.

The horrible moaning continued; plaintive, sounding human-like. It carried on the wind, through the campsite, piercing Marcia's body, causing cold shivers, echoing through her head.

She put her hands to her ears to try to block out the noise, but that didn't help. If anything, it made things worse. She had trapped the wailing. It was like the noise was inside *her*.

Finally, the wailing stopped. Marcia sat there, all fire doused with icy water, the echoes of the creature like an imprint that took a long time to fade.

———

"It's okay, girl. Nothing to worry about."

The ugly bleating sound had stopped, but Cricket was still spooked. She stood among the shady woods, looking back towards the ocean. Her ears were pricked, her tail down.

"Come on, Cricket." Peter continued walking.

Cricket turned around and trotted forward.

Peter didn't understand why the sound so unnerved Cricket. Sure, it was odd and a little unsettling, but it was probably just a whale or maybe a dugong, some sea creature. A mating call, perhaps. Nothing for land dwellers to be concerned about.

Peter was more concerned with the interlopers. The land dwellers who had intruded upon his land. He trekked through the scrub with caution. Every so often he gazed through the binoculars, but nothing yet showed in the distance.

When he started smelling smoke, he stopped. Looked again through the binoculars. This time, he saw something. Through the trees, past what looked like a freshwater lake, he saw colour, unnatural items: tents, a folding table, a white camper van. He heard voices, faint, but unmistakably human.

Suddenly Cricket took off.

"Hey!" Peter cried in a hushed but forceful voice. "Come back here!"

But Cricket wasn't listening. She bounded through the heavy scrub, in the direction of the stranger's campsite.

Shit!

He took off after her. Charging through the scrub, he felt on the verge of tripping and falling on his face. More than some bruises and scratches, he didn't want to alert the campers of his presence. He wanted to remain unseen, spy on them, and see who they were. But his presence would surely be compromised the way Cricket was bounding towards them.

He couldn't understand Cricket's behaviour. Cricket was usually a wary mutt, scared of anything unfamiliar, including people she didn't know. Now, all of a sudden, she felt the urge to run over to some strangers.

Soon, he saw her true reason for taking off and galloping through the bush.

When he caught up with her, he found her by the small lake, lapping at the water. So definitely fresh water. Out of breath, mouth dry, Peter considered joining Cricket. The water wasn't exactly pristine, but it looked clear enough, and was probably lovely and cold. It was cooler out of the direct sunlight, but it was still humid even in the bush, and after the run, he was roasting and raining sweat. He dipped in a hand. It was indeed lovely and cool. He splashed water over his neck, his arms, and on his face.

Sufficiently cooled, he straightened. Over on the other side of the lake, a black swan glided across the surface. A mother duck pulled her train of ducklings. Breaking the relative peace, he heard shouting close by. A male's voice, booming through the woods.

"... too soft on her! Christ, we came here to spend time in the outdoors, not to sit in the goddamned tent!"

"Just leave her alone!"

A female's voice, not as loud but still full of tense anger; shrill, quivering.

Peter raised the binoculars and took a look. He saw a man wearing Bermuda shorts and a colourful shirt. He was a bear of a man, about ten or fifteen years older than Peter, with a thick moustache below a fat nose. His round face was red. Peter moved his view a short way across the campsite to the woman. She also wore shorts, a loose-fitting blouse, was a lot shorter than the man, and had long, wavy blonde hair. As the two continued to argue, the man appeared in the frame. He hurried past the woman. She fled after him. Grabbed him by one of his thick, hairy arms. "Frank, leave her!"

The man whirled around and smacked the woman in the face with a fierce backhand. Peter heard the slap, even at this distance; it sounded almost like the crack of rifle-fire (or the snap of a spear being shot out of a gun). The woman staggered backwards and tumbled to the ground.

She sat there, holding her face. Peter finally saw the woman properly. She was plain-looking, middle age, with a flushed face that was teary and smudged with dirt; or what he took to be dirt, but might have been old bruises.

The man shook his head and continued stalking towards a small one-man tent on the edge of the clearing.

He disappeared inside.

The woman got up, took a few steps forward, but stopped short of the entrance of the tent. Peter heard the man's voice. Mostly low mutterings of indecipherable words, except for when he yelled: "Get out!" and: "Don't you say no to me!"

Soon the man emerged from the tent, body hunched, and face creased. "I give up!" he bellowed. He stalked towards the fire, picked up a stick from the woodpile and began poking the fire with force. Sparks flew. Peter flashed across the campsite in time to see the woman duck into the tent.

Something familiar about them, Peter thought as he lowered the binoculars.

Finished drinking, Cricket jumped into the lake. At the sudden intrusion, the swan took flight, the ducklings and their mother scattered, frightened by the splashing.

"Cricket," Peter muttered.

Cricket dog-paddled, what looked like a grin on her face. She loved the water. And the coolness must have been heaven for her. The duck quacked on the far shore and soon the scattered ducklings joined their mother.

Peter caught movement through the trees.

He looked up. The man from the campsite was moving towards him. He still held the stick. About twenty paces away, he stopped.

"Hello," the man called, voice deep.

Peter, armed only with a pair of binoculars, which he kept behind his back, held up his free hand. "Hi there. My dog was hot and decided to take a swim."

Cricket paddled back to shore, hopped out, and shook. Peter turned away as water sprayed.

The man laughed politely. "Well, it's a hot one, that's for sure."

Peter turned back around. His clothes had been sprinkled with water thanks to Cricket. "You camping around here?" He didn't want to let on he had been spying, or even that he had heard the man and his wife arguing.

"Just back there." The man, Frank, hooked a thumb behind. "Camping with my wife and kid."

Peter nodded. "Sorry if my dog bothered you. Has the social grace of a... well, a dog."

Frank smiled. "Not at all. I heard the splashing, the ducks, thought I'd take a gander and see what all the fuss was about."

Peter saw the strain on Frank's face; the painted smile, the anger still simmering behind the eyes.

"Well, better get back." Peter made to leave, but Frank said, "You camping around here?"

Peter hesitated. "Yeah, about twenty minutes back that way."

"You look hot. Want to come over and have a drink?"

Peter swallowed at the mention of a drink. Saliva slithered down his throat, thick and slow. "Thanks, but I wouldn't want to impose."

"Don't be silly. Be good to have another bloke to talk to. I'm surrounded by females, and you know how that can be."

Peter smiled back. "Yeah, I do."

"I have beer, softies, whatever you like."

"That does sound good. Been wandering around for over an hour, so I could use a cold one."

"Camp's just through these trees. I'm Frank."

Peter nearly said, "Yeah, I know." But he caught himself and said, "Peter." He started forward. Cricket hesitated. "Come on, girl."

She looked up at him. He couldn't read doggy minds, but he knew Cricket as well as any human, and to him she looked wary, like how she acted around the mouldy doll.

"Come on," Peter said, voice stern.

Finally, Cricket started walking. She padded forward, slowly, like a kid being made to go to school or the dentist.

"She a female?" Frank said as Peter drew closer.

Peter nodded.

"Figures. Stubborn, like the rest of 'em."

Peter smiled. "Yeah."

———

The fire was hot, the beer cold. Despite the searing temperature of the day, the campsite was well shaded, so it wasn't stifling being near the fire. Both men stood by the fire-pit clasping their cans of beer beneath the shade of a gum, close enough to feel the flames but not so close as to be roasted.

The site was smaller than his and Marcia's, the tangled brush closer, giving the place a sense of claustrophobia. But it was nearer the beach, the bluff within spitting distance, the surf a lot louder. On the opposite end of the campsite, at the back of the larger of the two tents, Peter saw a road leading through the woods. The track was mostly grass; the tyre ruts were barely visible, and it looked narrower and less used than the one leading to his campsite.

"How'd you find this place?" Peter asked.

"Friend of mine told me about it. Used to be a surfer, but he... well, he doesn't surf anymore. Told me about it a while ago, said it was a good spot if you want to be left alone. Difficult to find from the highway, hard to spot from the beach. Here, you're essentially invisible." Frank took a good slug of beer.

"It is private."

"No one to hassle you."

"Is it even marked?"

Frank grinned. "No. You have to know where to look. Helen, my wife, was scared when we arrived last night. Thought I was trespassing on private property, or in the wrong area. I showed her."

"You arrived last night?"

"Yeah, late. We got going later than I'd hoped. Bloody women, there's always something else to pack. And then traffic was a nightmare. Didn't get here till... oh, probably sometime after midnight."

Peter glanced at the camper. He had a flashback to last night, of almost running into the back of the white camper. The blonde-haired girl in the back. The man and woman arguing up front.

Were these the same people? The same white camper? The people last night were driving a white camper. Frank looked similar to the man, and the wife had wavy blonde hair, like the woman in the passenger seat.

And Frank and his wife were fond of arguing, much like the couple in the camper.

Christ, what were the odds?

Peter must have chuckled, or at least made some kind of noise.

"What's so funny?"

Peter looked over at Frank. "Huh?"

"You snorted, as if you just thought of a joke."

Frank was smiling, but it was lopsided, and his small, dark eyes, creased from the smile, still carried some residual anger.

"Did I? Oh, well, I guess you just reminded me of me and my wife. We got stuck in traffic, too, and didn't get to the beach till late. Slept in the car, made camp this morning."

"Is that right? Hell, maybe we passed each other on the highway."

Peter cleared his throat. "Yeah, maybe." He downed more cold beer. It felt wonderful.

"So, what is it you do, Peter?"

Frank picked up a stick, looked like the same one as earlier, and with his free hand, started poking at the fire.

"I'm a suit and tie guy. Boring, really. Work in advertising."

Frank huffed. Sparks jumped up from the pit. "So, you lie for a living."

"I said I was an ad man, not a lawyer."

Frank laughed a full belly laugh.

"Shit. You're not a lawyer, are you?"

"Me? Christ no." Frank's laughter died. "I worked in..." He started poking at the logs harder. Flames danced, smoke drifted sideways, towards the two men and also towards

Cricket, who was sitting close to Peter's legs, so close she was touching.

"I was a customs broker. I was retrenched last week." Frank took a violent swig from his beer. "This country's going down the toilet. Fraser bringing in all those fucking boat people. He'll turn this country into a second Asia before long. Which means fewer jobs for the Aussies, more people like me out of work because those Gooks will work for less pay."

Peter suddenly felt uncomfortable. He had voted for Malcolm Fraser; thought the man was doing a decent job. But he kept quiet.

"Sorry, Peter. Didn't mean to turn political. Nothing kills a party faster than talking about politics."

Is this was this was? Peter thought. A party?

He was just having a quick cold one before heading back. "It's all right, Frank."

"I'm just... still raw from being sacked, you know? What's a man worth without his job? That's a man's role in life, to provide for his family. Without that he's..."

Frank sighed, staring into the fire.

"I haven't even told Helen. Far as she knows, I'm just taking some time off work."

Peter looked sideways at Frank. Up close, he appeared older than initial impressions. Both his moustache and his short hair were flecked with grey, and his face was marked with lines, his hands with spots. If Peter had to guess, he'd put Frank at mid-fifties, though he looked like he was either ignorant of his age or trying in vain to make himself appear younger, trimmer; his shirt was maybe two sizes too small, so his gut stretched like a dead animal left out in the sun to bloat. And Peter now saw the tiny red veins like miniature rivers of blood that cut across his nose and cheeks. The vessels seemed to disappear up his face before reappearing in his eyeballs.

He looked like a broken man, a haunted man. A man on the verge of losing it. Peter had seen similar haunted features in his father, once the cancer had taken firm hold and was eating away at him from the inside. Not long before he died, it began to show on the outside, the cancer having clawed its way to the surface. It revealed itself in his thin, papery skin the colour of spoiled milk; in his hair, like tufts of cotton wool, having lost all colour and vitality; in his eyes, bloodshot and staring at the darkness, knowing he was close to death.

Peter didn't think Frank was dying from cancer, but he was suffering all the same. Something was eating at him from the inside. Something toxic.

"Sorry to hear."

Frank nodded, slowly. "Yeah, well, it'd just be another thing to fight about. I wanted this weekend to be good. I wanted it to be fun, do something special together as a family. Christ, I should have known better."

Frank finally turned away from the fire, but held onto the stick, its pointed end charred and dusted with ash. "You have any kids, Peter?"

"No. No, I don't."

Frank made a face like he'd just sucked on a lemon. "Count your blessings. You think you've raised them right, but then they turn around and disappoint you. Kids are nothing but a pain, and that's the truth. Anyone who tells you different is lying. I bring my family all the way down from the city to this beautiful spot surrounded by nature, and what do you think Jessica wants to do? Play out in the water? Build sandcastles? Roam around the bush, exploring? No. She wants to lie in her tent and read." Frank shook his head. "Christ, you can do that at home. Kid's too pale, too thin. She needs to get out in the sun, get some fresh air. But you think she listens to me? Her father? Not a chance. She hates the bush, apparently. Everything scares her. Says she wants to go home. Can you believe that?"

Yes, Peter could.

"Just a fun weekend, that's all I wanted. A last holiday before..."

Frank looked past Peter. Peter followed his gaze to the single tent. His wife was coming out. She stopped outside the tent and gawked at Peter. Even from where Peter stood, he could see the dark smudge on her face, that her eyes were red and glistening. She turned her eyes to her husband, and then, without speaking, she walked over to the larger tent and disappeared inside.

"Damn her," Frank said, draining his beer. "Always sides with the daughter. Never backs me up, never on my side. No, she lets Jessica do whatever she wants. She's too soft on the kid."

Peter finished his beer. He crumpled the can.

"You done?"

Peter nodded.

Frank took the can off Peter, lugged the two empty cans behind him into the bush. "Benefit of camping in such an isolated spot; nobody can see your sins." He winked.

"Anyway, thanks for the beer. I needed it. I should be heading back; missus is probably wondering where I am."

"You're welcome to stay for a second. Wish I could offer you something harder, but sink enough ale and it does the job."

"There's a pub about fifteen minutes up the road. It's where I got my rum."

"You have rum back at your camp?"

"Sure."

Frank licked his lips. "That'd go down a treat. A pub, you say? Must have missed it. Maybe I'll go and buy me some real booze. I'll need it with what I have to deal with this weekend. Sure you won't stay for another beer?"

"Thanks, but I wanted to get some surfing in before the weather turns to shit."

"It is supposed to get bad later. You said you were camped about twenty minutes that way?"

"That's right."

"Maybe I'll stop by later. Have a taste of that rum."

"Of course."

Cricket started to whine. "Quiet," Peter said down to her. But she continued. She stood up and started making a move as if to say: hurry up and let's leave.

Frank smiled one of his sad, dejected smiles. "They never stop complaining, do they?"

———

Marcia awoke to a shadow standing over her. She must have sensed somebody inside the tent. Or maybe the person had made a noise when entering, alerting her sleeping mind; either way, she was awake and looking up at a dark figure standing just inside the tent, the sun bright behind them. Tall, dark, the shadow just stood there, unmoving, silent.

She lay frozen on top of her sleeping bag, body uncomfortably sweaty, the tent oppressive, airless.

The shadow stepped forward. Marcia's body tensed.

"Hi."

The shadow turned from a dark shape into a person with features, and she saw it was Peter. She relaxed a little. She sat up.

"Must have fallen asleep. What time is it?"

"Nearing midday."

Peter stopped by her side of the bed. He looked down at her. His eyes roamed over her body. Dressed only in the bikini, Marcia suddenly felt naked, and she wanted to cover up.

Peter sniffed. A look came over him, like a dog having sniffed out a bone.

"You have fun exploring?" Marcia said, unable to hide the slight quaver in her voice.

"I guess. Didn't catch any fish, sorry."

Peter dropped to his knees. He reached forward to her chest and slipped a hand beneath her top. He clutched her right breast and started fondling, roughly.

He smelled of sweat and beer and his touch made her squirmy and cold, even though it was humid inside the tent. She pulled away. His hand jumped out of her top. She rolled away, and sitting with her back to him, adjusted her top.

"Sorry," she said, even though she wasn't. It just seemed the thing to say.

"Yeah, okay," Peter sighed.

"Doctor Hargreaves said it could take a couple of weeks for me to... feel normal again."

"It's been two months."

"Has it?"

"I want to, Mars. Help me understand. Is it still painful? Do you feel... I dunno, broken inside?"

"I just... it's hard to explain. I guess I just don't have those feelings at the moment."

"For me?"

Marcia, still with her back to Peter, stood up. She couldn't look at him when she lied. "No, for anyone. I'm sure it's just temporary."

"I hope so."

"Want me to make you some lunch?"

"Not really hungry. Maybe later."

Marcia wasn't hungry, either. The thought of food churned her stomach. "Okay, maybe later," she said, and picking up her cheesecloth cover, she headed for fresh air, for open space.

"What's this?"

Stopped just before the entrance, Marcia looked over her shoulder. Peter was holding the egg.

"Where did it come from?"

"I found it, just sitting on the ground. I thought it looked interesting."

"Looks like an eagle's egg."

Marcia slipped on the cheesecloth cover and stepped outside, leaving Peter fondling the egg. The sun hit her like a slap, stinging her eyes, but the wind was wonderful, the air that smelled of the sea more welcome than the hot plastic of the tent. It was good to be out in the open air, away from the confines of the tent, away from Peter, but her head was pounding, probably from dehydration, being cooped up in a hot box for hours, so she started for the truck. She got halfway there when she stopped. She remembered her bag with the medicine was no longer in the Patrol but rather in the tent. She didn't want to go back in there; could still feel Peter's clammy hand on her skin. Her stomach roiled, and her head throbbed harder at the memory of his touch. Instead of heading back into the tent, she continued to the truck and grabbed her sunglasses from the glove box. She'd take some aspirin later. For now, shielding her eyes from the glare would have to be enough.

Peter came out of the tent, wetsuit clutched in his hand. He started stripping off his clothes. When he was down to his underwear, Marcia looked away. Still so much a boy in many ways; his body was pale, hairless. Formless, really, with hardly any muscle definition. She had found it attractive, once. Athletic; not the way a swimmer or a footy player was athletic, more like a long-distance runner, but sexy all the same. Now, it was like looking at a stranger. A stranger she felt no strong attraction to.

He stepped into the suit and zipped up.

"Going for a surf?" she said, turning back.

"Brilliant deduction, Holmes."

He walked over to her. With the sunglasses on, he couldn't tell she wasn't looking at him.

"Why don't you come in for a splash? Day's hot, but the water's nice and cool."

"Maybe. But I have a splitting headache, and the sun will only make it worse."

"The water will help clear it up. Come on, you're always saying you want to give surfing a try."

"No, *you're* always saying I should give it a try."

"And? Now's a good a time as any."

"Maybe I'll come down. I could do with a swim, at the very least."

"Thatta girl."

"I'm not saying I'll try surfing, just that I'll see how I feel."

Peter reached up and started untying the surfboard from the roof rack. Once he had it down, he stabbed one end into the sandy earth and then looked skyward. "Report said a storm is on the way, but still looks clear to me. Hopefully, the storm will bypass us. Starting to get windy, though. Which is a good thing."

Peter looked back down. He clamped the board under an arm. "You coming?"

"Give me a minute to get ready. I'll meet you down there."

Peter nodded.

Instead of leaving, he stood there, as if mulling something over. "There's a family camped a little way up the beach. About twenty minutes from here."

"Okay."

"Husband and wife, little girl. I think they're the ones we almost hit. Remember? Last night, almost ran into the back of that camper?"

"I remember. You spoke with them?"

"A little. Seem nice enough. I was surprised to see them. I thought we had the place to ourselves."

"This is a public beach. Isn't it?"

"That's right."

"Then you shouldn't be surprised."

"No. Not surprised. Disappointed, I guess."

"You don't own this land, Peter. Other people are allowed to camp here."

"I know that Mars. Christ, that's not what I'm saying." Peter shook his head. "Forget it. I'll meet you down there."

He stalked away. His four-legged shadow, who was preoccupied with something by the table, stopped what she was doing when she noticed him leaving, and took off after him. Soon, they were both out of sight.

Can't go two minutes without fighting, Marcia thought with bitter sadness. *What's wrong with us?*

The shit between them was piled too high. That was the problem. Too much pain and resentment, too much left unsaid.

Feeling like something hot and heavy was pressing down on her, stomach unsettled along with the headache, she trudged towards the tent to take some aspirin and to gather some things together for the beach. As she passed the table, she noticed the chicken. Bloody water covered the tabletop and was dripping onto the ground, forming puddles of pink chicken juice.

She touched the bird, which, up until a short time ago, had been completely frozen. It was completely thawed. Sure, it was a hot day, but the table was in shade. And even with the temperature soaring, a bird this big should take till the afternoon, at least, to thaw out.

She shrugged. Must have been only partially frozen when she took it out of the icebox. Although she recalled it feeling like a brick of ice when she handled it this morning.

She picked it up and placed it in the fridge in the back of the car to keep cool. Then she rinsed her hands with water and headed for the tent. Just before stepping back into the hot box, a bird screeched. The sound was sharp and loud, causing Marcia to flinch. She heard fluttering and felt the wind rush by her.

She whirled around, but the bird, or whatever it was, had gone. She gazed up, saw nothing except clouds that looked like dirty cotton wool in the sky.

She had a flashback of earlier, the spear shooting by her face. A shiver ran through her. No spear this time. No anything she could see. But the unnerving sensation of a close call, of something sharp and deadly almost ending her life, stayed with her as she entered the tent.

God, I fucking hate this place.

3

Marcia started down the sandy slope. The wind had kicked up; an angry, almost violent gust. She held down her wide-brim straw hat so it wouldn't blow away. Her cheesecloth cover flailed like the wind was trying to tear it off. And she kept a firm grip on her tote bag.

She made it down the hill and onto the beach, where the wind was less fierce thanks to the bluffs to the back and the cliffs over to her right. Peter was belly-down on his surfboard, about ten metres out, paddling with his arms. When he saw her, he waved. She waved back. Then, as if to show off, he jumped up, steadied himself, and rode a wave to the shallows. He stepped off, picked up his board and jogged over.

"See that?" he said between breaths. "Not bad for someone who hasn't surfed in about a decade."

Marcia knew next to nothing about surfing, so she was no judge of competency. But she nodded and said, "You're a natural."

"I don't know about that. But it sure is a lot of fun. You wanna have a go?"

She wrinkled her nose. "Think I'll just sit and read and watch for a bit."

"Water's lovely and cool. Just come in for a swim?"

"Maybe later."

Peter's shoulders dropped. His eyes narrowed. She could tell he wanted to say something, probably something biting, but instead he said, "Fine."

He turned and jogged back into the ocean. At waist level, he slapped down his board, flopped forward, and started paddling out.

Marcia set her bag on the sand. Within was a towel, her book. Chances were, only one of those items would get any real use. She thought about placing the towel down, but with the wind it'd only get blown away whenever she wasn't on it, so she decided to leave the towel bundled inside the bag. The sand was soft enough.

She was about to fetch her book and attempt to read, when she noticed Cricket on the beach. The dog had discovered something. She was sniffing at it, then jumping back, then moving forward again, tail wagging.

Marcia looked out at the ocean. Peter was a way out, board slicing against the water as he continued paddling. She looked back at Cricket. The dog was rolling around in the sand. She sighed. "What are you doing, you stupid dog?"

She set down her unopened bag, marched over to Cricket. She scrunched up her face at the sight of the brown Labrador playing with a dead seagull. The bird looked newly dead. There was no smell. Still, Marcia thought it disgusting.

"Get out of it, Cricket."

At the sound of her voice, the dog stopped rolling, but didn't get up. Feathers were scattered over the sand. Some were stuck to Cricket's damp, sandy fur. The bird's black pebble eyes were staring. She couldn't see any blood on the creature, so she figured Cricket hadn't taken the bird down.

"Cricket, get up."

Cricket, not normally one to obey Marcia, as she was Peter's dog, did as she was told. But she didn't leave the bird alone completely. She continued to paw at it. As she did, knocking against a limp wing, Marcia saw how the gull's head jiggled, like it was held onto its neck by string. She felt a wave of nausea jet from her stomach into her throat.

"Come on Cricket, get away..."

The plaintive sound she'd been hearing since before dawn rang out again, loud and horrible. The wailing hurt her ears, jarred her head, and shook her body. Cricket stopped pawing at the gull. Her ears pricked up; she steeled her gaze towards the ocean. Suddenly, she took off, galloping towards the water's edge. Then the dog stood there, just shy of the sea, and started barking. Her barking was nearly completely swallowed by the overwhelming sound of the wailing. But Marcia could tell it wasn't a playful bark, but one of fear, a warning.

While the inhuman crying continued, Marcia looked to where Cricket was aiming her barking. In the short time since arriving at the beach, clouds had collected in the sky, masking the sun, turning the world grimmer. The ocean looked like dark blue and silver mud had been disturbed and had floated to the surface. The ocean had turned sinister and looking out at the seemingly endless sea of murky, choppy waters, she realised she could no longer see Peter. Before, she could see him lying on his surfboard, the bright colours of the board and his dark wetsuit-covered form stark against the bright blue water. Now, there was only the water, a giant mouth of deep blue with lips of foamy white. Christ, had Peter been swallowed by the ocean?

"Peter!" Marcia called, her voice mute against the strong winds, the ghost-like wailing. "Peter!" she cried again, scanning the ocean, seeing just the waves rolling in, smacking against one another.

Soon the wailing faded, leaving her ears ringing, leaving her with an awesome sadness. She was sure she had lost Peter. That she'd find him washed ashore tomorrow, water-logged, body having been feasted upon by sea creatures; dead.

No, don't think that. He's okay, I just can't see him, that's all.

Marcia saw a dark shape moving through the water. She thought it was just the shadow of a cloud, but it was right where Cricket was looking, where the dog was spewing her deep, anxious barking. The massive shape glided through the water, darker than the deep ocean, about the size of a large truck, and she was certain it wasn't a shadow, but some creature, and fear seized her hard; real fear, similar to how she felt when the doctor confirmed what she already knew—that she was pregnant.

"Peter!" she wailed, forcing out his name through a tight throat and dry mouth. "Peter, where are you?"

She lost track of the shadow, the shape blending in with the dark water and the other murky shadows. When Cricket stopped barking and started to whine, the sound reminding her of the wailing creature, Marcia's fear increased.

The wind continued to blow, hot and briny. Was that blood she could smell, along with the salt water? She frantically searched for Peter. She caught sight of something on the shore about twenty metres away, an object about the size of a man. The object on the sand was unmoving.

Oh no!

She hurried over to it. Saw as she neared not Peter's prostrate body but instead his surfboard. There was no blood on the board, no chunks missing, which she took as good signs. But still, no sign of Peter.

"Peter!" she yelled, but the wind just threw her hoarse voice back in her face.

She ran a hand through her hair, a hand that was shaking. She realised she had lost her hat, but only gave that a moment's thought.

She gazed down at the water that lapped at the shore like it was trying to reach her, trying to wrap its cold tongue around her legs and pull her in. Maybe she should go in to try to find Peter? She wasn't a strong swimmer, and the surf looked intimidating, with its high waves like mammoth rolls of dark blue carpet, before the carpet exploded as it crashed to the surface. She imagined the waves were giant chopping blocks that cut you in half if you got caught by one of the silver blades.

Stop it! Stop thinking such silly thoughts. It's not carpet or a chopping block. It's just water. You can go in. You'll be fine. Peter needs you.

He hadn't needed her recently, the thought came to her. He hadn't been there for her, just like she hadn't been there for him. There were days when she thought: if one was on fire, the other wouldn't bother pissing on them, let alone dousing them with water to put out the flames.

Standing by the water's edge, feet sinking into the damp sand, she wondered: would Peter jump into the ocean to save her if she was in trouble? Or would he decide it was too late, she was probably already dead, why risk his own life?

She didn't move. Just stared out at the ocean, wondering. Up the beach Cricket was silent. She had taken the plunge and had at least gotten her paws wet. The dog was up to her belly in the shallows, but because of either the strong waves or fear, she didn't go any deeper.

Suddenly, Cricket started barking. The wind carried it across to Marcia. It was the kind of barking Cricket did when Peter arrived home from work: high-pitched, happy. Marcia looked at the water close to Cricket, and she saw a shape rising from the ocean.

As the shape waded out, pushing against the incoming tide, she recognised it as her husband. She raced over. He came out drenched and looking pale, but otherwise he appeared unhurt. Without considering her actions, she wrapped her arms around him.

Cricket yapped and jumped, glad to have her master back, and then took off, bounding onto dry land.

"What is it, Mars?"

Marcia's feet were getting wet, the water cold and prickly, but at that moment, she didn't care.

"I thought... I couldn't see you... I thought you'd..."

Peter placed an arm around her. To her, it felt tentative, almost as if he didn't want to touch her. Realising what she was doing, realising she was giving him all of herself, she pulled back, embarrassed.

A quizzical look crossed Peter's dripping face. Almost a smirk.

"I'm okay," he said. "I got hit by a really big wave, the cord snapped, and I lost my board. I was scared for a bit, thought I might get pulled under and swept out to sea, but I managed to find my footing and found the surface. Hey, it's okay, Mars. You're pale. What's really wrong?"

He reached up to her face. Was about to either touch her or maybe remove some strands of hair that were stuck to her cheek, but she moved away, out of the water and onto the beach.

Peter followed. "Mars?"

"I'm okay," she said.

Even though she wasn't. She hated him. Not for scaring her, but for making her scared of losing him. As ridiculous as it was, she thought maybe he had done it on purpose, breaking the cord and pretending to almost drown just so she'd panic and realise how much she really still loved him and didn't want to lose him. It was just like something he'd do; something a child would do.

She stopped far from the water's edge, the heat of the sand familiar and warming. She gazed up at the bluffs. She wanted to continue walking, back to the campsite, back to the truck, and drive away.

Hands gripped her by her arms and turned her around.

"What is it, huh?" Peter's hold on her remained. He stared at her with both concern and amusement. "You thought I was gone? I was only in the water for a few seconds, ten at most."

"It felt longer than that. Anyway, it wasn't just that."

"What then?"

"I saw something... in the water."

Peter turned and looked back. He scanned the ocean. "What?" he said, facing her.

"I don't know."

"Probably just a cloud passing over the water."

"No, it wasn't. I saw something. Cricket saw it, too. You should've seen the way she acted. She was frightened. And then I couldn't see you..."

Peter smiled. It was a cocky smile. "And you were frightened too?"

She wanted to slap the smirk off his face. She was annoyed at herself for getting so carried away, for running up to him and showering him with affection. He didn't deserve it. It was just the moment, a momentary lapse of reason.

She shrugged. "It could've been a shark."

"Did you see a fin?"

She shook her head.

"The ocean can be deceiving. All the shadows, the murkiness, it can make you see things that aren't there."

"Maybe."

"Well, I'm sorry for giving you a scare."

He moved in for what Marcia assumed was a kiss, but she turned away. "Your surfboard's over there."

Peter slumped forward. "Okay. I wonder if I can re-tie the cord and go out for another swim. Although it's getting choppy out there. I think the storm will be here soon."

"Look, Peter, I don't think..."

Cricket started barking again.

The noise, sudden and intrusive, took Peter's attention away from Marcia and she wished the dog wasn't here. The animal was an annoyance, a distraction. The barking was incessant and exacerbated the pounding in her head, which, up until she lost sight of Peter, had almost disappeared. Now the headache was back and with it, a heavy weariness, and a queasy knot in her stomach.

"Christ, doesn't she ever stop?"

"She's a dog, Mars. It's what dogs do. I think she's found something."

Marcia sighed. "Probably another seagull."

"No, I don't think so." Peter squinted up the beach. "What is that?" he muttered.

Marcia looked past the surfboard to where Cricket stood yapping. Close by the dog lay something a lot bigger than a bird. Darker, too; dark blue, like a portion of the sea had plopped out and become solid. Peter started towards Cricket and the object. Marcia followed close behind.

"Cricket, enough!" Peter ordered.

When Cricket didn't stop, he yelled, "Cricket, shut up!"

This quieted the dog. She took a few steps back as the humans approached.

"What is that?" Peter said again.

Marcia didn't know. About the size of Cricket, the creature looked like a giant slug. A slug with flippers and a tail like a dolphin. Its head and one of its flippers were tangled in a plastic bag, masking most of its top.

Peter looked around, found a stick and with it, managed to push the bag, which looked old and faded, white with a hint of blue, up enough to uncover the creature's face. The thing had a bulbous snout, tiny eyes, and looked like a hairless dog or cow on the body of a dolphin.

"God. What is it?"

"Dunno." Peter squatted and studied the creature. "Looks like a baby seal."

"It's not a seal."

Peter didn't respond.

"Is it... dead?" Unlike the seagull, there was a smell emanating from the beast, but Marcia didn't know if that's the way it always smelled. It wasn't horrible, but it had the whiff of death about it.

"Yeah, I think so." He prodded the portly creature with the stick. The creature didn't move. "Looks pretty dead to me."

"Poor thing."

Whatever it was, it most likely drowned, the way it had been caught up in the bag. What a horrible way to go. Looking down at the creature, Marcia felt lightheaded. The world went hazy. Her gut squirmed.

She turned away, thinking she was going to throw up. She bent over, staring down at the sand, and took deep breaths. Soon the dizziness went away, though the queasiness remained.

"You okay?"

She shook her head. "I heard it again, before, when I thought something had happened to you."

"Heard what?"

"That noise. Like something crying. That horrible wailing." She straightened, faced Peter. "You didn't hear it?"

"No. Guess I was underwater at the time."

"Peter, do we have to stay here?"

"I am. I want to try to get in another quick surf. But you don't have to..."

"No, I mean here, this place. I want to go home."

Peter huffed. "Go home? We only just arrived."

"I don't like it here."

"Yeah, you've made that perfectly clear."

"It's not just me being a spoiled brat, or whatever it is you think of me. It's more than that. I don't get a good feeling about this place. It... scares me."

Peter half-grinned. "You just hate nature, that's all. Never been camping. You'll see, this time tomorrow, you'll be sad to leave. You just have to get used to the outdoor lifestyle. Give it a chance."

She'd never get used to this place. As vast and open as it was, she felt trapped and as she moved away from the dead animal, the notion that they weren't ever going to leave this place crossed her mind. It was a silly notion, just part of her general unease at being here, being around Peter. It wasn't true. They could leave anytime they wanted. She could leave anytime.

But the feeling of dread stayed with her, as gloomy and menacing as the clouds above.

Peter glanced once more at the sea creature, clicked his tongue, then stepped over to his surfboard.

"I'm heading back up," Marcia said. She was too unnerved to remain on the beach. There was too much death on the beach. "Maybe read or have a lie down."

"Suit yourself," Peter said.

"Just... be careful." Without glancing back at the dead animal, Marcia marched over to her bag, gathered it up and left the beach.

Peter took the cord in his hand. The way the cord was frayed at the end, it looked like it had been chewed on by some creature with razors for teeth. He couldn't believe it had snapped so easily. The wave that had knocked him down had been big, but not *that* big. Maybe it had rubbed on some jagged rocks on the ocean floor. Whatever had happened, there was enough length for him to re-tie it to the board.

He looked out at the ocean. The wind played with the water like a child playing with play dough: it squeezed and rolled and pulled and flattened the water. The waves grew high, only to crash down with an awesome, roaring din. He gazed at the dark waters, at the many shadows that were probably just clouds passing by. Probably.

He thought about how panicked Marcia had been, how certain she was that she had seen something in the ocean.

Maybe there had been something with him in the water, something with sharp teeth that had cut through the tether, causing him to crash.

The thought unnerved him and heading back out, plunging

into the depths and skimming the waves suddenly didn't seem so inviting.

He looked up at the overcast sky, looking like a dirty blanket, and then turned back to the ocean. The deep, deep ocean, murky and hiding god knows what beneath its stormy waters.

Screw it, he thought. *I've had enough surfing for one day.*

He dropped the broken cord, and clutching his board under an arm, walked away from the ocean and the lurking shadows.

———

"What do you think?"

Marcia, sitting near the fire, turned and looked at Peter. He held two potatoes in his hand. "Baked potatoes for dinner? Go well with the roast chicken."

Marcia shrugged. "Sure, whatever. I'm not that hungry."

Peter put the potatoes on the table. "Still have the headache?"

Marcia took a few beats to answer. "It's not too bad. But it's not that. I was serious before. Do we have to stay here another night?"

Peter sighed. "Christ, not this again."

"We leave now we could be home by ten, eleven o'clock." She hooked him with her gaze. Attempted to smile, but faltered. "I'll make it worth your while."

He wanted to believe her. But he could tell—her heart wasn't in it. Nor, he was certain, were her other parts. It was a desperate move by a scared woman. "Home is where I hang my dirty socks, love. We can do that just as well in the tent as in our bed."

"No, we can't. I'm serious, Peter. I want to go."

Peter grabbed the foil, tore off two bits, and started wrapping up the potatoes. "You want to pack up and leave on our first night?"

"Yes."

"But we have the fire, booze, hell, we even have marshmallows. We haven't even properly camped yet."

Marcia turned back to the fire. She hugged herself. "Forget it."

Peter looked skyward. The late afternoon sky was still soiled with grey clouds, but so far, the rain had held off. The wind had even died down, leaving a relatively calm and balmy, if overcast, start to the evening. The only bit of colour was an orange hue, just visible over the treetops, over in the west, heading inland. The dying rays of the sun Peter surmised. "I think we're going to be okay," he said, bringing the wrapped potatoes over to the fire. "Looks like the storm might pass us by. It's going to be a warm, dry night. It'll be great, you'll see."

Marcia glanced at the foil-wrapped potatoes. "You prick them?"

"Huh?"

"You need to pierce the skin or else they'll explode."

"Oh, right."

"I thought you've been camping before."

"Not for a long time, Mars. Christ, can't a guy make one little mistake without you jumping down his throat?"

"One little mistake?" Marcia muttered. "You've made more than one, and they've been plenty big."

"I heard that," Peter said, as he stepped back over to the table. He unwrapped the foil, found a fork, and started stabbing at the raw potatoes. The table shook, but Cricket, sleeping a short distance away between the fire and the tent, didn't move. She was tuckered out from a long and busy day. It felt oddly satisfying stabbing the potatoes with the fork. The white flesh was firm but giving, juice flecked out, like white blood, and soon he had made tiny openings all over both potatoes. He wrapped them back up, stalked back to the fire, and dumped the shiny round balls into the coals. Then, using the shovel, he covered them with more hot coals.

"There. No fear of them exploding now."

"My hero."

"What did you do with the chicken?"

"Put it back in the fridge."

He started towards the truck.

"Mind grabbing the rum and some cups while you're up?"

"Gladly." At the back of the truck, he opened the portable fridge and took out the chook. The first thing that struck him was the smell: rancid. He stepped away and looked at the chicken under the dreary light. The bird was covered in a slimy, blue-green substance, a lot like the muck that was on the doll he found this morning.

"This chook's gone off," he called out.

Marcia looked over her shoulder. "What? It couldn't have."

He walked over to her. "Well, it has. In fact, it's gone bloody rotten. Look." He held it out.

"Ugh!" Marcia drew back and placed a hand over her nose. "It stinks."

"It's all mouldy. You must've left it out too long."

"No, I didn't," Marcia said, voice nasally. "I saw the chicken had thawed, so I put it straight into the fridge. It wasn't mouldy then."

"It is now."

"Maybe the fridge is broken."

"No, it's working just fine."

"Throw it out."

Peter dumped the rotten chicken into the rubbish bag. Then he wiped his hands on a towel, put the towel in the dirty washing bag. "Can't understand how it could have happened. If you say you put it in the fridge while it was still fresh, and the fridge is definitely working..." Peter walked back over to the fridge, opened it and stuck in a hand. His skin was met with cool air. "Weird. Well, guess we'll have to defrost the steak. Although that will take hours." He suddenly remembered the large egg Marcia found. A smile crept on his face. "Actually, I have a better idea. If we can't have chicken, then the next best thing..."

"Peter, we don't belong here!" Marcia exclaimed. "This place is... cursed."

Peter laughed. "Cursed? Come on, Mars. A little mould on the chicken and..."

"I'm not talking about the fucking chicken! That... thing in the surf..."

"Nothing. Just shadows. Or a dolphin."

"It wasn't a fucking dolphin, Peter. And that creature on the beach..."

"That's life, hon. Things die. Dead animals are always washing ashore."

"I just don't like it here. And if you still have even a bit of love left for me, you'd agree to pack up and leave." Marcia jumped up. She stormed over to the table, grabbed the bottle of rum from the box, a paper cup, and poured herself an almost full cup. She tipped some back, winced.

"You don't even like rum," Peter said, moving towards the tent.

"I do tonight."

As Marcia continued to down more rum, Peter ducked into the tent and looked around for the egg. He found it still on the floor next to Marcia's side of the bed. He picked it up. The thing was heavy and filled his palm. Still with a wry smile, he left the tent and wandered over to Marcia. She frowned over the top of the cup when she saw what he was holding.

"Wonder if you can eat eagle eggs."

Marcia lowered the cup, swallowed. "Disgusting."

"What? Might be delicious. A newly discovered delicacy."

"You're not serious?"

He set the egg on the table. Grinned at his wife. "Maybe. Maybe not."

Just then, he heard what sounded like flapping. High up. Just the sound of leaves fluttering in the wind, he figured.

Still sipping from the cup, Marcia stepped back to the fire.

"Take it easy with the rum," Peter said. "Leave some for me."

The noise grew louder. The flapping sounded close now, somewhere at the treetops. He gazed up at the deepening sky, saw nothing. Abruptly, the sound swooped down. He thought he caught movement out of the corner of an eye, but when he snapped around, saw only the cloud-choked sky, the trees, and the fluttering went away.

Not long after the sound faded, it came again. More cacophonous this time, like many wings beating.

The flapping noise grew until it sounded like a hundred birds all around them, surrounding the camp. The hair on his neck bristled, his skin prickled with fire. Marcia looked up, fear etched on her face. "What is...?"

An unholy screech drowned out the rest of her words.

Suddenly, there was a mass of feathers around Peter's face. He raised both arms as talons extended towards his eyes. Claws scratched at his skin. The bird squawked along with its avian brethren and then the talons went away, as did the feathers. But as quickly as it had retreated, the bird attacked again, this time with its beak.

The sound of feathers, of angry squawking, was thunderous in Peter's head. He thought he heard Marcia screaming, but he couldn't be sure the sound wasn't coming from the large bird. He tried batting the creature away, but the creature kept attacking. Every time he reached out, his hands caught the sharp ends of its beak or claws.

Then, as suddenly as it appeared, the bird flew away, up into the dark purple sky, and disappeared. Soon, all noise faded, until the flapping, the screeching, was a bad memory.

Marcia bounded over to him. "My god, are you all right?"

Peter looked at his arms, his hands. Remarkably, all the scratches were superficial. They hadn't even drawn blood. Somehow, he had come through the attack unharmed. He brushed off some black and white feathers caught on his shirt. "Yeah, I think so."

Marcia scanned the sky. The sound of fluttering had stopped.

"Bloody hell, I just got attacked by an eagle. Eagles don't attack people."

Marcia looked back down. "Probably after the egg."

Peter gazed at the egg, still on the table.

"Or wanted to get us back because we took it."

"*You* took it," Peter said.

"You were going to fry it up."

"I was only kidding around. I wouldn't risk cooking that thing. I don't even know if you can eat an eagle egg."

"It's this place," Marcia said. "It's this fucking place."

"Not this again. The curse."

"Spear guns don't go off with the safety on," she intoned. "Chickens don't go mouldy within the space of a day. Eagles don't attack people. Dead animals all around..."

She picked up the egg.

"Marcia, don't. The bird might still be close by..."

She threw it. A mean throw like she was pitching a baseball and the person at the plate with the bat was Peter. The egg sailed through the air. It smacked into a tree, cracking open and squirting red and yellow goo.

"Why the hell did you do that?"

Marcia stared at the broken shell, some of which clung to the tree, stuck there by the snot-like insides.

"It's just an egg."

"You didn't have to smash it. It was a living thing."

Marcia turned to Peter. She was smiling, although in the shadowy light, it looked more like a snarl. "And it was just an abortion."

Hearing those words was like a kick to the groin.

He watched her storm off into the tent. She angrily zipped

up the opening, shutting him out. He stood there for a good while, getting his breath back.

Somewhere, a bird screeched.

Sitting on the mattress, accompanied by the glow of the gas lamp, Marcia strummed the guitar. She barely knew how to play, wasn't even sure if the thing was in tune. It was Peter's toy, not hers. She knew only a couple of chords, the simplest of fingering, but it didn't matter. Playing soothed her, even if the sound she made was tuneless.

Peter had tried teaching her years ago. She wasn't musically inclined, so she found it difficult to grasp even the basics. Peter got too frustrated and gave up after only a few days. He could be capricious, and he possessed a temper, although it took a while to reveal itself.

Not like her dad. No, his temper was on a constant simmer and would boil over at the slightest irritation. Her childhood was spent on tiptoes. She and her brother learnt from an early age how scary their dad could be; that it was better to remain hidden in their rooms or play outside—wherever best they could avoid their father. But, being kids, they occasionally made noise, or played in areas in the house outside their bedrooms, forgetting for a moment they didn't live in a normal house with a basically good, pleasant father. Living in such an environment, Marcia's stomach was forever in knots; her younger brother was too quiet, too withdrawn; and her mother flinched when the wind blew, such was her frayed nerves. Marcia hated her childhood and was glad when her mother took her and her brother away from that horrible man.

Peter wasn't as bad as her dad. He had never struck her. Wasn't a heavy drinker. And he didn't tear through the house, yelling and screaming because dinner was ten minutes late. No, Peter wasn't the monster her dad was. He had the potential for violence, but it had never fully revealed itself. When things didn't go his way or they annoyed him, Peter was more likely to turn sullen than angry.

Still, his anger reared up sometimes. Like when he tried teaching her guitar. Fed up with her lack of progress, he had ripped the guitar out of her grasp and berated her about how a child could learn such simple skills. He used the words 'stupid' and 'hopeless' before storming out. She thought about that as she continued to pluck at the strings, enjoying the vibrations just as much as the sound.

There came a rapping on the door of the tent. She stopped and listened.

"Mars? Can I come in?"

She tensed. "Sure."

The zipper slid down, and Peter stuck his head through the opening.

"Want me to stop? I didn't damage it, I was just..."

"No, you can play it. It's all right. The potatoes are ready. And I've heated up some baked beans. It's no roast chicken, but it's better than nothing."

"I'm not hungry."

"Mars. You haven't eaten anything since breakfast. You gotta have something in your belly besides rum."

It was true, but she didn't feel like eating. And she was also feeling the effects of the alcohol. Nothing terrible, just a small headache, and her head and limbs felt floaty, like they were pumped with helium. She knew she should eat something, but the thought of putting food in her mouth made her stomach roil. "Maybe later."

"Okay."

Peter hesitated. Then he pulled back, closed up the tent. She listened to his shoes padding away on the ground, towards the fire.

She played around with the guitar for a bit longer before growing bored. Wasn't much fun when you couldn't actually make any music. She set the guitar down. With a heavy sigh, she fell backwards onto the sleeping bag and stared up at the ceiling. Not a real ceiling like back home, or at a nice motel room—all nice and solid. No, this was a fake ceiling, a thin fabric cover that could come down and smother her if an especially strong wind knocked the tent over. It wouldn't save her if a tree branch snapped off and landed on the roof; she'd be pummelled. The tent was no more a barrier than if she was sleeping in a tent made from tissue paper. She hated to complain all the time, knew that's all Peter thought she did, but there was nothing about this experience she enjoyed. She couldn't help that. She wasn't built for the outdoors, for roughing it, for any of it. Nature made her nervous. This place made her nervous. She felt a bad energy, like it didn't want them here. She imagined nature as some sentient being, and this was its house and they were trespassing, and it was doing everything in its power to get them to leave. As silly as it sounded, especially to Peter, that's how she felt.

Lying there, staring up at the flimsy ceiling, she thought about what she had said to Peter. She had never said the actual word to him, not in such specific terms. She referred to the act itself as 'the procedure.' Whenever Peter mentioned it, which was hardly ever, he usually stammered a vague string of words, keeping things general. Neither had used the actual word. It was too real, too concrete.

But she'd finally said it, and she was glad she had. If for no other reason than to see the look on Peter's face. He had been so smug these past few days—more than usual. He wanted to bring her here, even though he knew she didn't want to come. She sensed in him a kind of perverse enjoyment at watching her suffer. Throwing the egg at the tree had felt good, although it hardly felt like her doing it. She hadn't thought about it, had just done it, like she was being controlled by some greater force. But she had liked doing it all the same; it had felt cathartic. She liked the surprise on Peter's face. Liked the look of shock even more when she told him it had just been an abortion. He had hurt her too many times in the past, all his cheating and lying. Sneaking off to cheap motels to screw some cheap fling. She had hurt him by killing his unborn child and had shocked him by the explicitness of her words. That had wiped the smug look off his face. And she wasn't sorry. For any of it.

For the first time since arriving, she almost felt good. She felt relaxed, comfortable on the bed, the warmth of the rum flowing through her. However, her good feelings were shattered at the sight of the monster creeping across the ceiling.

Marcia lay there, near paralysed, as the huntsman spider, giant and hairy, scampered over the fabric, heading towards the bed. The thing looked twice the size of a regular huntsman: dark and ominous and straight from hell. Heart thumping, sweat beading over her skin, Marcia waited till the beast was halfway between the tent opening and her body before moving.

She meant to move slowly, deliberately, towards the opening. Instead, she jumped up and scurried towards the exit. With quivering hands, she sliced open the tent and tumbled out. "Peter!" she shrieked.

Peter, sitting by the fire with a plate balanced on his lap, jumped up. Cricket, beside him, also jumped up. The plate full of food tumbled forward and fell into the fire. "Jesus, what's the matter?"

"Spider," she said, scrambling to get up. "In the tent."

Peter eased out a breath, smiled. "That all? Christ, I thought it was something serious."

"It's a big bloody spider!" she cried, feeling ticklish all over her body, like a hundred of the monsters were crawling over her. "Kill it!"

"Okay, okay. Relax. I'll take care of it. Where did you put the spray?"

"Back in the truck," she said.

Peter headed over to the truck, started rummaging around in the few boxes still in the back.

While Peter looked for the insecticide, Marcia glanced back at the tent. To her, it was enemy territory now: inhospitable.

"Ah, here it is."

Peter came back with the insecticide. His stupid smile remained. "Wish me luck," he said with a wink. He stopped by the tent. "Just the one?"

"That I saw. A huntsman."

"Damn. Those things can move fast."

Spray bottle raised, he entered the tent.

Marcia waited outside, still feeling like hairy legs were scurrying over her. For a time, everything was quiet, except for the crackling of the fire, the soft howling of the wind. Then, like the hissing of a snake, she heard Peter emptying the insecticide bottle from within the tent. A long, continuous sound, followed by silence, and then Peter's voice: "Shit." More spraying, this time shorter bursts.

Soon, Peter stepped out of the tent. He was coughing. "I wouldn't go in there for a while."

"I'm not going back in there, ever," she said. "Well? Did you kill it?"

Peter was no longer smiling. He winced. "Sorry, love, I think it got away."

"What?"

"I found it; it was on the wall above the bed. I sprayed, but it was like the thing knew what I was doing before I did it. It scurried away just as I started to spray. I mean, I doused the wall so it looked like it was snowing. I fully expected to see it on the floor, dying, but it was nowhere. I sprayed some more where I thought it had gone, but the thing just... disappeared."

"Great. Just great."

Marcia had had enough. She strode over to the truck, hopped up into the driver's seat.

"Mars? What are you doing?"

"I'm leaving."

"Mars..."

"I've had it with this place. I told you I want to leave, but you won't listen. You can stay and play with the wildlife. I'll be at the motel, living like a civilised person."

She slammed the door.

"Look, I'm sure the spider's dead. I sprayed enough insecticide in there to kill twenty spiders. No creepy crawlies are going to scare you again, I promise."

Marcia looked at her husband through the half-open window. "Are you coming? Last chance."

"I'm staying right here," he answered defiantly.

He crossed his arms over his chest as the smugness returned to his face.

"Fine. Good. Maybe I'll pick you up Monday."

She turned the key. The engine clicked but didn't start. She tried again, pumping the accelerator pedal, but nothing happened. "What's wrong with you?" she growled at the car.

"I don't think you're going very far," Peter said, still grinning.

"What's wrong with it?" she said. "Why won't it start?"

"Maybe it's the curse. Or maybe it's spiders in the engine."

"Peter!"

"I switched it to the alternate battery to run the fridge."

"Switch it back."

"You want to leave? You switch it back."

Marcia glared at him. Unbelievably, he walked away, back to the fire, where he poured himself a slug of rum, sat down and started drinking.

With fire coursing through her body, she turned to the dashboard, looking for a switch. She fumbled around, flicked some knobs and levers, but they appeared to do very little. She tried the engine again just in case something she moved happened to be the right switch, but still the engine remained lifeless.

"Fuck!" she cried and hit the steering wheel.

She looked back. Seethed at the sight of Peter sitting there, cup in one hand, stroking a resting Cricket with the other.

What an arsehole, she thought.

She hopped out, slammed the back doors, and then climbed back into the cab, locked both the passenger and driver's side doors, and sat there, staring out at the dark bushland.

————

Finishing off his third cup of rum for the night, Peter felt good and relaxed. The fire was healthy. The storm that had been predicted had so far held off, and with Marcia still sulking in the truck, he had a good helping of peace and quiet. He didn't know if she was asleep or just sitting there, fuming. But she'd been in there for almost an hour and hadn't moved, so he figured she had most likely drifted off.

Early to be turning in for the night, but it had been an eventful day, so she was probably exhausted and needed the rest. Peter smiled into the flames. *So scared*, he thought. Like a child, Marcia frightened so damned easily. A few bugs, a couple of dead animals, and she was ready to bail. Wouldn't even give this place a chance. Here, out of her comfort zone, she had given up before it ever started.

Well, he wasn't about to let her spoil his fun. He had come here to relax, to be closer with his dad. To remember the good times. He wasn't about to pack up and leave just because his jittery wife was scared of a few creepy crawlies.

He was deciding whether to go for a fourth nip of rum, or just settle back with a beer, when the abominable wailing bleated through the night. He turned towards the path leading down to the beach. That's where the sound seemed to be coming from, the beach, but, like the fluttering of the bird earlier, it seemed to swell, as if the creature was above, all around, everywhere. The sound, so large and full of anguish, caused a ripple of sadness deep inside him. It woke Cricket, who pricked up her ears and started looking around at the black border beyond the light of the campfire, as if expecting the creature to come slithering into their world.

"It's okay, girl."

Cricket really hated that sound. Not that he blamed her. It was the kind of sound you might expect to hear bubble up from the depths of hell, as if some fissure had opened up, letting out all the pain and suffering from within.

Cricket got up. Even when the sound went away, leaving the world in a brittle silence, she stood there, ears up, tail stiff and facing towards the earth. "Cricket, you can relax now."

Instead of relaxing, she started barking. A wary barking, like a warning.

Peter frowned. He looked to where Cricket was directing her barking. She seemed to sense something, and Peter wondered— a wild animal? But there were no dangerous animals out here. Besides snakes.

Peter sat up straight. "What is it, Cricket?"

He thought about grabbing the torch and looking around the scrub. Or better yet, a stick from the fire. If there were any slithering serpents out there, fire would surely scare them away.

Then a light. Pushing through the bush, bobbing around the trees, the bushes. Small, but bright, and getting brighter.

What the hell?

Peter grabbed the shovel and rose up. Beside him, Cricket halted her barking and started growling. The light speared through the darkness as it drew closer. Over the crackling of the fire and the dog's growling, Peter heard twigs snapping, leaves crunching. He raised the shovel. "Who's there?" he said, voice less than steady.

The light halted. "It's me, Frank," came a booming voice. "I come in peace."

Peter eased out a breath. He lowered the shovel.

The light continued forward, becoming blinding as a shadow stepped out of the bush and into the clearing.

The light moved away and behind the torch, Peter saw the man he had met this morning, looking even bigger and somehow older than he remembered.

"Jesus, you gave me a fright. That weird wailing spooked Cricket, and I thought she was still reacting to that, or maybe some night critter, but then I saw a light and..."

"Said I'd come over and have a drink with you. Or did you forget?"

Frank laughed. It sounded like an engine running low on juice, trying to start.

Peter had forgotten, but he said, "No. I just... thought you'd come by the beach. Didn't expect you to traipse through the bush."

Cricket was still growling under her breath. "Cricket, quiet," Peter said, and Cricket stopped, but she remained on guard.

Frank switched off his torch, strode over to the empty deck chair and dragged it towards the fire. He fell heavily into the chair and then sat there, gazing into the flames.

Peter, still standing, set down the shovel and said, "Like a beer?"

"Sure. I'd love some rum even more."

Peter grabbed the bottle of rum off the table, along with a paper cup. As he did, he glanced over at the truck. Still no sign of Marcia. He brought the rum and cup back to the pit, filled the cup almost to the brim, and handed it to Frank.

"Thanks, matey." He took a big gulp. "Damn, that's good. I needed that."

By the look of him, and the smell, Frank didn't need it. The smell of beer oozed from his pores, wafted from his sweat like a drunken southerly. He'd probably already partaken in enough booze tonight to power a small car. He looked dishevelled, too. His salt and pepper hair was messy, like he'd taken a shower but hadn't bothered to comb it after, leaving it to dry where it fell. His shirt, still the gaudy Hawaiian he'd been wearing this morning, sat askance, as if buttoned wrongly—the few that were buttoned, anyway. The top and bottom of the shirt sat open, exposing a chest of wiry, gray hairs at the top, and below, a round belly covered in dark fuzz. Thankfully, his shorts were fully done up.

"Your wife and daughter didn't want to come?" Peter asked, picking up his cup and tipping a small amount of rum into it. The bottle was only a quarter full. Soon, it'd be empty. He had hoped this second bottle would last the rest of the weekend. He took a sip, welcomed the sweet heat.

Frank huffed, and it was a spiteful sound. "Nah. Left 'em back at the camp. Sick to death of 'em both. Needed a break. You know?"

"Sure, I get it."

Frank downed more rum and afterwards slumped down in the chair and set the cup on one thick thigh. "Where's your missus? Asleep in the tent?"

"Not exactly. She's in the car."

Frank looked over his shoulder at the truck. His heavy brow knitted; his dark eyes threaded with wry humour. "You two have a lover's quarrel? Surprised she didn't make *you* sleep in the car. I guess she knows who's boss, huh?"

Peter forced out a smile. "It's not like that. There was a spider in the tent. She got scared, so she opted to sleep in the truck."

"Women," Frank said with a shake of the head. "Christ."

He finished the rum and extended the empty cup. Peter liked to drink, mostly to get buzzed, not blind drunk. He usually sipped, especially when it came to hard liquor. This man guzzled. "You want a beer instead? Getting hot sitting by the fire. I was going to get one for myself."

"Sure, why not? The more the merrier."

Frank kept the cup extended, so Peter poured some more rum, but only half this time. He tipped what little there was left in his cup down his throat and got up.

At the truck, he opened the back doors. It was quiet in the

vehicle. He saw a dark shape up front. He opened the fridge and took out two cold bottles of Courage Draught.

"We have a visitor."

Marcia spoke softly.

"Yeah."

"The guy you met today, the one camping up the beach?"

"That's right."

Marcia fell quiet.

Peter closed the fridge. Waited. When it was clear Marcia was done talking, he closed the back doors and walked back to the fire. He opened the tops of both beers, the lids tumbling to the earth like tiny flying saucers crash-landing, handed Frank his bottle. Peter looked down into the man's cup, saw it still filled with dark rum, then he sat down and took a long drink. The beer was cool and refreshing, sliding down easily.

Frank gulped from his bottle, then let fly a burp that rumbled through the dark night. He followed up with a rum chaser. "You mentioned hearing a noise? What was it you said... a weird wailing?"

"Yeah, just before you showed up. What do you think it is?"

"Don't know, didn't hear it."

Peter, having just taken another sip of beer, almost choked on it as it washed down his throat. "What do you mean you didn't hear it? You must have. Thing's louder than thunder. I've been hearing it on and off since I got here." Peter looked hard at Frank. There was no humour in his face. No hint he was taking the piss. "You really didn't hear it?"

Frank shook his head.

Peter sat back in his seat. "Huh."

"I have heard a cackling, though. An odd sound. Probably just a bird. At least, that's what I've been telling Helen and Jessica. The noise freaks them out. Jessica thinks it's a ghost or some damned thing. It does sound creepy, I'll give her that. Like a witch's laugh. Sends the chills through your bones. But, like I say, it's probably just a bird, or some kind of creature."

"I've heard birds, day and night, but can't say I've heard anything resembling a witch's cackle."

Frank shrugged his beefy shoulders. "Must have a nest near our camp."

"So," Peter said after a brief silence. "Your family enjoying camping more than they were this morning?"

Frank didn't speak for a spell. He looked lost in thought, eyes glazed and transfixed by the flames. "No," he finally said. "They hate it here. I guess I can't blame them. This wasn't a planned trip. I sort of sprung it on them. Got the idea in my head, bundled them into the camper, and just took off."

An odd smile came over Frank. Thin-lipped, it looked more ominous than imbued with any humour.

"Yeah, I brought them here. Not against their will, no, nothing like that. But they don't know."

"Know what?"

Frank, still with that haunted grin, raised his beer. "The real reason for the trip."

Peter swallowed. He hesitated to ask. "And what's that?" he said, trying to sound light-hearted.

Frank took a long, deliberate drink from the bottle. "How old are you, Peter?"

"Twenty-nine."

Frank shook his head. "Not even thirty. Christ. Still have your whole life ahead of you. You happy?"

"I guess so. I mean, who's ever truly happy? But happier than most, not as much as some." He took a slug of beer. Considered pouring himself some more rum, but he was already feeling too swimmy, which meant he was close to becoming drunk, so he held onto the beer.

"Life goes too fast. Remember that. One moment you're young, wanting to play footy in the big leagues, become the next Gordon Coventry... the next, you're old and fat and settled into a nine-to-five job, married to a woman you don't love and stuck with a kid you don't understand who mostly disappoints you, and you look back on your life and realise you're a failure."

"You can't mean that," Peter said. "You really think your life's been a failure?"

"I was a good footy player. Full forward, just like my hero. I kicked plenty of goals. Could plough through a pack like a steamroller. I could have gone further, I know it, but my old man, he didn't think so. He thought I was hopeless. Slow and cumbersome, he used to say. A lead foot who couldn't kick a goal if the posts were twice as wide and I was standing three feet in front of them. He didn't encourage me, that mean old bastard. Told me I was wasting my time. He even laughed at me when I told him I wanted to play for Collingwood, like Nuts. Said I'd never make it, so why waste my time? So, I stopped playing. But I always wonder what would have happened if I hadn't stopped, if I had followed my dream. My life would have been better, I'm sure of it. I certainly wouldn't be here, on this beach, with no job, no future, nothing but a life filled with regret."

Frank had slumped lower in the chair. His face was creased, and there might have been a tear or two leaking from his bloodshot eyes.

"You can't think your life a failure just because you didn't become a professional footy player. Most men don't make it, don't live out their childhood dreams. Doesn't mean they've failed."

"What did you want to be when you were young?"

"A musician. A rock star."

"Why didn't you become one?"

"A rock star?" Peter chuckled. "I dunno... not talented enough, not good looking enough, not lucky enough. I guess I just grew up and realised that dreams don't always come true and at some point, you have to face reality."

"So, it had nothing to do with your parents? Your old man

didn't mock you, put you down, make you feel like a fool for even thinking about following your dream?"

"No. My dad, he was... a good guy. He wasn't big into music, couldn't stand the stuff I listened to, but he didn't discourage me. Actually, he bought me my first guitar. A cheap, second-hand thing, but still, it was the best present I ever got."

Now it was Peter's eyes that started to well up. His dad was a simple man. He didn't show his love easily, or give much affection, but Peter always knew he was loved. His dad was typical of the time, showing his love by working hard and providing for his family. That guitar, not a birthday or Christmas present, but something waiting for him in his room one day when he got home from school, was the ultimate display of that affection. Dad didn't understand music, but Peter sure as hell remembered the proud look on his dad's face when, after Peter taught himself to play 'I Don't Want to Walk Without You', he did a rendition of the song in the living room for his old man. It had been his dad's favourite song (he always said because it was the song playing when he and Mum first met; Peter thought Dad had a thing for Helen Forrest).

"You were lucky. Had good parents."

"I was mostly raised by my dad," Peter said, furtively swiping at his eyes. "My mum died when I was five."

"What did your old man do for a living?"

"He worked for Rosella in the factory in Richmond, making tomato sauce. Used to tell me how they brought in the oldest, nearly rotten tomatoes to use for the sauce, and how it put him off ever using the stuff. When he told me that as a kid, put me off too. Well, that and the smell. I could smell the sauce being made from our little cottage near the factory: sweet, sickly sweet, coupled with the smell of coal and a chemical type smell. I haven't touched tomato sauce since I was seven years old. The smell of it still makes me nauseous."

"No kidding? Me, I love the stuff. Can't eat a meat pie without a big squirt of sauce."

"How about your old man? What did he do?"

"Did odd jobs, but mostly he worked in abattoirs, around the Ovens Murray region."

"Dirty work, I imagine, especially in the old days."

Frank nodded. "He always smelled like dead animals. Had arms the size of bowling pins. Reminded me of Popeye, although I never dared tell him that. Died an old man, bitter and never shy about reminding me how much of a disappointment I was to him. Hated that I went into an industry that deals mostly in paperwork. Thought it weak. Manual labour, that was real work, according to him."

"And your mum?"

"Stayed at home, raised the kids, tended to her husband. A saint of a woman. It's how it should be. These women today, all that feminist bull, messes up the balance. The world is all messed up. Women want to work, men are all mixed up, don't know what to do, kids aren't being raised right. Your missus work?"

"No, she doesn't."

Frank raised his beer. "Good for you. How it should be. But you said you don't have any kids?"

"No, we don't."

Frank leaned over and nudged Peter hard. "But you're working on it, I bet, hey?" He winked.

Peter put the bottle to his face and waited until Frank had moved away before lowering it.

"Are we, Peter?"

Peter spilled beer down the front of his top upon hearing Marcia's voice. Frank flinched.

"Why don't you tell him the truth?"

"Mars, hey," Peter said, feeling his face go hot. She stood by the car, arms folded.

"Frank, this is my wife, Marcia."

"Pleased to meet you."

Marcia didn't smile. She didn't extend even a cordial greeting.

"I have to pee." She stalked over and collected the torch. Then she marched towards the tent.

Frank watched her as she walked, dressed as she was in shorts and a tight-fitting t-shirt. Peter felt a mixture of anger and pride at the older man gawking at his wife.

When Marcia reached the front of the tent, she halted. They had been using the bush behind the tent for their business. The bush back there wasn't as dense as other areas, yet there were still bushes to squat behind, and it was close enough that if they had to go in the middle of the night, they didn't have too far to trek. Peter had even dug a pit about ten metres away, although that had yet to be used.

But Peter figured the memory of the spider was still very much present, as she moved away from the tent and back towards the truck. She disappeared from view, but Peter could still make out the glow of her torch, a little way behind the truck.

"Got yourself a pretty little lady there."

Peter turned back. Frank's eyes were back on the fire.

"But I get the feeling she doesn't want me here. You two have something going on that's personal."

"No, we... just typical husband and wife problems. She doesn't like it here either, wants to leave. She's just annoyed at me, that's all. Nothing to do with you. Stay, have some more rum."

Peter picked up the bottle.

"I won't say no," Frank said, and handed Peter his empty cup.

Peter poured three fingers of rum for Frank, the same for himself.

"Cheers," Peter said.

"What shall we drink to?"

"How about... men being men?"

"I'll drink to that. Cheers."

They knocked their cups together. Peter took a big swig of rum. He glanced back at the truck, at the white glow, and swallowed the liquid fire with relish.

———

The bottle of rum was empty. Beer bottles lay scattered on the ground, looking like the empty shells of dead critters. Peter sat by the fire, smoking. He wasn't drunk, but he was close. Frank, a non-smoker, instead of a cigarette, held a stick. On the far end clung a marshmallow. He held it close to the flames, rolling the sweet treat gently to cook all sides. After a short time, he took the stick from the fire, studied the marshmallow. He hadn't managed an even roast: one half was blackened. Smoke drifted from the white ball of sugar. Before the marshmallow melted and fell off the stick, Frank popped it into his mouth. His eyes widened. He fanned his mouth with his free hand.

"Forgot how hot they get," he said once he'd swallowed. He swallowed some beer. "But man, as tasty as I remembered."

Peter said, "Have another. Hell, have as many as you like."

"Yeah?"

"Can't see me and the missus finishing the bag this weekend."

"Thanks, matey. This means more than you know."

Frank dipped into the bag of marshmallows, took out another white one, and stuck it onto the gooey end of the stick. "I haven't done this since I was a kid," he said as he started roasting his second marshmallow of the evening. "We didn't get many treats in my household. The only times I got to roast marshmallows was when I went camping with my best mate and his dad. Those were good times. Pity they had to end. Nothing in my life since has come close to capturing the fun and... hell, magic, of those times."

"Nothing?"

"You spend most of your adult life trying to recapture your youth, trying to find that spark, that sense of wonder. But it's a fool's game. That's what growing older does. Kills any bit of magic you used to have, and replaces it with cold, hard reality. There's only so much room in your soul. It's like an audio tape; you record something new, it replaces the old. It's like that throughout your life."

"A depressing thought," Peter said. "You believe in the soul?"

Frank sat there, not turning the stick, just breathing heavily, staring at the fire. Finally, he said, "Maybe. I used to believe in heaven and hell, and that if we do bad things, we go straight to the bad place. But I don't believe that anymore. If the soul does exist, I think it just... dissipates when we die, like a puff of wind."

Peter drew on his cigarette and looked at the grey, gloomy sky. No stars were visible with all the cloud cover, and the moon was hidden. He didn't believe in the existence of the soul, just like he didn't believe in God. But he nonetheless imagined all those human life-forces drifting into the air upon death, floating up like balloons, before popping into nothingness, the essence of each person snuffed out forever.

He thought about the wailing. Maybe that was the sound of a soul, but one caught in limbo, for some reason unwilling or unable to pop out of existence. Maybe it wanted to move on but was instead stuck up there in the sky in a kind of purgatory, and the sound he and Marcia had been hearing was its anguish.

Despite the heat from the fire, despite the heat from the rum, Peter shivered, and he recalled what his friends used to say when he was young about a shiver—it meant someone just walked over your grave. It used to freak him out thinking about that, even though it never made complete sense to him. After all, he wasn't dead; he wasn't buried, so how could someone walk over his grave? And why did it make you shiver?

"Aw, shit."

Peter looked down to see Frank lifting his stick out of the fire. The marshmallow was gone, dropped off his stick and was now a blob sizzling in the flames, a black ball growing smaller and smaller, disintegrating to nothing.

"Take another."

Frank grabbed a fresh marshmallow, stuck it on the blackened point of the stick, and propped it just above the flames.

"I hate when that happens," Peter said. "Feels like a waste, a failure of sorts. My dad showed me how to roast them without it happening. First, you have to make sure the marshmallow is firmly on the stick, not half hanging off the end. Then he said to cook it over the coals, not the flames. Takes longer, but it won't burn, and you get a more even char. Still have to be quick to eat it once it's toasted, though, because all that heat melts the inside. After he showed me the proper way, I never lost a marshmallow into the fire."

"Hmm." Frank moved the stick away from the flames to the outer rim of the pit, where hot coals sat simmering. "Your dad sounds like a good man."

"He was. Firm, sure, could be hard on me, but he was always fair and took good care of me."

"He still around?"

Peter felt like he had been shot in the chest with the spear gun. "No. Died about ten years ago. Lung cancer."

"Shit. Sorry."

"Our last camping trip together was to this spot. He was already sick, although I didn't know it. I don't think he knew for sure what was wrong, only I'm sure he knew it was something serious. Looking back, I remember he had a haunted look in his eyes, and he had grown thinner. He didn't move as easily as he once did, and he coughed more than usual. As a teenager, I didn't take much notice, just thought he had a cold, or it was the price of getting older. He got worse not long after, went to the doctor and was given the news. We never went on another camping trip. I promised him we would, that before he died, I'd take him on a last trip. He wanted to come here. He always liked the beach, the ocean. We never got the chance."

"I can understand why your old man liked coming here. It's peaceful, and pretty in its own way. Funny, I've never been here before, but it feels like I have. I felt a connection to it the moment I turned off the highway and started down the track. Like I belong here. Being here feels right. Silly, I know."

"No, it's not."

The marshmallow looked good and toasted. Frank removed the stick from the coals and inspected the treat. "Hey, look at that, perfectly cooked all over. And it hasn't fallen off."

"Better eat it before it does."

Frank pulled the marshmallow off the stick with his teeth and chewed. "Tastier, too. Your dad was a smart man. Ain't that the way of the world?"

"What's that?"

"My dad, a mean old bastard who didn't deserve to be spit on if on fire, dies in his sleep an old man, none the wiser. Yet your dad, kind and warm and decent, dies of cancer before his time. The world really has a sick way about it. People pray to God because they think He rules over everything; I say the devil is in charge. And you know what I say? Fuck the devil. Fuck the world."

A sentiment Peter didn't wholly disagree with.

"You go camping a lot as a kid?"

"Yeah. Dad loved the outdoors. He took me camping all over country Victoria. He took me to this spot a few times, the farthest north we ever got. It was his favourite place to camp. It's why I wanted to come back here. To remember. To see if it's the same as what I had in my memories."

"And is it?"

"Smaller than I remembered. More overgrown. It's lovely and all, but it doesn't quite have the same magic as it used to."

"That's what I was getting at before. You can't go back. Who you were as a kid, that's gone, erased by the harsh realities of adulthood. And when you try to go back, whether it's your childhood home or a campsite, it's never the same. It can't be. You're a different person. You're seeing it all through different eyes. Sucks, but that's the way of the world. The world doesn't want you to be happy. It wants to grind you down, take away all the happy and innocent parts. It wants you miserable. It wants to be your master."

Peter sighed. "Yeah, I'm beginning to see that."

Frank huffed. "You're young. Wait till you get to my age. Youth seems a million miles away, like it happened to some other creature in some other galaxy."

"I get it, I do. It isn't just that this place looks smaller. That, at least, I can understand. When you're small, the world seems huge from down there. But it's more than that. The landscape itself looks different. Still familiar enough, but changed, like it's an approximation of the place I used to camp at with my dad. Does that make sense?"

"Sure."

"Or maybe I'm just drunk."

"Could be that too," Frank said with a warped smile.

"In a way, it is like I'm seeing it all for the first time. It's so different from what I remember as a kid."

"Adult eyes. It's a curse. When you start seeing everything through adult eyes, it's the beginning of the end."

"This place meant so much to me when I was young. It was like another world, a world just for me and my dad. He could do anything. He cleared this site. It was an overgrown field when we first got here. It was Dad who scythed the grass and made a spot to set up our tent. He cleared a path down to the beach. In a way, he had settled this spot, like the explorers of old. He caught fish using just sticks he had whittled. No hi-tech spear gun for him, no, not even lures and fishing rods. He was the master of this land; here, he was king. He even built me a treehouse, using just what he found. He created a paradise here, for himself, for me. Now, it all feels... empty. Changed. Even the bay looks smaller. Hell, there's not even a trace of the treehouse. It's like my favourite memories have either been altered or erased."

Peter sucked the last of the cigarette. It sizzled, the tip glowing. He exhaled a dense cloud of smoke. "What you said about the past being like a cassette that's being constantly taped over, that's kind of what it feels like. A hint of the old life remains, but it's faint and fuzzy beneath the newer stuff. The louder adult stuff."

"Sometimes, that adult stuff can become too loud. Sometimes, the tape breaks or becomes unspooled until it looks like a plate of black spaghetti and is impossible to set right."

Peter glanced at Frank. In the glow of the firelight, he looked haggard and haunted, eyes dark and deep-set. Peter suspected there was more behind his words than mere regret, an older man looking back on his life and wishing things had gone differently.

There was deep sadness there. Anger, too. Christ, Peter hoped he never grew that bitter. Longing for the simple joys of childhood was one thing; feeling as if your life was at a breaking point, that it had come undone and could never be made good again. That was a position Peter hoped he never found himself in.

Peter flicked the cigarette butt into the fire.

"Things may have changed for you here," Frank said, "which is sad but inevitable, but not everything has been erased. On the way here, I passed a tree with planks of wood nailed to its trunk. Looked old. Looked like a ladder. I didn't stop to inspect it, just noticed it as I passed by with the torch. I think it was your treehouse."

"I looked all around when I first got here. I couldn't find even a rotted plank on the ground."

"Well, I definitely saw something that looked like a ladder. Only about a five-minute walk."

Peter smiled, but it was crooked. "Five minutes? I remember it being a lot closer to the campsite. Think you can find it again?"

"I think so."

"You up for a late-night stroll?"

"Sure. Why not?"

Peter jumped up. He grabbed his torch, switched it on. Frank rose up out of the chair, taking the bag of marshmallows.

"In case you get hungry?"

"That, and to use as a trail. Work better than breadcrumbs, I reckon."

Frank popped a couple of raw marshmallows into his mouth.

"Trail? How far away is this ladder?"

"Not that far," Frank mumbled around gobs of stickiness. "But I'm even more inebriated now than when I trekked here, so..." Frank grinned after he had swallowed.

Peter looked down at Cricket, curled but not asleep between the fire and the tent. "You stay here."

Cricket aimed her eyes at Peter. She didn't move, just looked at him with wariness. Peter guessed he didn't have to worry about her wanting to come with them.

With Frank leading the way, they walked out of the clearing. Peter glanced at the Patrol as they left the campsite. It was dark within, and he saw no sign of Marcia, not even her shadow. Must be asleep in the back, he figured. He considered waking her to let her know what they were doing, but he decided best not to disturb her. Anyway, he was a grown man. He didn't need to tell Marcia his every move.

They left the relative warmth and brightness of the clearing and stepped into the cool darkness of the bush. Two spears of light cut the path ahead as the shrubs and gum trees closed in around them. Peter's memory had the treehouse maybe fifty metres away, at most, from the campsite. During the day, you could see it while sitting outside the tent. The gum tree, a towering beast of a tree, had limbs lower down the trunk, thick ones that allowed his dad to construct a small wooden room in its arms. Peter hadn't seen him do it, but thinking back, his dad must have cut back the bushes and branches to make a clear path so he could keep watch on his son while at the campsite. A long time had passed since then, so the foliage would naturally have grown back, but still, as Peter trailed Frank, not only was there no signs that any of the bushes or trees had been, at some point, cut back, but when they passed roughly the fifty-metre mark, Frank kept on walking.

They continued deep into the bush. After a few minutes of weaving around bushes, around trees, Peter began to wonder if Frank was either lost or simply mistaken. That he hadn't actually seen a ladder nailed to a trunk; his intoxicated mind, along with the shadows, had simply tricked him.

Because they were far from the camp. Too far, in Peter's estimation. Sure, he was young back then, and the world seemed bigger, wilder, and he certainly hadn't timed how long it took to reach the treehouse from the campsite, nor had he measured the distance. But he definitely remembered it being just a short walk from the camp. He remembered being up high and looking down through the bushland to see his dad building a fire or cooking lunch or just sitting there, whittling sticks into spears.

"Frank, are you sure we're going the right way? Are you sure you actually saw a ladder?"

"Pretty sure. And yes, definitely."

Frank, the bag of marshmallows tucked under an arm, dug into the bag, and popped a few more into his mouth.

"Maybe dropping some of those isn't such a bad idea," Peter said, glancing around. No longer any sign of the fire, or the moon-lit ocean. No sign of the white sandy beach. Just dark bushland.

"This is the way, I'm sure of it," Frank said around the treats.

In the dark, everything looked the same. Peter wondered

how Frank could be certain.

They trudged through the bush for another minute or two, cracking twigs and crushing dead leaves. Peter heard, or thought he heard, things scampering around the earth. Above, leaves shook, and branches creaked.

Finally, Frank stopped.

"Here it is."

Peter took a few steps forward and cast his torch to where Frank was aiming his light. There, attached to a large trunk, were numerous planks of wood. Peter moved closer. The planks were old, weathered from sun and wind and rain, but they didn't appear rotten. The nails holding them in place also looked like they'd been there for almost two decades: the thick nails looked rusty. Peter angled his light up, tracing the rectangular boards, all six of them—the same number his dad had attached to the tree—until he hit the treehouse itself. His throat tightened. Just as he remembered: long wooden planks stretching from one limb to the other making up the floor, with gnarly branches for the walls. Simple, but for a teenage boy, oh so effective.

"So, is it yours?"

Peter felt Frank's weight come up beside him, bringing the smell of beer, sweat and the sickly sweet aroma of puffed sugar.

"Has to be, right? Unless someone else's father built them a treehouse in this area, which seems bloody unlikely."

"No," Peter pushed out, voice high and whispery. "This is it."

His dad had used a dinghy he found on the beach to partially construct the treehouse. Old, with a large hole in its hull, the dinghy looked long abandoned. But most of it was perfectly healthy, so Dad had dismantled the small boat and used the planks for the flooring of the treehouse and steps for the ladder. Peter noticed the same watermarks, the same type of wood, as he remembered; there was even the faded lettering on one of the steps, part of the name of the boat, Peter assumed. In faded red, the letters EMM. This was his treehouse all right. Weird, how far away it really was from the campsite. He just hadn't searched deep enough this morning, that's why he hadn't found it. Must be the age difference, he figured. The difference between himself as a fit, spritely teenager and himself now as a slower, more cumbersome man just ten years shy of forty. What had seemed like a short skip away back then now felt like a slog.

He reached out and touched the plank directly in front of his chest. A familiarity struck him; the cool feel of the wood, not hard or splintery, but almost soft and rounded. He tugged. The wood was still intact, the nails still had a tight grip. He tried a few more planks. They also felt sturdy. Amazing, after all this time, the wood hadn't rotted; the nails hadn't come loose. That some delinquents hadn't decided to tear it all down.

"You going up?"

"I don't know," Peter said. "These steps feel strong enough. But who knows what the wood is like in the tree house."

"Come on, relive your youth. Climb up."

Peter turned and faced Frank. "I thought you said you can't recapture your youth."

"You can't. But then you don't have many opportunities to even try. It won't be the same as when you were a kid, but so what? It'll still be a memory you'll have for the rest of your life. You probably won't get many chances to do something like this."

Peter nodded. "Yeah, you're right."

"Think of it this way: you remember what it was like to be up there when you were young. It won't be the same now, okay, but now you get to see what it was like through your dad's eyes. He built it, right? He was up there, hammering away. Now you're closer to his age, you might see what he saw."

"Christ, that's deep," Peter said with a curled smile. "You always like this?"

Frank shrugged. "Mostly when I've been drinking. Want me

to climb up first? If these old planks can hold an old fart like me, they can sure as hell hold you."

Peter shook his head. "No. No, I'll go." He turned around and shined the torch up. The house was high, higher than he remembered. Funny, but he would have expected the opposite. He switched off his torch and once again gripped the fourth step from the bottom. Tugged. Still held strong. He put one foot on the bottom rung, took a breath, stepped up with the other. Now, with his full weight on the two planks, he remained there and waited. When neither plank broke apart, he reached up to the next highest and pulled himself up, moving his feet to the second plank from the bottom.

Half expecting either the fifth plank to come unstuck in his hands or for the lower one to break, he was relieved when neither happened.

"Your old man sure knew how to build things to last," Frank said from the safety of the ground.

"I don't think he built this thinking of it holding for almost twenty years. Two, three years, sure."

Swallowing his nerves, Peter continued climbing. He reached the floor of the treehouse and then, perched on the ladder, looked at the wooden structure before him. Only scant moonlight lit the treehouse. From what he could see, the floor looked intact. "Hand me my torch."

Peter looked down. He was never fearful of heights, and he wasn't that far up, maybe three, four metres, but he suddenly grew lightheaded. Frank picked up Peter's torch and extended it up. Peter, frozen on the spot, waited till the dizzy feeling started to abate.

"You okay?"

"Just got hit with a touch of vertigo."

Peter leaned down and grabbed the torch. Then he straightened back up and, keeping firm hold with his left hand, clicked on the torch and scanned the light over the treehouse.

The light revealed a carpet of dead leaves, fallen twigs, an old bird's nest, long since abandoned. He saw no major damage. He set the torch on the floor and tested the flooring with his hand. The planks felt tight. He called down, "I'm going for it."

"Good luck."

He pushed himself up over the lip of the floor and climbed the rest of the way into the treehouse.

Not just any treehouse. The one his dad had made for him. The one he had spent long days and occasional nights up in. He scooped up the torch, eased his body up. Slowly took it all in. Frank had said you couldn't go back, but my god, he almost felt twelve again. All those old feelings of freedom came flooding back. It wasn't just about being up among the trees, or the spectacular view overlooking the bush, the beach, the ocean. It was that this was his. No one else's. Down there, it was a shared place: his and Dad's. Up here, he was King.

He remembered all the stories he had concocted. All the fantasies of being lost at sea like Robinson Crusoe and being shipwrecked on this uninhabited beach. Sometimes he was an explorer. Other times he was a baddie: a pirate, or a bushranger. This was alternatively his home, a lookout tower, a place to stash treasure, or a place to hide from the bad men or from the coppers (depending on which side of the law he was on).

On his last trip to Moondah, when he was maturing and had discovered the opposite sex, he fantasised about finding a native girl, or someone lost in the wilderness. He'd rescue her, take her up here to his home, and they'd... do things. Sometimes, when he was the baddie, it'd be a girl he had kidnapped. Then he'd take her by force. He'd tie her to the branches and have his way with her. Those he felt guilty about, especially afterwards, but they filled him with a different kind of a thrill than the adventure stories. Because he had discovered something else by the time of that last camping trip with his dad; and had done that, too, while alone up here—numerous times.

"How's it looking?"

"Looks good. At least, so far."

Carefully, he moved away from the opening. The wooden floor felt sturdy underfoot, but he knew there was a chance of hitting a piece that had rotted away. He kept the light trained on the floor as he moved around the small area. He tested the walls. Miraculously, they all seemed strong, like the treehouse had been built only yesterday, not back in nineteen-sixty. The boards creaked as he trod with caution, but nowhere did he sense them bowing or loose.

Starting to relax, he moved over to the side that faced the ocean. When he was young, the ocean had been so close he felt he could jump off the railings and dive into the water. Now, the white strip of sand and the dark void looked far away, like the large gum tree had been pushed back about a thousand metres. He couldn't reconcile the difference between his memory and the reality of now. The long traipse through the bush to get here was odd, but he put that down to being young and not perceiving distance like you do when you were older. This, though, was harder to explain away. He distinctly remembered the beach being close, so close he could make out individual shells on the sand, could hear the waves as if they were just beneath his treehouse. Looking out this night, he'd be lucky if he could spot a clump of seaweed, and the surf, though audible, was a distant sound.

A strange feeling came over him. A dark feeling, like he was in a dream but was acutely aware he was in a dream. An odd feeling of being out of time; things were familiar, yet different.

Looking out at the distant ocean, he saw a dark shape in the water. Even though the ocean itself was dark, compared to the truck-sized shape, the water looked lighter. The massive sea creature—that's what he thought it was, not merely a reflection —was a black shadow within a shadow. He watched the shape move through the waters. The creature moved fast for something so huge, yet whatever it was, it didn't seem to be going anywhere in particular. It moved in the same general area, as if contained. The shape frightened Peter, though he didn't know why. He couldn't see it, it couldn't harm him, yet it filled him with dread, similar to how he felt on that long walk down the hospital corridor all those years ago, knowing what was waiting for him in the small room that smelled of sickness, yet not wanting to ever reach it.

The dizziness returned.

He moved away from the low railings. Which, unlike when he was a teenager, and the railings had come up to his chest and there was no fear of him falling over the edge, not unless he was being silly or deliberately climbed over, the railings now came only to his belly button. If an especially strong wind were to blow, he could conceivably be knocked over and plummet to the ground below.

As he moved away, he noticed, through the long sea of treetops, hovering over the ocean, a group of birds—or were they bats? They were large and black and circled in the sky like a gathering storm. A smell like wet mould, of things rotting, started to overpower the sweet earthiness of the bush and the fresh, briny ocean air. The stench had a dark quality, and it added to Peter's unease, the dizziness.

Peter turned from the ocean, from the deep, dark shape and the circling birds. He wanted to stay up here longer. This was the closest he had felt to his dad so far this trip, the strongest tie to his youth, even if it was tainted and askew, like everything else. But the dizziness, the rank smell permeating the air, was becoming too much. That, and the bubbling concern over the soundness of the structure. Deciding it was time to head back down, he started back towards the ladder. As the light from the torch moved across the treehouse, something glinted. It was a dull glint, like a coin being struck by a dying candle flame, but it had a yellowish tint. Curious, Peter altered his course and started towards it. Whatever had glinted in the torchlight was tucked in one of the corners. He kicked away dead leaves as he moved carefully across the small confines of the treehouse. The boards underfoot felt sturdy, but he was still mindful of the nearly two decades of rain and salt winds assaulting the wood, the bolts, the nails that had held the structure up for so long.

Just as he reached the corner, he heard something behind him. The sound of huffing, of wood creaking. He crouched, aimed the light in the dark corner choked with dead leaves and twigs. He saw a knife blade. Large, about fifteen centimetres in length, one edge serrated, the blade was coated in rust. The dark, yellowish brown encrusted the blade. An overwhelming familiarity crashed through Peter. It was his blade, the one he had found on the beach when he was a teenager. It hadn't been quite so rusty then, but he knew it was the same blade; the size, the shape, that it was up here, where he had hidden it from pirates in the course of his fantasies, meant it had to be the same one. He thought he had lost it; had been dejected on the drive home that final trip to Moondah. But he had found it.

More sounds behind of someone clambering up the trunk.

Frank.

Oh shit!

Peter rose up, turned around. Saw Frank pulling himself up onto the floor of the treehouse, his round, sweaty face creased from the strain. Once upright, he stood there and heaved a sigh. "I'm too old and fat to be doing this, but fuck it, I wanted to see the view."

There was the strain of the climb writ large across his face, but there was something else, too, something more subtle that Peter noticed. Something dark and troubled, like the climb or maybe the tree itself, had reminded Frank of something sinister, perhaps a bad memory from his past. But the look drained away, leaving his wet, pudgy face soft and pale once again.

Frank started walking across the treehouse.

"Frank..." Peter started to say, but it was too late.

He was going to tell him to stop, go back. He doubted the treehouse could hold two adults, especially one as solid as

Frank. Frank got a little over halfway when the boards started crying and groaning. Sharp wooden shrieks and the sounds of old planks bending under the weight. Trying to hold on, but unable to stop from breaking.

Frank's eyes widened as the realisation hit him.

Peter looked over at the narrow opening leading to safety. The small enclosure suddenly seemed as wide as the ocean. He looked behind. Considered moving back to the edge and gripping onto the wall made from fallen limbs. Before he could, the floor broke apart. There was a cracking sound and then dust and leaves and old wood flicked into the air and Peter felt his world tilting towards a hole that was now before him, where planks of wood had been just moments ago.

He felt himself start to drop. Frank plummeted forward as a section of the floor gave way. He landed hard on the floor with a whooshing sound punched from his gut. He was showered with leaves and dust, but he remained there, his side of the floor basically level. Peter yelped as he was sucked down towards the gaping maw. He raised his arms to try to find purchase, something, anything, that might stop his tumble to the ground below.

What he found, just as he fell through the hole, was something soft and sweaty. He didn't know what gripped him, just that something did and that whatever it was had stopped him from crashing to the ground. He looked up and saw a hand clasping his, and above the hand an arm pushing down through the gap. Beyond the arm was Frank's face, straining. Frank had managed to grab hold of Peter just in time and was clearly using all he had to stop Peter from falling.

Peter felt movement as Frank tried pulling him up, but the movement was slight. As he attempted to pull Peter up, Peter saw Frank slipping farther towards the hole. Could feel his own hand slipping out of Frank's grasp; there was too much sweat between them for him to hold on much longer.

Dangling like some vine, Peter heard more sighing of wood.

With the already fractured floor and the weight still on it, he knew it wouldn't be long before the rest of the floor buckled and then both men would fall.

"Forget it," Peter said. "No use you falling, too. Get down the ladder."

"No, I can pull you up..." Frank said through gritted teeth.

"It's not that far down. I'll be okay."

Peter looked past his shoes. The ground didn't seem that far away, maybe four metres. He just had to remember to bend his knees as he landed and roll with head tucked under his chin. He'd be fine.

"Let go."

Frank eased his grip. Peter's hand slid out of Frank's and the ground hit him a moment later.

He managed to bend his knees, tuck in his head. Still, the jarring as his legs hit the earth was brain-rattling, the roll not nearly as smooth. It was more of a ragged tumble, and his back got bitten by jagged rocks and stabbed by twigs. He came to a stop on his back and then he lay there, staring up at the broken bottom of the treehouse, wondering if he had broken something of himself. He felt no great pain. His ankles hurt, as did his backside, but they felt minor, just the after-effects of the jarring fall, and the scrapes and bruises from the roll.

He was starting to feel like he was okay, that he was lucky. Turning to his right, he saw how lucky he was. Less than ten centimetres away was one of the treehouse floorboards. The broken piece had landed with two long, sharp nails sticking up. A slight change in direction and he could have been stabbed by the old, rust-bitten nails. Rolling over that with his back would have been horrible, painful, and without a tetanus shot in the near future, potentially deadly. But if he had rolled onto it with the back of his head, well, he'd be as dead as the baby dugong.

He sat up, slowly. Looked up. Couldn't see Frank. The floor hadn't continued to collapse, but still, Peter wanted to move away just in case. He had narrowly dodged a sharp pair of bullets; he wasn't about to risk more nail-studded planks falling down and piercing him. He stood up. His ankles, particularly his left, felt weak and painful. It hurt to put weight on it, but he didn't think it was fractured. Just strained.

He heard the sound of Frank climbing back down the ladder. There was a gasp, a shriek, followed by a heavy thud of something big hitting the earth.

Peter hobbled around the tree and saw Frank sprawled on the ground. His eyes were open and wide in his red, sweaty face. One rung of the ladder rested on his belly, the plank rising and falling with his panting.

"You okay?"

"Damned thing just came off in my hands."

Peter saw the third rung from the top was missing. All that remained were the ends of two thick nails sticking out of the trunk.

Frank sat up. The plank fell off him onto the ground. "How about you?"

"Ankle's a little sore, but otherwise, I'm okay."

Frank got to his feet. He took in a deep breath. "Sorry I couldn't pull you up."

"Don't worry about it. Probably best you didn't. Who knows what would've happened? I don't think the treehouse could have lasted much longer with both of us up there."

Peter gazed up. The treehouse appeared to be settled after its small implosion. There was now a sizeable hole in the middle of the floor, a hole with jagged edges. Seeing it broken, Peter felt dispirited.

"I thought it would hold. I thought it was strong enough."

"Yeah, well. Like you said, you can't go back. Wasn't like I remembered, anyway."

"Still, it was yours. Your dad built it, and now it's ruined."

Peter thought about the rusted blade, still up there. Once, he thought it was a treasure. But it was just an old blade missing its handle that was being slowly eaten by rust.

"No, it's not."

Peter sniffed the air. The dark, rotting smell was gone. Just the scent of the woody bush, tinged with salt.

"Let's head back," Peter said. "I think we've earned some beers."

"Here, here."

———

Back seated around the campfire, Peter and Frank thirstily drained a few more bottles of beer each. Both were reserved with their conversation. Peter's mind was too filled with drastically divergent memories: the good of the distant past butting heads with the bad of the recent past, the present. Peter's body was still sore, but it wasn't nearly as bad as it could have been. He hadn't broken any bones or suffered any major external damage; however, his body would be sore with bruises come morning. His ankles were tender. He had hobbled back through the bush with the aid of a stick, but they were already feeling better, with a little help from some liquid courage. He didn't know what occupied Frank's thoughts—Peter was hesitant to probe. Whatever it was, it had darkened his countenance like when he first climbed up in the treehouse, just before it all came crashing down. Frank, normally a loquacious sort, had been noticeably quiet on the trek back to the camp. And now, nursing his beer, he looked sullen, like something truly deep was troubling his mind.

He hadn't even noticed that he had left the bag of marshmallows behind in the bush.

They continued to sit and brood and drink, and Peter wondered if Frank would ever leave and go back to his camp.

Just then, light speared into the campsite. Peter saw it first. It came from the path leading down to the beach, a pale, yellow light bobbing in the darkness. When Frank saw Peter looking intently away, he turned and saw the light.

"Aw, shit," he groaned.

Soon, two figures emerged behind the light: one taller, the other shorter. In the dim light, Peter saw the blonde woman from the campsite, Frank's wife. Beside her, clutching her mother tight, was the thin girl that had stared out at them from the back of the vehicle.

"Why are you here, Helen?" Frank said. "I said I'd be back when I'm done."

"I know, but you've been gone a long time. We heard that noise again, and Jessica got scared. She didn't want to stay at the camp, so we came to find you."

Frank looked at Peter and rolled his eyes. Then, with exaggerated effort, he pushed his bulk out of the chair. Peter stood up, walked up to the two females, trying hard not to show his pain. "I'm Peter. Nice to meet you."

"Helen. This is Jessica."

Jessica remained clinging to her mum's side. Gone was the forlorn expression on her slim, pale face from the previous night and in its place was a look of fear.

"Want something to eat? Drink? We have marshmallows, if your daughter wants to... wait, sorry, I just remembered we're all out of marshmallows."

"Thanks, but we're fine."

The sound of a car door opening caught Helen's attention. Peter turned and saw Marcia step out. She moved towards the mother and daughter. Though Marcia had spent the past few hours in the car, she didn't look sleepy, and her hair wasn't mussed as if having just woken. Peter wondered: Had she been awake all this time, listening in on his and Frank's conversation? Did she know they had left the camp and were gone for over half an hour?

"Hello, I'm Marcia."

Helen flashed a polite smile, but it died soon after it was born. "Just come to fetch Frank. It's getting late, and I'm sure you two want to turn in for the night."

"It's not that late," Frank said, his words sounding every bit as drunk as he surely was. "If they want to go to sleep, then they'd tell me. I'm not overstaying my welcome, am I, Peter?"

"Not at all."

"See? Stop assuming, Helen. It's embarrassing."

Cricket stood and tentatively sidled over to the girls. They stepped forward to greet the chocolate lab. In the glow cast by the fire, Peter saw their faces properly. The woman's was bruised and puffy, especially on her left side. She had a black eye, and her lips were swollen and split. The girl's face wasn't as bad as her mother's, but she had a red welt on her right cheek, as if slapped by a big hand.

"Is he friendly?" Helen asked. "Is it okay if Jess gives him a pat?"

"Of course," Marcia said. "It's a she, and her name is Cricket. She's very friendly."

As the girl reached down and gently petted the top of Cricket's head, Peter noticed the dark ring on her left forearm, on her wrist. Peter glanced back at Marcia. She was staring at the two females with sadness written over her face. When her eyes flicked to Frank, who was clumsily retrieving his torch from off the ground, the sadness changed to spite.

"She likes you," Marcia said, turning back to the girls. "Cricket's a good judge of character."

The girl, not exactly smiling but still looking happy petting Cricket, squatted, and started scratching the dog under its chin. Cricket sat there and ate up the attention.

"Come on then, let's get going," Frank said. "You barged in on a perfectly good time, ruining my night, but okay, so what else is new? You want to head back to camp? Let's head back to camp." He looked down at his daughter. "Don't get too attached to the dog. She ain't coming with us."

The girl stopped scratching Cricket and straightened.

As Frank staggered towards his wife and daughter, Cricket turned and scampered away.

Peter heard Marcia laugh; it was a soft, barely audible huff, but he knew that sound well, so his ears were well attuned. It was a smug laugh, one of triumph.

"You're welcome to stay," Marcia said, ostensibly to the three of them, but Peter knew it was really meant just for the two girls. "It's late, silly to walk all the way back."

Helen glanced at her husband. For a brief moment, Peter detected hope in her eyes.

"No, we have to get back," Frank answered. "All our things are there. And we have to get up early tomorrow. We have... things planned."

The hope dropped from Helen. She took hold of her daughter's hand and together they stood there like bruised statues.

"Well, thanks for a swell time," Frank said. "I really appreciate the company, the rum and beer, and the... marshmallows."

"It was my pleasure," Peter said. "Maybe I'll see you tomorrow. Teach you to surf if you like."

An even heavier darkness came over Frank, as if the grey clouds in the sky had turned black. "Yeah, maybe. Well, bye."

"Have a good night," Peter said.

Frank turned on his flashlight and trudged towards the path leading down to the beach. Only when he was ahead of them did Helen and her daughter start walking.

"Bye," Marcia called, but no one replied, and soon all three were gone.

Peter faced Marcia. She had a look of contempt. "Don't start," he said.

"Some friend you made. A real top bloke."

"Look, it's none of our business. I can't control what happens behind closed doors... or closed tents, as it were. We don't know the full story. We shouldn't judge what we don't know."

"I know he's a fucking coward who beats his wife and daughter."

"Mars..."

"And sending them back with him feels wrong."

"He's the girl's father, the woman's husband. What did you want me to do, restrain the guy, tie him up?"

"That'd be a good start."

Peter sighed. "I don't want to start another fight. I'm tired and..."

"Drunk."

"Not quite drunk, but darn close. Look, how about we go see them tomorrow? You and me, together, make sure the girls are okay?"

Marcia's hard features softened a little. "Yeah, that'd make me feel better."

"Okay."

"I'm going to brush my teeth and then turn in. Can you get my sleeping bag from the tent and put it in the back of the truck?"

"Really, Mars? You're going to sleep in the truck when there's a perfectly good tent available?"

"I can't sleep in there. Not with that... thing in there."

"We went through this. It's either dead or..." Peter sighed, too tired, too full of booze, to argue. "Okay, you want to sleep in the truck and have an uncomfortable night's sleep, fine. Whatever."

They parted, Marcia towards the toiletries bag and the water, Peter limping towards the tent. If she insisted on sleeping alone, that was fine by him. He'd have a better night's sleep without her, anyway. Hell, he was used to it.

———

Marcia climbed into the back of the 4X4. It was hot and stuffy in the truck with the windows opened, only a slice so not even a mosquito could fit through (but it meant no spiders could fit, either), so she opted to lie on top of the sleeping bag. Dressed only in bra and underpants, she felt comfortable enough. She lay on her back in the close quarters of the cargo area and stared at the ceiling and thought about that repulsive man and what he'd done to his wife and daughter.

He'd done a number on his wife's face. Marcia felt sorry for her, but she felt even worse for the daughter. The bruises on her arms. The frightened look in her eyes. Marcia knew about bruises. And her eyes were well acquainted with fear. She empathised with the girl—in some ways, they were the same. Same blonde hair. Same thin, haunted look. Same abusive father.

Marcia touched her left arm; wrapped her fingers around her biceps.

Her arm was long healed, but once it had been broken, the bones snapped in two places. All because she reached up for a plate to make herself a sandwich. She was eight, wanted to be a big girl, a responsible girl; wanted to make her parents proud. But she was clumsy. Knocked down some cups while getting down a plate, including her dad's favourite mug. She had watched them fall in slow motion. Her brain screamed at her to catch them, but of course, before she could put her body into action, the cups had already hit the floor and shattered.

Soon after, it was her arm that had shattered when her dad saw what she had done. Just an accident, she wanted to plead with him. She didn't mean to...

But the words never came out. They got stuck in her throat, like glue. From panic. From fear.

Even now Marcia remembered the force of her father, his massive hands, rough as bark and fingers hairy like caterpillars, as they grabbed her around her biceps and pulled her towards him. Mouth yelling, spit flying, words pummelling her. The force of him, the white-hot pain as she was tossed across the room. For a moment, she thought her arm had been ripped from its socket. That if she were to look at the left side of her body, she would see a space where her arm used to be, blood would be gushing, and looking over she'd see her dad holding her arm like some ghoulish cricket bat.

But she stumbled and fell to the kitchen floor, and she knew her arm hadn't been pulled off because there was unbelievable pain as she landed hard on her left side. She heard the sound of bones cracking, fire shot up and down her arm, then spread through her body. Lying there on the cold tiles, screaming, she wished her dad had ripped off her arm as she couldn't imagine a worse pain than what she was feeling.

Bastard, Marcia thought, hating her father now, maybe more, than when she was a kid.

Bastard, she thought, hating Frank, and hoping the girl and her mother would be okay.

She kept her hand on her arm and looked out the back window at the tent only a few metres away.

Bastard, she thought.

———

Sitting cross-legged on the air mattress, Peter re-tuned his guitar.

Damn her, he thought, the joint that dangled from his mouth sending gentle curls of smoke that spread through the tent, creating a haze. *Why can't she leave my stuff alone?*

The instrument was well out of tune, all six strings, and he spent a while with the knobs.

Once he was happy with the way it sounded, he tested it out with a Gordon Lightfoot ballad.

Not bad. Not perfect, but better than what Marcia had left it.

He closed his eyes as he played. He knew the fingering by heart. Along with the booze and the weed that flowed through his body, the music calmed him.

Unlike Frank, Peter was mostly content with his life. He

liked his job; he worked with a good group of people, and he had a small but close circle of friends. He didn't spend a lot of time mulling over his life; what could have been, what he lacked in his present lot. He didn't have time to dwell. But, on the occasions he had time to sit and ponder, he always thought about his dream of becoming a musician. He always felt a small twang in his gut, an ache in his heart, and he thought of that simple two-word question that held so much pain and could turn a person mad if he let it: *what if?* What if he had devoted his time and energy into music, would he have made it, become famous, rich?

Like so many before him, he had let fear win. The fear of rejection. The fear of failure. Going into advertising had seemed the better option, a more certain future. Still, he wondered: *what if?*

It's Marcia's fault, really, he thought as he fumbled with the tune. Stopped, repositioned his fingers, then continued. *If I hadn't married at such a young age, maybe I would have pursued a career in music.* It was the need to support a wife that made him go into full-time work, become another nine-to-fiver.

He had been a good guitarist, and a more than competent singer. He probably could have made it, been another Dylan or Lightfoot, Denver or Cat Stevens, if only things had worked out differently.

He stopped, took a deep drag of the joint, and then changed to a different song.

Without meaning to, he started playing 'I Don't Want to Walk Without You.'

He guessed it was because of the conversation with Frank. He hadn't thought about the song in years, hadn't played it since he was eleven years old. But he still remembered all the notes, the chords, the melody.

He was transported back almost twenty years. Young Peter standing in the tiny lounge room one cold, wet day. Dad sitting in his favourite chair, pipe affixed to his mouth. Peter had played the song he had been learning for a week. He had been nervous. His hands shook. It was the first time he had played the guitar in front of anyone. Sitting in his room, practicing, was one thing; standing there with someone watching was an altogether different beast.

He had made it through with only a few mistakes. What he remembered most about that day wasn't the rain pattering against the windows. It wasn't the smell of Dad's pipe tobacco. And it wasn't the notes he had bungled. No, it was his father's face as he sat there and watched his son play his favourite song. He had rarely seen his dad look so happy; his eyes even had a sheen to them. He had looked proud. He had clapped after, which was fine, that was to be expected. But it was the look on his face that Peter remembered, a joy that couldn't be faked.

Dad was so good to me, and I didn't pay that back, Peter thought as he neared the end of the tune.

He had lied to Frank. Made it seem like his dad died before they got the chance to come back here. Which was true, in a way. But he wanted Frank to think there hadn't been the time, that the cancer had taken Dad too quickly before they were able to make the plans. Truth was, there had been time. Dad had been sick, sure, but the cancer had worked its evil slowly. If Peter hadn't been so preoccupied with work, he could have made the arrangements. He kept holding off on planning the holiday. *Soon*, he'd tell Dad. *I'm just busy at work, it's a bad time to take time off, but soon, I promise, soon...*

Peter never intended to take Dad out of the hospital and back to this spot. It was all talk. An empty promise. He had been a young man, just starting out in the company. He hadn't wanted to disappoint his boss, the company. He wanted to show them he was a hard worker, harder than anyone else. Everything else—his wife, his family, his terminally ill father— took a back seat.

So, the promised camping trip never happened, all because Peter was too scared.

He wasn't even there when Dad passed. He chose to work late instead of heading over to the hospital. He knew how sick his dad was at that point, how close to the end. Yet, he had elected to stay back and work. Dad had died alone.

The strumming had become hard, almost violent.

Tears stung his eyes.

Suddenly, the high E string snapped. It struck him on the cheek like a thin metal whip. Cricket, asleep on the empty side of the mattress, woke and raised her head fast, eyes springing open.

"Hell," he muttered, dropping the guitar and putting a hand to his cheek. Blood smeared his finger. The cut stung.

He looked down at the broken string, curled on the fretboard, dead, a ruined thing.

He moved the guitar onto the bed and sucked in a good helping of smoke. He held it in until his lungs started burning, then he exhaled, blowing smoke into the already dense fog inside the tent.

A noise outside startled him. Startled Cricket, too.

Sounded like something had fallen to the ground.

Maybe Marcia sneaking out for a late-night snack. Or a night cap. If she was after a sneaky nip of rum, she'd be severely disappointed. Or maybe she was stepping out for a late-night visit.

Part of him hoped it was Marcia coming over to the tent. Still wearing only her underwear, she had decided she'd had enough of sleeping alone in the car and was creeping over to surprise him. It being dark, the fire having dwindled, she knocked into the table or a chair.

He waited, but the tent didn't open.

Hope and desire turned to anger and disappointment.

What did you expect? he asked himself. *We've barely looked at each other for the past few months, let alone slept together. And we're fighting, like always, so there's no chance of her coming over in the dead of night to fool around.*

He had given up on the noise being Marcia when he heard more sounds coming from outside. Rustling, banging, like someone rifling through their food boxes, knocking into the plates and cutlery.

Peter reached for his torch. Cricket was now on full alert. "You have my back, girl?"

Cricket, standing facing the front of the tent, looked at him.

"No, you're a scaredy-cat."

Cricket whined, as if in objection.

Peter crawled up to the opening. Took hold of the zipper. Open slowly, or quickly? he wondered.

There's nothing out there, nothing dangerous anyway.

With that in mind, he zipped open the tent with his usual speed when leaving, in an effort to convince himself nothing bad was out there making the noise.

He slipped out, stood up, and aimed the torch at the table. Many pairs of glowing eyes stared back at him. The small, furry creatures were on the table, and on the ground by the boxes of food. At his presence, the possums and bandicoots fled, tipping over boxes, knocking over cups, plates.

"Goddamn it," Peter sighed.

He sucked on the last of the joint, flicked it into the fire, which consisted mostly of coals and low flames. Walking over to the table, he barely hobbled. Either the weed helped to cover the pain, or the strain was simply healing on its own.

He started cleaning up. Had just put the cans and food items not ravaged by the creatures back into the boxes when he heard movement on the outskirts of the campsite. He shot the torchlight towards the sound. A snake was moving through the grass, heading away from him.

"Jesus Christ."

He didn't know much about snakes, had no idea if this one was venomous or as harmless as one of the bandicoots. He kept the light trained on the serpent and watched it slither away into the surrounding bush.

When it was gone, he eased out a breath.

He moved the torch to the area the snake had been. Saw the broken remains of the eagle egg: the shattered shell, the glistening embryo, looking like a wad of red snot.

He continued cleaning up the mess. He picked up the cups and plates, the fallen cans, and intact packets of food, and placed them all back in the boxes. The partially eaten food and leftover scraps he threw into the fire. When he was done, he stopped by the truck and shone the light into the cargo area. Marcia was sound asleep on top of her sleeping bag. Though sleeping, she looked far from restful. She had a pinched expression, like she had fallen asleep in an anxious state of mind.

Leaving her to her troublesome rest, Peter headed back to the tent. Cricket stood outside, looking out at the darkness.

"Thanks for the help."

Cricket glanced at him, cocked her head, then returned her gaze outwards.

Just before he entered, he stopped and looked out at the surrounding bush. Weird, but the campsite seemed smaller, as if the bush had grown within the space of a few hours, encroaching onto the clearing. *Just the darkness, the shadows, makes everything appear distorted*, Peter thought, and he slipped into the tent. "Cricket," he called.

She didn't follow. Instead, she continued to stare at the bush; specifically, where the snake had vanished.

"Cricket," Peter called again.

His dog looked back. She didn't seem spooked or wary, as if the snake was still out there. She had an almost... hungry look, like when they had chicken for dinner and Cricket sat by the table, a longing in her eyes.

Cricket looked back to the bush one last time, then turned around and padded into the tent.

4

————

Marcia had just finished her second cup of coffee and was munching on toast with jam when Peter emerged from the tent. Dressed only in boxers, body sheathed in sweat and looking wan, he crawled out and then staggered to his feet. Cricket appeared soon after, panting and looking hot and fatigued. She went straight over to the tub filled with water they were using in lieu of a proper water bowl and began eagerly drinking.

Peter shuffled forward. The way he moved, his body looked stiff and sore. He stopped by the fire, opened his mouth, but clamped it shut. He looked terrible. Face as pale and slick with perspiration as his torso, eyes like tiny red pebbles. He had a single scratch on his cheek that looked red and angry.

"Want some coffee?"

Peter nodded.

She poured some of the instant coffee into a paper cup and handed it up to him.

He took it sluggishly and sipped. "I feel like... death."

Marcia tried not to smile, but she couldn't stop herself. She put the cup to her mouth so Peter wouldn't see her gloating. She swallowed the bitter drink, along with the smile. "Drank more than you thought, hey?"

"Yeah, I guess. Didn't sleep well, either."

"Me neither. What happened to your face?"

"Huh?"

"That scratch on your cheek."

Peter reached up and fingered the mark. "Oh, that." He looked at the ground. "I, ah, stepped into a low-hanging branch last night. The result of too much booze and not enough light."

"Want me to clean it? Put on some cream, a band-aid?"

"It's just a scratch."

"Might get infected."

"I'll be fine."

Peter took a few more swallows of the coffee and then squinted upwards. "What time is it?"

"Just after ten."

"That late?"

"I only woke up half an hour ago. Managed to get the fire going, surprisingly. I remembered what you said about the coals, about finding some that were still hot and using tinder and dry leaves to get it going, before putting on the bigger bits of wood. But we're running low on firewood, just so you know."

"Okay," Peter sighed.

Marcia munched the last of her toast. It tasted of ash, which wasn't unpleasant. Cooking it in the wire rack contraption over the flames gave it an earthier, more rustic taste, much different than at home using the electric toaster.

Don't tell me, Mars, that you're beginning to enjoy this camping business?

Not a chance. She admitted, the open fire was nice: the natural heat, the sound of the wood burning, the smell of the smoke, there was something beautifully simple yet powerful about it. But hell, they could install a wood heater at home and enjoy it just as well there. Didn't mean she liked the overall camping experience. They were going home tomorrow, and she couldn't be happier. If she had her way, they'd pack up and head home today. But she knew, unless a miracle occurred to radically alter Peter's mind, she would have to suffer through another whole day and one more long night.

"Want some toast?"

Peter made a face. "Nah, I'm good."

"You sure? Some food might help to soak up all that alcohol. Vegemite on toast is good for what ails ya."

"Please, Marcia, stop talking about food."

Peter practically fell into the second camping chair. He held his cup with both hands. Steam curled up into his face.

"Campsite looks different," Marcia said. "Tidier. Also, and maybe I'm going loopy, but there seems like less food than there was yesterday."

"We had some visitors last night." Eyes once again closed, Peter looked ready to fall back to sleep.

"Visitors? What do you mean?"

"Animals. Possums, bandicoots. Must have smelled the food. We were careless and left some out. Had to throw a bunch into the fire. I spent some time cleaning up, so they wouldn't come back."

Marcia suddenly felt icky, like her personal space had been invaded. She glanced around the campsite, half expecting to see some critters sitting there, staring at her, waiting for more food.

She looked down at her cup. Had the creatures been at the dinnerware too? Maybe their filthy paws had climbed over the cups, their diseased mouths sniffing around the spoons.

Christ, how she hated camping.

She tossed the paper cup into the flames, watched it blacken before catching fire.

"So, what are we doing today? More sitting around on the beach, getting sunburnt? More surfing in shark-infested waters, trying to avoid the dead things floating in the ocean? More eating baked beans and shitting in the bush?"

"Come on, Marcia, my head's pounding. Do we have to get

into it so early? Can't you let a guy wake up and deal with his hangover?"

"Or we could go home," she said, quietly, but not too quietly. "I mean, animals invading the campsite, eating our food...?"

"That's just a part of camping, Mars. We're in nature, it's to be expected. Besides, as long as we remember to pack up our stuff at night, make sure there's no food left out, we shouldn't attract animals."

"Maybe you should leave Cricket outside at night. Scare away the possums and whatever else is lurking out there."

Peter downed some more coffee. He opened his eyes. "No, she's safer in the tent with me."

"Look at you, you're sweating worse than a pig in a sauna. It's too hot in there. Cricket will suffocate. Look at her, she looks sick."

Peter glanced back at Cricket. Finished at the tub of water, she just stood there, mouth dripping, still panting and looking exhausted.

"I forgot to open the windows last night. That'll help cool things down."

"Why are you so against Cricket staying outside? Not like she's going to run away."

Peter dumped the remainder of his coffee on the ground. "Just leave it alone, Mars."

She eased forward and looked hard at her husband. "Why, Peter? What are you afraid of?"

"Nothing."

She could tell he was lying. He tended to cast his gaze down whenever he lied. Nursing a wicked hangover didn't stop his unconscious giveaways.

"Lie, just like you always bloody do. I don't know why I bother." She jumped up. "Is everything out of your mouth a lie? Can you ever tell the truth?"

"Oh, for crying out loud..." Slumped in the chair, Peter

looked like a living skeleton. "Fine. Okay, I saw a snake last night. That's why I didn't want Cricket out at night."

Prickles ran up and down Marcia's body. She scanned the ground. "A snake?"

"Probably wasn't dangerous. Most snakes aren't, you know. It was just sniffing around the eagle egg. It took off when I shined the torch at it. Don't worry, I'm sure it won't bother us again."

Marcia gazed over at the tree where she had thrown the egg. All the bits of shell were gone. Nothing remained except for some dried mucus on the trunk.

"I put what was left of it in the fire, too. Look, Mars, people go camping all the time. Most aren't bitten by snakes or attacked by wild animals."

"You were attacked by the bird," she reminded him.

"It was after the egg. The egg's gone. As long as we keep the place clean, we won't be bothered. Animals are more scared of us than we are of them. Honest, Mars, you don't have to worry. I'm not lying."

She whipped her head back around and stared at Peter. "If you're so sure the snake won't return, why won't you let Cricket stay outside at night?"

Peter almost managed a smirk; his cheeks wobbled, his lips curled, but then it all collapsed. "Just a precaution. Dogs are inquisitive creatures. If a snake happens to wander close to the campsite, Cricket will go and investigate. But we have nothing to worry about."

"We wouldn't if we packed up and left. Hell, maybe we could head over to Portsea, spend the last bit of the weekend with Mark and Carol."

Peter leaned forward, closer to the fire. Even though he was wearing only his boxer shorts and looked to be sweltering, he seemed to savour the small fire Marcia had made. "Maybe," he said.

Suddenly, all fears of snakes and bush creatures drained

away, and in its place a sense of hope (along with images of Mark walking around in nothing but shorts). "Really?"

"I'll think about it. I hate to leave this place, but give me a chance to get over this hangover and then we'll talk about it later. Okay?"

Marcia smiled, for perhaps the first time in days, weeks even. "Okay."

"I'm going to scrounge up some more firewood. How about you take a morning walk, enjoy the sun, the salt air?"

She suddenly felt more buoyant, happier. The thought of taking a stroll along the beach didn't cause a heavy weight of dread. She didn't feel trapped in a place she was unable to escape.

"Take Cricket with you. She could use a run after being cooped up inside the tent all night."

For once, Marcia didn't mind Peter's mutt tagging along. She whistled. "Come on, Cricket."

Cricket hesitated. But then, as if doing so out of obedience, not any real desire, she walked slowly towards Marcia.

"Take your time," Peter said. "Enjoy the scenery. You haven't stopped to really appreciate this place yet."

"I'll try. Oh, I still want to check up on the mother and daughter."

"Mars..."

"You promised we would."

Peter sighed. "Okay, when you get back, we'll take a drive over."

"Good. Just no 'hair of the dog' with that Frank bloke, okay? You're wrecked enough."

"Don't worry, just the thought of alcohol..." If possible, Peter turned even greener.

"See you soon."

With Cricket in tow, Marcia headed for the path leading down to the beach.

He had only just started scouting for dead wood when Peter heard Marcia call out. Her voice was faint, but clear.

"Peter!"

Still feeling like crap, like his insides were slowly dissolving and would come pouring out of his mouth, like his head was a speedball that was being repeatedly hit, he turned and started through the bush towards the beach.

What now? he thought as his shoes snapped twigs and crushed fallen leaves. Fortunately, he had slipped on a pair of shorts and a t-shirt before looking for firewood, so the spiky branches and prickly bushes didn't scratch him as he pushed through the dense bushland. *Probably found a dead fish and thinks the world's ending,* he thought derisively. Use it as further proof this place is evil, only strengthening her resolve to leave.

He was going to let her think he was considering leaving, at least until sometime after lunch. That way, he'd have some peace, some time without her constant bitching and begging to get away. They were staying until tomorrow; he was adamant about that. He wanted to stay for as long as possible. But he wasn't about to tell her that.

When he broke through the brush and stepped out onto the soft sand, he saw the distant figure of Marcia near the water's edge. Something large was on the beach. Looked like some kind of sea creature, smaller than a whale but bigger than a seal. "Marcia!" he called.

She turned and waved. He started jogging, but doing so made his insides feel like jelly and that his head would pop, so he slowed and walked the rest of the way.

Marcia stood about a metre from the dead animal, hand over her nose. Cricket remained back, oddly docile.

"It's another one," Marcia said. "Another dead animal washed ashore."

The strange-looking creature had a thick, brownish-grey

body that was slimy and partially eaten away. Drooping folds of fat framed a squat, gorilla-like snout. It had squinty, pig-like eyes. Whatever it was, it looked—and smelled—like it had been dead a while.

"What the hell is it?" Marcia said. "It's not a dolphin, and it's not a shark."

Peter looked back at his wife, and despite the queasiness churning up inside, he grinned. "I think it's a Bunyip."

"Peter, be serious."

"I am. At least, that's what the blackfellas thought, back in the day." He turned back to the weird-looking animal, fat from bloat and courting an ever-growing number of flies. "I'm pretty sure it's a dugong. A sea cow, as it's sometimes called. Used to be thousands of 'em all up and down the coast, but they've been killed off for their meat and oil. Poor old bugger. Ugly thing. Sorry, mate."

"I don't think it's a male."

"Why do you say that?"

"Looks like a bigger version of that other dead creature we found yesterday."

Peter nodded. "Yeah, maybe."

"It is, I know it! It's a she, Peter, and she's probably that baby's mother. That was her baby we found, and she was trying to get to it."

"I highly doubt that. This animal's rotting. I reckon it's been dead for at least a week. We only found that baby yesterday."

"I don't care. This is the mother, I'm sure of it."

Peter looked up the beach, to where the smaller sea creature still lay, tangled up in the plastic bag.

"It would explain those noises we've been hearing. The mother mourning her dead..."

He stopped and looked at Marcia. Her face was stony, but her eyes held tears. When she blinked, they trickled down her face. She hurriedly wiped them away.

"Well, anyway, I don't think that's what happened."

"It is. She died trying to get to her baby. Christ, Peter, if this is nature, I don't want any part of it."

She stormed away, trudging along the beach towards the bluff.

Cricket remained standing, head ping-ponging between Marcia and Peter.

"What are you doing out here, you poor, ugly thing?" Peter muttered down to the dugong carcass. "You don't belong here; you belong in the water."

Despite Marcia's hysterical insistence, Peter leaned towards a shark attack. The two dead dugongs—if that was what the smaller creature was—were unrelated, except for being the victims of a more vicious predator.

Any other explanations simply didn't make sense.

———

Once her emotions had settled from finding the dead dugong (she didn't care what Peter thought, it was the baby's mother; she knew it), once Peter recovered more wood and built up the fire (which she protested against, why bother building up the fire if they were going to be leaving soon?), and after they had nibbled on some grapes, slices of bread and honey, and some cheese and crackers—it was all either of them could stomach for lunch—they headed off for the neighbour's camp.

Peter wanted to walk, even though his energy was still depleted from last night's over-indulgence. She wanted to get to the campsite as quickly as possible and then (providing the mother and daughter were fine) get back to theirs and start packing. So, she had suggested driving. Peter had thought her silly—they were in no rush, so said King Peter—but in this instance she had won out. She had hurriedly brushed her teeth, her hair, grabbed her hat and sunglasses, and by the time she was ready, Peter was already in the car, waiting. Though rather than sitting behind the wheel, he was in the passenger seat. He insisted she drive. Wasn't feeling up to it, he said. She had hopped up behind the wheel, started the engine (which was working again, sneaky Pete had evidently worked his magic while she was busy getting ready) and had made the bumpy journey out of the clearing, skirted around the bluff, and down onto the beach.

Perched up in the driver's seat, the sand brilliant in the afternoon light, Marcia wondered if she was doing the right thing going over and checking up on the family. It wasn't any of her business, not really. It wasn't her job to make sure everyone she encountered was safe. What she wanted most was to leave. She didn't even care about the tent or the boxes of food or any of it. She wanted out of here. It was starting to get late as it was. By the time they got everything packed and ready, it would be dark when they reached Portsea, after midnight if they headed straight home.

You're doing the right thing, she told herself. *I'm sure they're fine. Yesterday was just an especially bad day, the result of one—or five—too many drinks, an argument that flared into something more. Just a one-off.*

She wanted to believe it.

"How far up?" she asked, glancing across at Peter. He was slumped against the door, eyes half-closed. For some reason he had brought along his old slingshot. He sat there, holding it, lazily pulling on the rubber sling.

"Not far. Just around this next bend."

She continued driving along the beach. In the side and rear-view mirrors she saw clouds of white sand being kicked up by the tyres. To the right, the ocean was oddly calm. She was used to the surf wild, great waves leaping up and crashing. Seeing it so flat was eerie, like some giant beast lying in wait, waiting to pounce, to kill.

She steered the Nissan Patrol around a sharp, rocky bank.

"See those high bluffs ahead? Camp's somewhere up there. Just pull over close to the bluffs."

As she manoeuvred the car over, Peter stopped fiddling with his toy and ducked forward. "Strange," he said, gazing through the windscreen.

"What?"

He shrugged. "Probably nothing. Just... yesterday, there was smoke drifting in the air. It's how I discovered there were others camping in the area. There's no smoke now."

"It's a warm day. They probably didn't bother lighting a campfire."

Peter sat back. He looked distracted. "Yeah, that's probably it."

"Or maybe they left. Decided to leave early and head home."

Lucky for them, she thought.

She pulled the car to a stop. Opened the door and started to hop out.

"Maybe you should stay here."

She pulled her right leg back in and gazed at Peter, who still held a slightly troubled expression. "What? No. It was my idea to check up on the mother and daughter. I'm coming with you."

"All right. Suit yourself."

Marcia jumped down and met Peter on the other side. He was still holding the slingshot. She followed him towards the bluffs, towards a narrow path winding from the beach to the top of the cliff. Peter started up first. The path was steep and sandy. The walk up to the top strained Marcia's leg muscles and caused her lungs to burn. She wasn't as fit as she used to be. She was glad when they reached the top and flat ground.

Through the trees, the white camper, tents and other things like tables and chairs could be seen.

"Still here," Peter muttered.

He stopped and looked at the ground. Bent down and snatched a small pebble from the earth.

"What's that for?"

He nestled the small rock in the leather pouch of the slingshot. "Just in case."

"In case what? You think Frank is dangerous?"

Without answering, Peter continued forward. With nerves pecking at her insides, Marcia walked behind, onto a narrow path that led into the bush.

As they edged closer to the campsite, one thing struck Marcia as odd: the utter quiet. It was around two o'clock, so even people who went to bed late should be up by this time. There was no noise from a radio, no talking, no laughter. No sound of dishes being washed, or games being played. Not even the sound of people arguing, which, at this point, she'd take.

Maybe they're all sleeping, she thought. Spent the morning at the beach, swimming, playing, and now they're all taking a nap. But as they wound through the thicket of trees, vines and bushes, and came up to the camp, Marcia saw how odd things truly were.

The site was overrun with thick flora. Strangle vines and creepers had seemingly poured out of the surrounding scrub to form a dense blanket. Vines had clawed their way over the tents, the table, and chairs. The badminton net was strangled with green creepers. Even the camper was starting to be consumed by the tentacle-like growth. The area was so overgrown with foliage it was difficult to know where the bush ended and the campsite began.

In Marcia's mind, there was only one explanation. "This is an old campsite. Looks like it's been here for years. We've come to the wrong place."

Standing at the end of the path, Peter surveyed the site and shook his head. "No, this is their site. That's their camper. Their tents. I remember. I was just here yesterday."

"But that's impossible. Look at this place!"

"Hello!" Peter called. "Frank? It's Peter."

They listened. Heard only silence. Even the ocean behind

them was hushed. Except for a strange noise, like the creaking of a rusty door hinge or the constant squeak of a rocking chair. The sound was repetitive and seemed to move in time with the wind.

"What is that?" Marcia said.

"Don't know. Sounds like it's coming from the bush on the far side of the camp."

Peter proceeded forward. Marcia followed, and together they battled through the thicket. The vines were thick and hardy, and the longer ones that had slithered down from the trees threatened to trip them. The creepers, spindlier, were no less problematic. They covered the ground like long curls of green thread, threatening to catch you in its web. Peter and Marcia moved cautiously through the overgrowth. They came first upon the campfire, which was cold, just a pit of grey ash and half-burned logs. The large, white camper sat off to the side, looking like some animal that had been trapped by the tangle of vines.

"I really think you have the wrong camp," Marcia said again, more to calm her increasingly frayed nerves than any real belief in the statement; a vain attempt to convince herself it was the truth. However, when they passed the table, Marcia saw food spread out, including a loaf of bread. Aside from a line of ants running up the table and spreading over the loaf, the bread looked fresh, which unsettled her almost as much as the strange creaking sound they were heading towards. And the backpacks and tote bags on the ground, gripped by the vines, looked new; at least, not ones abandoned years ago, left to rot and gather leaves and dirt. None of it computed in her mind. Her head swirled with questions and emotions, crashing together in a mass of white noise.

They continued through the campsite. Instead of stopping at the tents, which were closed up, Peter moved beyond the clearing—or what was once a clearing—to the opposite end of the site. The creaking grew louder. Another sound joined the creaking. This one more familiar. The sound of birds, a kind of cackling, the sound not dissimilar to laughter.

A short distance from the tents, where the vines weren't as crowded, not far into the dense bush surrounding the campsite, hanging from a gum tree, was Frank.

Peter gasped. Marcia didn't move or make a sound. For a moment, she thought (hoped) she was looking up at a mannequin that someone had strung up for a laugh. An overweight mannequin wearing a Hawaiian shirt and Bermuda shorts, sporting a purple face and fat tongue that poked out the side of the mouth like some slug had crawled in and made itself at home.

Not a mannequin, a small, child-like voice whispered. *A person. A human. A dead human.*

Unlike some plastic dummy, the thing hanging from the tree had the smell of death about it, much like the animal on the shore. Along with the stench of death, there was also the pungent aroma of urine. Marcia noticed a stain on the front of the shorts, and there was a puddle on the ground just below the feet, which swung back and forth barely half a metre up.

Birds were perched on the branch above Frank's head. Big, black ones. They pecked at the face, tearing chunks of flesh, and Marcia saw, just before she turned around and vomited, the twin sockets where the eyes used to be.

As she bent over and emptied what little food and drink she'd downed at lunch, she heard the birds, their horrible laughing squawks; and worse, the silence when they weren't cackling but feasting upon the carcass.

"Go on, get!" Peter shouted.

Marcia caught sight of him fire the pebble up at the birds, and a moment later, she heard sharp squawking and the sound of flapping.

"You okay?" Peter asked.

Marcia straightened, wiped her mouth with the bottom of her top. "No."

Peter, if possible, looked even more wan. His eyes darted around, as if unable to settle on any one thing.

"Peter," Marcia said, voice brittle and quivering. "The girls."

Peter's eyes closed. He held them that way for a good ten seconds before he opened them and managed to focus on Marcia. "I'll take a look."

"I'm here too. I was the one who insisted we come, see if they were okay. I want to see it through. I *have* to see it through."

Peter nodded.

She pointed to the tent closest to her: a small, one-man tent. "I'll take that one."

"You sure?"

"Yes."

"Okay."

He turned and started towards the larger of the two tents.

Marcia faced the small tent. Her palms were sweaty, her mouth tasted sour. Her head throbbed, like she was the one with a hangover. She could only take in short breaths, as if winded.

Maybe they're okay, she thought, even though it was a stupid thought, the thought of a child. *Maybe Frank kissed them both once they had laid down for their naps, closed up the tents and then climbed the tree, secured the rope to the limb, made a noose, and...*

The terrible creaking sound persisted as she stepped over to the tent. It echoed around the overgrown campsite, scratching at her ears, worse than nails down a chalkboard.

She stopped by the entrance. Noticed a thin line of ants marching along the ground, making their way through the campsite and into a tiny opening in one corner of the tent.

Oh God...

Heart pounding, Marcia gripped the tent flap. More than anything else in her life, she didn't want to pull back the flap and look inside. But she had to. She had to know.

Movement behind her. She glanced back and saw Peter

stagger out from the bigger tent. He stopped, bent over, and retched. Not much came out, mostly bile. He straightened and, looking over, said, "Marcia, don't. Don't look."

She nearly asked what he had seen, but didn't. She didn't need the details. She could guess well enough what he had seen inside that tent.

She almost took Peter's advice and left the tent to its secrets. But she felt she owed it to the girl. Someone had to know what had befallen her. She turned back around. Took a deep breath. Swallowed. Peeled back the flap. Bent over, took a few steps forward and gazed into the darkness.

"Get them off me!" Marcia kept repeating.

Peter tried talking to her as they hurried away from the dead campsite. He asked her what she had seen inside the smaller tent: was the girl dead? (Almost certainly, Peter knew—just like the mother; Christ, he couldn't get what he had seen out of his mind... the mess, the blood...). And he asked her what was on her she wanted off? Because he saw nothing on Marcia.

But she was insensible to his questions. To even his presence. Peter had wanted out of the vine-choked camp, too, but Marcia fled like she was on fire. Slapping at her body, a panicked look on her ashen face, screaming the same four words, over and over again.

She moved down the path with such force, Peter thought for sure she'd fall and tumble to the beach below. He wanted to tell her to slow down but knew it would go unheeded. So, he just ploughed down with her, trying to keep a sure footing, trying not to let the grisly find inside the tent play over in his mind.

When they reached the beach, Marcia continued to flail and cry.

"Marcia! What is it? What's wrong?"

She looked at him with wide eyes and screamed, "Get them off me!"

"Get what off you?"

"These... things! These ants!"

Peter looked, couldn't see even a single ant.

"They're crawling all over me!"

Marcia suddenly took off, bolting towards the ocean. "Marcia!" She crashed into the water and disappeared beneath the waves.

Peter knew Marcia wasn't a fan of the water. She rarely swam, even in friends' pools when they went over for summer barbecues. She must really be out of her mind, Peter thought as he made his way down the beach. Standing on the shore, ignorant of the water lapping at his shoes, he waited for her to emerge.

Ten seconds clicked by. Twenty. No sign of Marcia. Panic started to simmer. He was close to diving in when Marcia popped out of the surf and stood there, waist deep in the ocean, looking scared and lost and confused.

"Mars?"

She turned to him. Her eyes held pain and sadness, but no longer the blind panic. She looked down at herself. "I thought..." she began, as waves broke around her. "I thought I was covered in ants. I could feel them all over me." She scanned the water around her.

"You weren't, Mars," Peter said.

She raised her hands, cupping them over her face, and began to cry.

Peter didn't know what to do. What she wanted him to do. So, he just waited in the shallows for her to finish.

Finally, she lowered her hands. Tucked wet strands of hair that looked like golden seaweed behind her ears and started wading out of the ocean.

She was almost out, the water only licking at her knees,

when she cried out. She sucked in a breath through her teeth and immediately began hobbling.

"What happened?"

"I dunno. Think I stepped on something."

Peter saw red floating to the surface, looking like red tendrils. He helped her out and sat her on the dry sand and lifted her bare right foot. Blood flowed from a long, thin cut.

Peter winced.

When Marcia saw the blood, she said, "Oh my God. It's bad."

"Maybe not," Peter said, nausea rolling through him. The sight of the blood recalled the scene inside the tent: walls and ceiling spattered with blood, soaking into the sleeping bag. Unlike Marcia, who had no problem with blood, he hated the sight of it; his, hers, anyone's. When he cut himself, he got Marcia to clean and bandage the wound.

"Often it's the superficial cuts that bleed the most," he said, not sure if that was true, but it sounded about right. At least, it was something to say to try to keep his mind from thinking about the horrors he had seen. "Back in a sec." He took off his shirt, stepped down into the ocean, and dunked his shirt in the water. He hurried back up to Marcia and gently washed the underside of her foot while trying not to look at the blood.

"God, Peter, this place! I hate this fucking place! What next?"

Peter held the wet ball of fabric in place. "I don't know."

"There's something wrong with this place. I've been trying to tell you. It doesn't want us here."

He took the shirt away from her foot. Blood still trickled out, but nowhere near as voluminous as before. Steeling himself, he looked at the wound.

"Bad?"

There was a gash about five centimetres long on the bridge of her foot. Though it was hard to tell, it looked fairly deep. "Not too bad," he said, looking down at the sand for a moment and taking some breaths. "It'll need to be bandaged."

"What the hell did I step on?"

Peter shrugged. "Whatever it was, doesn't look like there's anything imbedded in your foot, which is good."

He put the wet and bloody shirt back on the wound.

"You lost a thong," he said, trying to lighten the dark mood. The other thong was still on her left foot. "Want me to try to find it?"

"No. I don't care about a stupid thong."

In short time, Peter took another look at her wound. Blood no longer seeped, but the cut looked worse without the curtain of blood. "You okay to move?"

Marcia wiggled her foot. Doing so made the wound start to weep, but only a little. He made a tourniquet with the shirt, wrapped it around Marcia's foot. He helped her up. When she put pressure on her right foot, she winced.

"I'm okay," she said. "I can manage. I just want to get away from here."

She glanced towards the high bluff. "We have to notify the police."

"Yeah... of course."

"Why would a man bring his family out to a place like this and..." Marcia turned away. "Let's go," she said, flatly, and holding onto Peter for support, they walked towards the truck.

———

"Can't we go any faster?"

"Last thing we need is a broken axle."

Peter, in the driver's seat, powered the truck down the beach. Now they were a distance from the campsite, the true weight of what they had found fell down on him. Christ. He couldn't believe what Frank had done. Killed his wife, his daughter, and then hanged himself. He thought about what he had found inside the main tent. It wasn't just that Frank had ended his wife's life—it was the manner in which he had done it; he had split her face apart. Caved in her head so it resembled a watermelon that had been beaten with a hammer.

Only it wasn't a hammer, but a rock. A rock about the size of a softball, and it sat beside the ruined head of Helen, blood and bits of flesh or brain stuck to it. Helen, naked from the waist down, was lying face up, so she had probably seen her husband when he attacked her. Rock in his hand, murder in his eyes.

How could a man do that? Just bash in his wife's face. What could push a man to do such a thing?

Peter couldn't imagine. He wasn't capable; didn't have that violent, animalistic side to him.

Maybe she was asleep when Frank came into the tent, armed with the rock. Maybe she didn't know it was coming. Maybe the first blow had knocked her unconscious, and she felt very little as Frank continued to pound, splattering blood and matter all over himself, the tent.

Then, when he was finished, he stalked over to his daughter's tent (or had he killed her first?), and when that was done, had climbed the tree, rope in hand...

Peter blinked against the bright sand, glinting like a million tiny shards of glass.

He looked over at Marcia. Still wet, still looking painted with white, she stared out the windscreen at the beach.

"What happened back there, Marcia?"

Marcia didn't blink. "I can't..."

"She was dead, though, right?"

"Yes."

"Was she... bad?"

"Bad? Of course, she was bad. She was a dead child, Peter."

"I know. But I mean... was she... could you tell how she died?"

Marcia snapped her head and stared daggers at Peter. "She didn't die. She was killed. Murdered by that bastard. And no, I couldn't tell. She was too covered with..." Marcia shivered; her body jerked as if itchy. "I didn't look too hard. But I could tell she was dead, okay? Her face was... blue. Jesus, I don't want to think about it!"

"Okay, I'm sorry. I just had to know."

"I just want to leave. I just want to leave," she repeated, softly.

Soon they came upon the dead baby dugong, which meant they were close to their campsite. Up ahead, Peter saw the big, dark shape of the adult sea cow, but he barely took any notice of it. He started to steer the truck away from the ocean, towards the bluffs and the track leading back to camp.

"Peter," Marcia said.

"Hmmm?"

"Peter, stop!"

Peter stamped down on the brakes, the truck jerked to a halt. "What?"

Marcia was looking out the passenger window, across the beach at the adult dugong. "That... thing, it's moved!"

Peter gazed over at the large dugong. Now he looked at it properly, the dead mammal did appear to be farther up the beach.

"It's still alive."

Peter huffed. "It's fucking dead, Marcia. Look at it; it's a rotting corpse."

"You're wrong. It has to still be alive. There's a trail in the sand where it's dragged itself."

"It's... the tide," Peter said, stumbling over his words. "It's going out, so it gives the illusion..."

"No! It was after her baby, but now it's after us."

"Marcia, you're being ridiculous."

"Trust you to think that," Marcia said.

Peter gave the dead dugong one last look (*it certainly looks like it has moved. No, surely not*), and then continued towards the bluffs.

———

Once Marcia had changed into dry clothes, Peter dabbed some cream onto the wound, which caused Marcia to whimper and tears to well in her eyes. Then he put some butterfly stitches over the cut before finally wrapping a bandage tight around her foot.

"Thanks," she said with little warmth. "I'm going to pack my things, and then we can leave."

"It'll take a while to take down the tent, pack everything up. It's getting late, why don't we..."

"No," Marcia said, face creasing. "You said we could leave. Fuck the tent, fuck the food, fuck everything. I'm getting my stuff, then we're leaving. Okay? We head straight to the nearest police station and tell them about... what happened."

With lips trembling, she hobbled away into the tent, where her bags were still housed. She hesitated before going in. Peter doubted it was fear over the huntsman still being inside that was the cause of her hesitation. She had probably completely forgotten about the spider. No, the memories of Frank's campsite were the greater monster now. Marcia broke through and entered the tent.

Peter wandered over to the fire. Picked up a stick and poked at a log. Sparks jumped into the air. As he idly poked at the fire, he thought about everything that had happened this morning, and about what they were going to do about it—if anything.

Soon, things started becoming clear. He knew what had to be done.

He glanced over at the spear still stuck in the tree trunk. A weird determination pulsed through him. He dropped the stick, walked over, and took hold of the metal rod with both hands. Expecting the spear to put up fierce resistance, he pulled hard. The shaft came out easily. He stumbled backwards, nearly tripping. When he regained his balance, he stepped back up to the tree. There was a gap where the point had been lodged; the bark around it had crumbled away. He fingered the trunk. The wood felt papery and broke away in his fingers. The tree was rotten, as if dead.

Peter frowned.

Only yesterday it had been solid, unyielding. A perfectly healthy tree. Now, the tree looked like it had been standing there dead for years.

His mind reeled. He thought about Frank's campsite, the thick vegetation that had grown overnight, almost like it was trying to conceal the crime that had taken place.

The spear suddenly felt hot in his hand. Not scalding, like it had been resting in the flames of the campfire, but pulsating, almost soothing, like a hot drink on a bitter winter's day.

"Peter, I'm ready."

Peter whipped around. Marcia stood there, clutching her suitcase in her right hand. Her tote bag was looped around her shoulders.

She noticed what he was holding. She stared at it for a few seconds before looking back up. "Are you packed and ready?"

"I was thinking, maybe it's best we don't go to the police."

Marcia stared at him and didn't speak for a few moments. "We have to. We can't just leave them there."

"They might think we had something to do with it."

A strained laughed leaped from her mouth. "That's absurd. Why would we go to the cops if we had something to do with it? Anyway, it's pretty clear what happened."

"Is it, though? Marcia, you don't know this area. I do. The people around here, they're a strange lot, suspicious, particularly of outsiders. That includes the police. I remember what it was like. Dad even warned me when we would head into the nearest town for supplies; be on guard, he used to say, don't engage with these people."

"That was decades ago, Peter. Times have changed."

"How about, when we're far away, we find a payphone and make an anonymous call?"

Marcia sighed heavily. She looked spent, like she hadn't slept in a week. "Okay, fine. Can we just go now?"

Peter moved over to the table and placed the spear on top. He looked around the campsite. "Where's Cricket?"

Marcia shrugged.

Peter whistled. "Cricket! Here, girl!"

He waited, expecting her to come bounding in from the bush. When she didn't, Peter called again. He listened for a bark, something to signal she was around and okay.

He heard nothing. "Was she with us when we drove up the beach?"

"I don't know. I don't think so."

"When was the last time you saw her?"

"I don't know. Maybe... this morning?"

"Christ, Marcia!"

"What? She's your fucking dog! You're the one who let her come. She was supposed to stay home."

Peter thought back, but couldn't remember seeing Cricket since around lunchtime, just before they left to go to Frank's campsite. And he wasn't even completely sure she was around then. Maybe he just assumed she was, as Cricket was always around when there was food. The last time he definitely remembered her being around was when Marcia discovered the adult dugong on the beach.

"I'd better go look for her."

Panic shot into Marcia's face. "It'll be dark soon. I want to leave before sunset. I want to be far away from here by the time night comes."

"We can't just leave her. Look, it won't take long..."

"For Christ's sake, she's dead!"

The words felt like a shot to the head. Peter almost staggered backwards. "You're lying."

"No, she is. I... found her in the bushes, before we drove up the beach. When I was going to the toilet."

Peter felt a rush of emotions; he held them back, like a thick dam wall. But they were strong and would soon break through and come crashing at full force. "What happened to her?"

"I don't know. I think, maybe, a snake."

Peter swallowed. "Where is she?"

"I buried her. Just leave her, Peter. Let's just go and..."

"I'm not leaving her, Marcia. If she's dead, then I want to bring her back home and bury her in the backyard. But I don't think she's really dead. Is she, Mars?"

"God! Why can't you listen to me for once! I want to go; we *need* to go. If we stay here another night..."

"What? What will happen? Nothing. It's just your paranoia, your selfishness rearing its ugly head again."

Marcia gaped at him. "*My* selfishness? You want to talk about selfish behaviour?"

"Yes."

Marcia dropped her bags to the ground. "Fine. Let's talk."

"You're being a selfish bitch, as usual. You've done your best to ruin this trip, which was important to me."

"I told you I didn't want to come here! You practically forced me to come along."

"Force? *Force*? I forced you to come to a beautiful camping spot near the beach? What a horrible person I am. *Forcing* you to spend a bit of time in the wilderness, getting back to nature. Christ, Marcia, why can't you appreciate nature like everyone else?"

"You self-centred prick. You drag me along to this awful place with your thousands of dollars' worth of camping equipment, including a fucking fridge, and you have the nerve to call it getting back to nature? Really? Get a reality check. You're a city dweller who came here to stick his head out of his fancy tent like a tortoise and pretend he's a bloody survivalist or something. It's a joke. *You're* a joke!"

"Reality, huh? You want to talk about reality?" He took a breath. "Is reality murdering the unborn? Is that reality for you, Marcia? Because it's sure as hell reality for me."

"You're unbelievable," Marcia said, voice hoarse. "Fuck you. It wasn't... murder."

"If it wasn't murder, then why didn't you tell me about it? Why did I have to hear about it from Mark?"

"He wasn't supposed to tell. Carol wasn't supposed to tell *him*."

"But they did. You want to talk about reality? You told fucking Carol about it, but not your own husband. Why were you ashamed to tell me you were pregnant? Huh? Why did you go ahead and kill our unborn child without telling me? My child, Marcia! Mine!"

"You really have to ask?"

"I want to know!"

"Because I don't love you!" Marcia was crying. But she didn't look sad; if anything, she looked relieved, like the tears were her soul finally breaking free. "Because I didn't want to bring an innocent being into... whatever toxic thing this is between us. We're no good together. Whatever we used to be, whatever love we had, is dead."

Marcia took a breath, wiped her eyes.

In the silence that followed, Peter heard a bird screeching. The image of Frank, swinging by the rope, birds pecking at his flesh and cackling, stormed into his brain; followed by the memory of Frank's wife, head bashed in, dead and dirty with ants and flies.

"You're a liar and a cheat," Marcia continued, husky voice soft. "I've known it for years. Put up with it for years. You think I couldn't have screwed around? I had chances. I had offers, but I chose not to take them up. But I was close. I fantasised about being with Mark. You wouldn't believe how many times I imagined us together. That's the real reason I wanted to go to Portsea this weekend. Not because I love it so much there, or even to spend time with Carol. It was to be near him, to watch him. But I've never cheated on you, Peter. Not in the flesh anyway, not in the real world. But you have, so many times.

Well, I'm sick of it. I've had enough. I can't take this any longer. I want a divorce."

Peter felt his body tense up, like it was made from coils of red-hot anger. He tried smiling his anger away, but he ended up snarling instead. "Bullshit," he huffed. "This week it's a divorce. Next week it's news drapes and a facial at Pepe's."

"No bullshit, Peter. We're over. I want out."

The coils grew even tighter. Heat washed over his body. "How we love to tear each other apart. Oh, how we relish the taste of human flesh. We're the neo-cannibals."

"*Estranged* cannibals," Marcia said, eyes starting to dry up. "Filing on Monday."

Peter smiled, coldly. "Long weekend, love. You'll have to miss tennis and do it on Tuesday. But by then, you'll have come to your senses. You won't leave me."

Marcia looked at him with hard eyes, bitter eyes. Eyes heavy with contempt. She stepped closer. "I killed our unborn child, yes, because I wanted to punish you. But mostly because I cared more about it than I cared about you. Because I didn't want it growing up with *you* as its father."

The coils finally released. Peter lashed out. He backhanded her across the face. Startled, Marcia stumbled backwards. If not for slamming against the side of the truck, she would have fallen. Shocked, Marcia put a hand to her right cheek, which was marked with red.

Peter stood there, also shocked. But not sorry. The anger he felt for his wife in that moment—really, an erupting volcano with years' worth of bubbling magma just waiting to explode— was potent and all-consuming.

"You bastard," she said.

"Frigid cunt," he growled back, and gave her an even harder slap, this time on her left cheek, and this time she was knocked to the ground. She yelped as she fell into one of the camping chairs. The chair rocked but held steady. She landed on the earth with a grunt.

After taking time to collect herself, she pawed at the ground in an effort to get back up. Her hand found the spear gun, minus the spear. She took hold of it and used it to help push herself up.

Once standing, she swung the spear gun at Peter. Peter was unprepared for the attack, but he responded with frightful speed. He managed to grab the gun before it hit him, and with force, wrenched it out of her grip.

Grinning at his victory, holding the spear gun and wondering what to do with it, he didn't see Marcia bring up a knee. Pain shot through his groin. He doubled over and only when he saw Marcia lower her leg did he realise what had happened. Before he got his breath back, while his groin still felt ablaze with a pain akin to pins and needles, just sharper and more intense, Marcia turned away and fumbled at the driver's side door. She opened it and climbed up into the cab. Slammed the door, then locked it.

When she tried to start the car, and failed, Peter grinned through the pain.

"Dammit, Peter!" she cried. "Start this fucking car!"

He slowly rose as the pain started to subside. "Sorry, love. Switched it back to the alternate battery when you weren't looking. Must keep my beers cold."

Marcia screamed; a wild, gut-wrenching scream. Then she looked out at him, her angry breathing fogging up the window.

Peter gazed up at the sky. It was still afternoon, still relatively bright, but it was turning. The clouds were starting to gather.

"Be dark soon," he said, looking back down and smiling at her.

"I hate you," she said, voice muffled but clear enough.

Just then, the sound of barking. It was distant, maybe down at the beach, but it was unmistakably Cricket.

Peter's grin widened. "Well, well. Who's the fucking liar now?"

Marcia turned away.

"Bitch," he muttered. Holding a hand on his tender groin, he started for the beach.

———

Marcia felt trapped. Cooped up in the truck, unable to start the engine, she couldn't leave this godforsaken place. She could walk, she supposed. Her foot was wounded, but she'd push through the pain if it meant salvation. Trouble was, she wasn't sure salvation awaited her, not out here in the middle of nowhere. She was scared. She just wanted to drive away. Leave this place and not stop until she reached home.

She looked up in the rear-view mirror. The red marks on her cheeks reminded her of a bad sunburn.

Can't believe he hit me! Twice!

Can't you? a little voice asked. *You knew it was coming. Someday. Just not so soon. After all, don't they say girls always marry men who remind them of their father?*

The sudden intrusion of Frank hanging from the tree caused her skin to prickle.

The memory of his fat, dead body, face like a purple balloon, kept repeating in her head like a broken reel from some ghoulish film. But as bad as he was, it was nothing compared to the girl in the tent. Lying there, arms splayed, hands curled into fists, face staring up at the ceiling with eyes half closed as if in the midst of falling asleep. But she hadn't been drifting off to sleep. No, she was dead. Face colourless, lips parted, tongue pressing against her ocean-blue lips like it had died trying to escape. Flies buzzing around, looking for places to lay their eggs. And the ants. So many tiny black ants, thousands of them, a mass of miniature moving parts, making it seem as if the girl was moving.

Marcia still felt like she was covered with ants. The logical part of her knew there weren't any on her body, but she could feel them tickling her skin all the same. Could feel them marching up her nostrils, into her mouth, even into the corners of her eyes.

Stop it! Stop it!

For no better reason other than desperation, she tried starting the car again. Again, it gave her nothing.

Damn him, she thought, hands clasped on the wheel.

The late afternoon sun shone through the windscreen, glinting off her wedding ring. She took her hands off the wheel. Started pulling at the ring. She wanted it off. It meant nothing to her; *he* meant nothing to her. She had thought, maybe, they could work things out. Now, in her heart, she knew it was over. She wanted it to be over. She could admit that now. Their marriage had been over long before she found out she was pregnant.

The gold band held tight to her finger. She wiggled it, breathed hot air onto it. She felt it start to move. She gritted her teeth and tugged hard. Finally, it came off. She breathed out and sat there, holding the ring between her thumb and index fingers.

Such a small thing, she thought. Yet, in a way, its own kind of prison.

Fiddling with it, she fumbled, and it dropped onto the seat. She reached out to try to catch it, but the gold ring bounced into the narrow space between the seats and disappeared.

"Shit," she muttered, no longer wanting to wear it, but not wanting to lose it, either. If nothing else, she could pawn it, get some money.

She stuck her hand down into the narrow space. Felt around. Her fingers touched wrappers, coins, and dry, crumbly things she thought—hoped—were old chips or crackers, but no ring. She pulled her hand back out, got on her knees and turned around, facing the back of the vehicle. She looked down at the floor of the cargo area, but couldn't see any sign of her wedding band. Her eyes fell to the passenger seat, specifically to the space beneath the seat. She didn't know if the seat could be moved, pulled forward to get a look underneath. She never had any call to do it. She figured it must, and not thrilled with the idea of pawing blindly in such a dark recess, not if she could help it, she took hold of the backrest and pulled it towards the windscreen. To her surprise, the backrest folded inwards. There, resting on a metal tray, was her ring. But that wasn't what most captured her attention. It was the dial on the metal tray and plate above that read: battery/alternate.

She stared at it, first with puzzlement. But soon that puzzlement turned to a smile as she realised what she had uncovered.

———

Peter stood at the crest of the bluff and looked down at Cricket on the beach, jumping around and barking madly. "Cricket, you dope, where have you been?"

Peter delighted at the sight of his beloved Labrador.

Dead my arse, he thought with vitriol.

But the happiness at finding his dog alive and well dwindled when he saw the reason for Cricket's behaviour. She was barking at the large dugong, which, unbelievably, appeared to have moved even farther away from the water's edge and closer to the bluff. Closer to the campsite.

But that was impossible. The beast was dead. A fly-blown, rotting carcass. It made as much sense as Frank suddenly opening his eyes, reaching up and pulling the noose from around his neck; or the mother and daughter rising up and crawling out of their tents...

But he couldn't deny; the sea cow was closer than before. There were drag marks along the sand. And Cricket certainly seemed to sense something odd about the creature.

"Cricket!" he called. "Get out of it! Leave it..."

He was startled by the sound of an engine. The deep

grumble sounded close by, just a short way behind, in the vicinity of the campsite. Peter's first thought was: *someone's here!* Another camper had entered the wilderness, *his* wilderness.

Worried, he turned away from the beach and the undead dugong and bolted back up the path.

He was getting it sorted in his head, what he was going to say to the interlopers, how he was going to proceed—and importantly, how he was going to deal with Marcia in her distraught and illogical state—when he arrived back at the camp and saw the Nissan finishing up a three-point turn. He halted, not quite believing what he was seeing.

Cricket came running up behind him, tore past, jumped, and barked at the back of the truck.

Marcia was behind the wheel. Marcia had gotten the vehicle started. Marcia was driving away.

He found his legs and ran after the truck. "Marcia!" he bellowed. "Marcia, wait!"

The truck came to a stop as she righted the wheel. Peter managed to catch up and, with Cricket at his heels, he grabbed for the back doors. His fingers almost got a grip on a handle, but before he was successful, the car jerked forward, kicking up sand and dirt. He chased the truck for a bit longer down the narrow road, but the Patrol gained speed and it pulled away, disappearing around a bend like it was swallowed up by the bush.

"Marcia!" he screamed.

But he was left with the dying dust clouds and the sudden silence.

———

Night came too quickly. One moment it was light, and then dusk fell, stayed for a brief visit, only to be taken over by inky darkness. Maybe it was just the thick bush cutting out the light, as the deeper into it she got, the denser the foliage became.

Although she didn't remember it being this bad on the drive in. Bushes seemed to lunge at the car, scraping the sides with ear-splitting screeching noises. Branches appeared like arms grabbing at her. Trees grew at angles, the tops meeting in a leafy embrace, forming an archway of green. She still felt trapped, even away from the horrid beach and rotten campsite.

But she kept going. She powered down the sandy track, following the bends in the road, moving the wheel madly, weathering the bumps, her foot on fire, wet with fresh blood and cutting a rod of pain that extended up her leg. Pain she could deal with. It was the fear that threatened to overwhelm her; the claustrophobia, the thought of never finding her way out of the woods, even though she knew the highway was nearby.

To have some noise, some company, and in an effort to stave off the growing storm of fear, she turned on the radio. The signal was weak. She flicked through the channels, hoping to find something—music, talkback, it didn't matter—that she could listen to. All she found was a man talking. She figured a news report. The voice flickered between spurts of static: "... road between... mbula and Tathra... temporarily closed... bushfires burn... of control in the... district... started because of... dropped by a careless... advised that drivers should... diverted... be careful..."

The voice bled out, static took over, so she gave up and turned off the radio.

She considered putting on a tape, but she would have to stop to do that, and she didn't want to stop, not even for a minute. So, with nothing but her own thoughts to occupy her mind, she continued along the rough, bumpy road. At each junction, she took the leg she thought most likely led to salvation. Some tracks clearly curved back around towards the ocean. Those she avoided. She continued on the road she thought would lead the way out of this hell. She had to be on the right track. She just had to be.

As she hammered down the present track, headlights pushing through the darkness, through the trees and bushes that looked like they were trying to stop her from leaving, she remembered a time when she was young. One night, when her dad was passed out in front of the TV, her mum had crept into her room and told her to come quietly. They were going on a late-night trip.

Marcia, having just drifted off to sleep, sat up, confused. "Why?" she had asked.

"Never mind why," Mum had said. "Just because. Now come on, get your dressing gown on and let's go."

"But I have to pack," she had said, rubbing her eyes and reaching over to turn on her Mickey Mouse lamp.

"No," Mum had said, slapping her hand away. It was the first and only time her mum had hit Marcia. "No lights, no packing. We have to go now."

"What about Duffy?" she had asked.

She always carried her stuffed elephant with her.

"You can bring Duffy," Mum had said, and so Marcia, eight years old, had got out of bed, slipped on her dressing gown, her slippers, and hugging Duffy to her chest, followed Mum downstairs.

Mum had told her to be quiet. Being a naturally quiet person, it wasn't hard to do. Holding Mum's clammy hand, they had crept carefully past the living room, where her dad was snoring in his chair. The TV gave off stark black and white images, burnishing the room, and they left through the front door, Mum being extra cautious to make as little noise as possible when opening and closing the door.

Fully awake now, Marcia had started feeling excited. This was a game. She didn't know exactly how to play, or what the prize was, but it was fun all the same. Sneaking out at night, hopping into the car, and taking a drive, it all felt strange and daring and even a little scary. But fun.

Billy was already in the back of the car. He didn't look quite as excited. He had a firm, serious look on his face, but then her eleven-year-old brother was usually solemn; his gaunt, pale face hardly ever smiled. And Marcia knew, even at her age, that her brother still wet the bed. She had seen Mum furiously washing his sheets, had smelled the unmistakable tang of pee in his room.

Still, Marcia had thought it all thrilling, so she figured she'd be excited enough for the both of them. That sense of adventure remained until Mum hopped into the car. The overhead light came on. Marcia saw Mum's face. Inside, the house had been too dark to see. Mum had mostly been in shadows. But Marcia saw Mum's face then: puffy and bleeding. One eye completely closed like it had been stung by a bee. Lips cut and bleeding, jaw and throat marked with angry red straps.

"It's going to be okay," Mum had whispered. "Lock your doors."

They locked their doors. A hot, squirmy feeling began in Marcia's belly. She hugged Duffy tighter. Mum started the car and, opposite of how she had acted earlier and told Marcia to act, moved furiously, like she couldn't get out of the driveway quick enough.

Marcia was pushed back against the seat as the car fled backwards down the drive. She and Billy were hurtled forward as the car stopped in the middle of the road just long enough for Mum to whip the gear into drive, and then they shot forward down the street, away from their house.

Marcia had looked out the back window and as her house grew smaller, she saw the door fling open and a figure ran out onto the road, and stood there; a dark shadow watching them drive away.

They drove for a long time that night. Billy remained his usual sullen self, hardly speaking. Marcia asked questions. She had an inquisitive mind, something she knew annoyed her dad. Mum didn't have many answers for her, though. She didn't know where they were going. They were just driving. She had no destination in mind, other than away from *him* (that's what she called their dad—him). No, they weren't going home tonight. Maybe never again.

Marcia fell quiet after that, the game no longer fun, and she sat there, unable to fall asleep, just watching the world flash by, the darkness thicker and heavier than normal, and wondered where exactly they were, how long till they reached somewhere, and what was going to happen when they arrived?

Marcia felt that way now, twenty years later. The darkness was too thick, too heavy. She knew where she was headed but was fearful she would never get there.

Because she knew things didn't always end well, the way you hoped.

They had finally reached somewhere, a dingy motel far from home. They ended up living room to room, day to day, for a while, mostly at motels, sometimes in houses where they had to share rooms and bathrooms with smelly, dirty people. Mum did odd jobs. They ate lots of food from cans and bread and butter. Eventually, they were found by *him*. They were taken back home. Things turned from bad to worse. It didn't end well for any of them. Billy left home at sixteen, addicted to drink, and killed himself in a road accident when he was twenty. Mum grew old before her time and hardly ever smiled for the rest of her life, which was cut short when she died from brain cancer at age forty-nine, three years ago. Her dad was still alive, last she heard. Living in some dingy one-room flat with only his anger and regret for company.

Sometimes, Marcia felt like she had spent her whole life in that car, driving down that dark road, unsure of her destination, fearful of what she'd find when she arrived. In many ways she was still that scared eight-year-old girl. The only difference was, she no longer had Duffy for comfort. She had nothing.

The track kept going, seemingly never-ending. Then something struck the windscreen. Marcia thought it was an especially low-hanging branch, or maybe a rock kicked up by the tyres. But it happened again, and this time she saw a bird, white and large, its wings stretched and flapping angrily.

"Get away!" Marcia screamed, and just as it flew up and disappeared, another bird, smaller, grey, crashed against the glass, causing a small crack, which soon splintered into many fissures.

She honked the horn. Put on the wipers. Still, they came. Flying at the windscreen, beaks like arrows. Banging against the driver's side, claws scraping the glass. Landing on the roof, their scratching loud, like they were trying to cut open the metal.

With vision obscured by the avian onslaught, she weaved like a drunk on a slip and slide, crashing the car through bushes, rolling over roots or rocks that sat on the shoulder. She tried pulling the car back onto the road. As she slowed to get the car righted and back on the track, she realised the birds had vanished, leaving the windscreen and driver's side window cracked.

What the hell was that about?

Since when did birds attack cars?

When do spears fly out of guns... when do fathers murder their family... when do dead animals move...

Like that night when she was a kid, when Mum told her and her brother to lock their doors, she felt all hot and squirmy in her belly. She wished Mum was with her now. She wished she hadn't come along on this infernal weekend trip in the first place.

Her vision was skewered so she didn't see the large rut in the road. As she ran over it, the car jumped and bucked. The sun visor dropped down. She noticed a dark shape scurry out, but her mind took a few moments to catch up with her peripheral vision. The dark shape dropped down onto her lap and she saw what it was: a large huntsman, as big as her hand.

She screamed. Lost all focus on driving. She sat frozen in her seat; the spider, too, sat there, as if sizing her up.

A sudden jolt. She was pushed forward, hitting her head on the steering wheel. Pain like a lightning bolt shot through her forehead. She sat there dazed for a few moments. When she came back, she realised two things: one, the car had come to a stop; and two, looking down, there was no sign of the spider, which, in a way, was worse than when it had been on her lap. She took her foot off the accelerator, the clutch. The car stalled. She punched open the driver's door and jumped out.

On the road, she vigorously brushed at her clothes, her hair. Fear like electricity coursed through her. Like with the ants, she could feel the huntsman all over her, scurrying up her shirt, down her pants; on her legs, tangled in her hair.

Somewhere deep in her mind, she knew the spider almost certainly wasn't on her, but that didn't stop the sensation, or her panic. When she was sure the spider wasn't anywhere on her, she started to calm down. She looked over at the car. She had run it off the road, into a ditch, straight into a tree. The headlights speared the bush. The driver's side door hung open, the inside dark, like an open mouth. A mouth with a spider waiting for her inside.

She shuddered. The spider may have scuttled out, but she wasn't about to take the chance. She couldn't go back in there. Anyway, the front looked well banged up, probably was unable to run. Even if it could still drive, the car looked stuck in the ditch. With no other option, Marcia took off down the road, hobbling, foot feeling like scorched earth.

Away from the car, the world grew intensely dark. Without the headlights, and with no torch, she was nearly blind. There wasn't even a moon to help guide her. The world was full of shadows, the track a dim path she had no choice but to tread on.

A dark road with no end in sight. Always a dark road.

Help me! she cried to no one.

From above, she heard flapping.

5

MARCIA HAD YET TO RETURN. He expected her back, either from remorse at how she had acted, what she had said, or because she got lost among the maze of sandy tracks.

Peter waited, but the truck didn't appear.

Even when night dropped, and the world grew cool and stark in its utter lack of light. No headlights, no truck rattling into the camp. No Marcia, face broken with guilt or disbelief.

Maybe she had made it out. Maybe right this moment she was at the pub, unloading to the barman, and soon there would be flashing blue and red illuminating the darkness, along with the wailing of sirens. Or would she not even bother telling anyone about him? Would she just mention the three dead bodies and conveniently leave the fact that she had left her husband stranded in the middle of this lonely place, with only a tent, a box-worth of food, and barely two litres of fresh water to last him?

Maybe she hadn't even stopped at the pub or a police station or anyplace. Maybe she just put her bandaged foot on the pedal and drove. Maybe she was already halfway home and had put him completely out of her mind.

Peter reached down and scratched Cricket behind the ears.

She didn't close her eyes and make a rumbling sound as per usual; she just sat there, staring at the wilderness, on guard.

"You won't leave me, will you, girl?"

Cricket didn't respond.

"We'll be okay, won't we? Doesn't matter if it's just us, we'll be fine."

But Christ, he could do with a beer. Rum would be even better. Something to help take the edge off. All he had were some crackers, bananas and grapes, bread, some spreads, a few cans of baked beans, and a couple of bars of chocolate. Nothing substantial to curb the rumbling in his gut. Nothing to drink except tepid water. He didn't even have marshmallows to roast.

He looked out at the darkness and roamed the scrub for glowing orbs, the high branches for hungry eyes. He couldn't see anything other than thick darkness. But he felt a presence out there. Many things watching, waiting.

This night felt different from the others. It wasn't just because he had been abandoned by his wife and was now alone, aside from the dog. There was a sinister quality about the place. The wind was cooler, but also heavier, and smelled not of the ocean or the bush, but of rotting flesh and spoiled food. The surrounding vegetation seemed alive, even if Peter's rational mind knew it was just the wind surging, moving the branches and leaves, so it appeared as if the trees and bushes were shaking, reaching out to him. It seemed like the vegetation was creeping closer, continuing their march forward, gradually constricting the ring of cleared space. Bushes were widening, trees extending their arms, vines snaking towards the centre. It was just his imagination; it had to be. The shadows playing tricks. But he remembered Frank's campsite and suddenly it didn't seem so unbelievable. The sky offered no illumination, no respite from the oppressive darkness. Because of the wind, the clouds resembled waves in the ocean; dark grey crescents linked together to conceal the moon so no light could break through. Even the fire was against him this night. The wood he had collected earlier must have been too green or rotten, as the flames were muted, the smoke thick and choking.

With the air dropping in temperature but increasing in violence, Peter left the relative warmth of the fire and headed into the tent to retrieve his jacket. He stopped and looked down at the empty side of the mattress, at the scattered remains of Marcia's items she'd left behind, apparently deeming them not essential enough when she hurriedly packed to leave: a pair of jeans, a long-sleeved top, suntan lotion, her lone thong. Seeing these caused a mixture of anger and sadness. But the sadness quickly dissipated when he thought about how she had driven away, leaving him behind, and all the things she had said just before.

"Bitch," he muttered, kicked at her things, and then left the tent.

Striding back towards the fire, he noticed something dark fluttering in the wind. He stopped, heart kicking up a gear. He heaved out a breath, nearly cut a thin smile, at the sight of his wetsuit, hanging on a coat hanger from a branch. The dim shape, looking human, continued to flap as the chilly wind, heavy with smoke and the smell of death, continued to blow.

———

By the time ten-thirty rolled around, Peter had given up hope that anyone was coming, Marcia or otherwise. He guessed Marcia really had meant it when she said she hated him. She had lied about many things, but not, apparently, about that. Hated him so much she had chosen to ditch him like a piece of rubbish.

Or nature had claimed her.

The suggestion would have sounded absurd a week ago; hell, even a few days ago. Now, it seemed not only a possibility, but a likelihood. This place didn't want them to leave, Peter knew that now, and he suspected Marcia had fallen prey to the vengeful whims of Mother Nature. Maybe she was driving around in circles, on an endless loop of tea trees, scraggly brush, and towering gums.

Peter laughed, a high, cackling sound.

Somewhere, a creature laughed along with him. Then others joined in, but to his ears, they were mocking him. Taunting him. They were harsh, bitter sounds.

I've done nothing to you, he thought. *I've been nothing but good to you. I came here; I felt your calling, and now I'm here, you laugh at me, treat me like your enemy? Why? What do you want?*

But he got no answers; none he could understand, anyway.

Soon the cackling went away, leaving just the sound of the wind and the sound of tree branches creaking mournfully. He gazed up, half expecting to see the figure of Frank swinging by the rope like a human pendulum. Thankfully, he didn't, but he thought he saw other shapes moving about.

He picked up his spear gun and rested it across his lap. It was already loaded. He made sure it was cocked and ready to fire, and then he settled back into the folding chair—as settled as he could be.

He munched on some water crackers, chewed on a banana, washed the food down with warm water. He opened a bar of chocolate, ate it lifelessly. The sugar rush was needed, but there was no enjoyment in the gooey combination of chocolate and caramel. He considered cracking open the baked beans, but he couldn't be bothered getting the pot, setting up the tripod, and heating them up. He could always eat them straight out of the can, but the thought of cold beans didn't appeal. He wasn't that hungry, so he settled on a box of sweet biscuits, ate most of what was left in the box, which was less than half full to begin with, and tossed the last bits down to Cricket, who sniffed at them, nibbled, but apparently it wasn't to her liking, as she turned away and left the biscuits on the ground.

"You're not hungry?" he said down to her.

Cricket sighed, as if in response. She continued to look out at the bush.

"You feeling okay?"

It wasn't like Cricket to refuse food. She'd eat the snot out of a dead man's nose, such was her usually voracious appetite.

"I understand," Peter said, sitting back and staring at the limp flames. "I feel it, too. You're on edge. I get it."

He looked up into the trees again. With the wind and the murky light creating shadows, it was difficult to tell whether the shapes were just branches and leaves moving, or bushland creatures. He could see no eyes glowing, so it had to be just the trees, but he couldn't stop the feeling of being watched. A hot, prickly sensation, as if the unseen eyes were light globes that emitted heat but no light.

Maybe it was spirits. Those passed on, but still stuck in this world. Unable—or unwilling—to make contact. Instead, the disembodied souls just watched.

Not that Peter believed in such things. At least, not in his normal life. His hectic, clock-run life, a life ruled by steel and concrete and routine and bright artificial lights and choking smog and dinners at fancy restaurants and boozing it up with clients and locked behind the wheel of a car, stressed and eager to get to point B. In that life he hardly had time to scratch himself, let alone ponder the world beyond this one.

Even if there were such things as spirits, they would be blocked out, shunted aside, unable to be seen in today's modern world. But out here, such things did seem possible.

Maybe all it took was to get back to nature, to sit in the darkness of the unspoiled wilderness, in the clear air, to see them. To feel them.

Maybe this was a special place. A magical place. A place where the fabric between their world and the spirit world was paper thin or broken. A fissure in the space-time.

Christ, he thought, eyes scanning the shadows. *And you're not even drunk or high.*

Still, he couldn't dismiss the concept entirely. He had seen things he couldn't explain, felt things he had never felt before. Tonight was especially potent, but perhaps that was just an emotional response after what they had discovered at Frank's campsite, and with Marcia ditching him. He had rarely been alone in his life; *truly* alone. Even when his dad died, he had work friends, a girlfriend, even the idiot box, to distract him. Now, he had nothing except himself and the world, and he was beginning to realise how small and insignificant he truly was.

He was reminded of the last time he went camping with Dad. It was the summer holidays before starting high school. They had stayed here a week, and it was on the penultimate night that Peter had woken to find his dad's bed empty. It being early January, and exceptionally hot, the tent flap was left open to let in the ocean breeze. Going by what he saw outside, it was sometime in the early morning as the campfire was mostly glowing coals, and there was the utter quiet that only came in the hours before dawn, when even the night creatures seemed to grow weary and silent. Peter, sleepy and unsure why he had woken in the first place (he was usually a heavy sleeper), gazed squinty eyed at his dad's cot and figured he had just stepped out for a piss. Peter had learnt that older people tended to wake in the middle of the night to use the bathroom. He closed his eyes but hadn't fallen asleep. Tired though he was, now he was awake, he wanted to wait for his old man to return. He didn't like being in the tent by himself. He liked falling asleep knowing his dad was in there with him, at worst, out by the fire.

He lay there, waiting, more annoyed than worried, as he just wanted to get back to sleep. His body wrestled him. It wanted to rest, but he fought to stay awake. When, after what felt like ten minutes and Dad still hadn't returned, he started to grow concerned. The times Dad had woken during the night to go to the toilet, he wasn't gone for more than a few minutes. Peter listened for any telltale sounds—the sound of someone walking back from the bush, the sound of urine hitting the dry scrub like someone had turned on a hose. But he heard only the quiet; the suddenly horrible quiet.

Peter, on his left side, wanted to turn onto his back, but he was too scared to move.

Soon, he felt the need to urinate, but he didn't dare move, let alone get out of his sleeping bag and make his way outside. He couldn't pinpoint why he was so afraid of moving. Why Dad not being back made him so nervous. Dad probably had to go number two, and that was why he was taking longer than usual. Or maybe he was down at the beach, enjoying the night-time view. Dad loved staring out at the ocean at night, thought that's when the beach was at its best. Or maybe he was sitting near the campfire, somewhere Peter couldn't see from his view inside the tent. Dad had simply fallen asleep in the chair, lazing in front of the dying flames.

If you weren't such a scaredy-cat, you'd know, he thought to himself. *Just take a look outside and you'll see him dozing just outside the tent, and you'll laugh at yourself for being so silly, and then you can fall back to sleep.*

But he couldn't move. He was too frightened.

What if something has happened to him? he wondered. What if he's gotten lost, or a snake bit him while he was peeing?

After another ten minutes or so had gone by and Dad still wasn't back, Peter thought it his duty to go out and look. Take his Wham-O and be the big, brave boy his dad thought him to be—that Peter wanted to be.

But he didn't move. Even when the urge to pee grew forceful and uncomfortable, he didn't get out of his sleeping bag and unload his bladder. Lying there, he started hearing things. Not the usual night-time sounds like a bird cawing, an owl hooting, but strange whisperings like the wind was talking. And he saw things, too, out of the corner of his eye: shadows flitting about like birds flying around the campsite. But there were no flapping noises, just silent motions of darkness.

Close to an hour after first waking, he heard the sound of

footsteps coming towards the camp. Twigs snapping, followed by the softer padding as the person moved from the bush into the clearing. Peter, positive it was some stranger and not his father, held his breath and, though he wanted to squeeze his eyes shut, he didn't even want to make that movement, so he lay still, eyes glued to Dad's cot.

When the tent flap rustled and someone entered the tent, Peter thought he was going to wet himself. But he smelled the familiar smell of his dad—pipe smoke, muskiness of his body, the faint hint of soap—and when Dad stepped into Peter's field of vision, Peter wanted to cry, not from fear but from relief. His dad quietly sat on his cot and as he started taking off his boots, Peter finally shut his eyes and despite everything, despite his full bladder, he quickly fell asleep.

It was a memory seared into Peter's brain, and he felt cold at the remembrance of his utter fear and hopelessness, lying in the tent that early morning, sure his dad would never return, sure the wilderness was conspiring to get him, too. He jabbed at the logs, trying to produce higher, stronger flames, but all he managed was to create more smoke.

Nature can make you think—and feel—some pretty strange things, he thought, gazing around at the surrounding bush. He tightened his grip on the stock of the spear gun; not because he felt in danger, just to make sure it was still there, and still real.

Because when morning broke and he rose out of bed, finding his dad already up, cooking bacon, toast and scrambled eggs over the fire, the day bright and sunny, the birds singing a pretty morning song, Peter had decided the previous night was just a dream. A bad dream, but something not real. And he continued to think that for the rest of the day, swimming in the ocean, paddling on Dad's surfboard, whittling pieces of wood into spears so Dad could catch fish and other small bush animals, and helping Dad collect and chop more wood for the fire.

It wasn't until that evening, sitting by the fire after dinner,

Peter toasting marshmallows, Dad smoking his pipe, that he learnt it hadn't been a dream after all. Well, part of it may have been. He didn't know what to make of it at the time, and almost twenty years later, he still didn't know. However, having experienced what he had (although still not quite believing it all) and feeling what was he was feeling, he was starting to wonder if everything that had happened that night at Moondah Beach had in fact been real and not part of a dream.

Mostly out of curiosity, but also to assuage the small bit of lingering dread, Peter had said, off handed to his dad, "Did you get up during the night and leave the tent? Or was I dreaming?"

Expecting—hoping—he'd say no, you must have been dreaming, Dad instead said, "Yeah, I did."

All the memories of the night came flooding back; the fear, the inability to move, the strange noises, the flying shadows.

"Oh," Peter had said.

Maybe it was the way he had said it, or perhaps Dad saw his son's face, which no doubt would have turned pale and pressed with fear, because his dad laughed softly, lips around his pipe. "You look like you've seen a ghost, Petey. Why do you ask?"

Peter shrugged. He wanted to tell his dad everything, but knew it might all have been his imagination. And not wanting to look like a silly, frightened coward, he answered, "Nothing. It's just... you were gone a long time."

Dad stopped laughing and continued puffing on his pipe. And then he said something that made the already odd situation even more baffling. "No, I wasn't. I was only gone... five minutes at most. Too much beer tends to wake you up from a good sleep. But when you have to go..."

"You were only gone five minutes?"

Dad nodded. "Were you awake?"

Peter took his stick from the coals but didn't eat the browned marshmallow. He just held the stick like it was a fishing rod and he was angling. "Yeah," he said, barely audible.

"Well, sorry if I woke you, kid. Did you get back to sleep easily enough?"

He had, but that wasn't what bothered him. He distinctly remembered lying there for ages and ages waiting for Dad to return. He hadn't looked at the time. He couldn't be completely sure how long it was. His watch had been on the floor on the other side of the cot, along with his shoes, slingshot and penknife, but he knew it was a lot longer than five minutes.

Maybe he had fallen asleep soon after waking? Maybe he had woken, saw Dad was gone, and then promptly fell asleep until shortly before Dad arrived back, and everything he had seen was conjured up by his mind and Dad was telling the truth.

It was possible. It made the most sense. Because why would Dad lie about something like that? For what reason would he be gone for an hour in the wilderness in the middle of the night, leaving his son all alone? There could be no reason for such behaviour, and so Peter had decided that it had been a dream. That was the easiest, most sensible, and least unsettling answer. And that's the way he had left it, the night slowly receding from memory until it became just one of many. A strange blip that he mostly forgot about, occasionally remembered, mostly with a smile. Just the wild imaginings of a scared child, even if the fear associated with the memory never totally went away, nor the strange whisperings and shadows.

Just a dream, he had always told himself. If there was doubt, he quickly quashed it and tried to forget about it.

But he couldn't ignore the doubt now. He felt sure what he had heard and witnessed hadn't been conjured up while dreaming. Maybe what he had heard were the whisperings of spirits, the dead trying to speak. What he had seen were the spectres moving about the bush.

"Frank?" he called, voice tentative. "Frank, is that you?"

Suddenly, tears stung his eyes. He swallowed what felt like a hard lump of coal and said, "Dad? Are you out there?"

He waited, but he got no sign; no whisperings like he had heard that night as a boy. Saw no strange, soundless shadows moving through the trees. Still, he felt something was out there. Maybe Dad had heard or sensed it, too. Maybe that's why he had woken up and left the tent, the reason he was gone so long. The more Peter considered it, the more he thought he was right. Dad had seen or heard something that night. That something— ghosts, spirits, the essence of nature itself—had called out to him and he had gone out to see what it wanted.

Shortly after that last trip to Moondah, Peter started noticing a change in his dad. Nothing too drastic, at least not initially, but he became more distant, more inward, reflective. In hindsight, Peter had put it down to his declining health, which soon would be given a name: cancer. Specifically, lung cancer. Now, Peter wasn't so sure. Maybe it had more to do with this place, and what his dad had seen that night. Somehow, this place had gotten into him, had affected him.

Dad always wanted to come back here. He said he felt at peace here. That he wanted to pass away while on the beach, at night, staring out at the ocean. Well, Dad never got to come back for one final trip. Never got to carry out his dying wish, instead passing away in the sterile surrounds of the hospital, with bare, white walls instead of gum trees, the smell of disinfectant instead of the ocean, on a hospital bed encased in starched-white sheets, instead of lying on the soft sun-blessed sand.

As crazy as it sounded and would no doubt sound even crazier in the cold light of day, Peter was certain this place had called to Dad, just like it had called to Peter. Maybe it wanted his dad, his soul, but when it couldn't have him, it sought out Peter as an alternative. This was a haunted place, ruled by things Peter didn't understand. It infected people, only by the time they realised it and wanted to get away, it was too late.

It was too late for Frank and his family. He wondered: was it too late for him? For Marcia?

The wind changed; smoke started drifting towards him. Before he started to choke, he moved his chair around, away from the waft of grey smoke.

"What do you think?" he said to Cricket. "Do you think this place is haunted, or do you think I'm crazy?" He looked down, but Cricket wasn't by his side. He looked over to where he had just been sitting, but his dog wasn't there, either. Just the uneaten biscuits on the ground. "Cricket?" he called, gazing around the campsite. "Where are you?"

He heard the sound of barking. Like earlier, the barking was coming from the direction of the beach.

Damned dog, he thought. *What's she doing down there?*

He knew the most likely answer, even though he didn't want it to be the case. He retrieved the torch from the tent and, taking the spear gun with him, trudged out of the clearing and down the path. He stopped when he reached the bluff overlooking the beach. With the moon trapped behind the thick wave of clouds, the beach was in almost total blackness. He shone the light towards the barking. He found Cricket on the beach below. But instead of finding her near the large mummy dugong, the spotlight found her by the smaller baby.

"Cricket!" Peter shouted. "Leave it!"

But Cricket ignored his instruction. She continued barking at the calf, stopping every now and again to rush towards it, growling, like she was testing whether it was alive or dead.

"Cricket, come here!"

Cricket either misunderstood his command, or she deliberately disobeyed; either way, she lunged once more towards the dead baby dugong and bit down on its tail. With the dugong between her jaws, she started dragging the sea creature along the beach, away from the ocean, which was invisible beyond the spray of light, just part of the darkness, though it crashed and roared with fury.

"No! Leave it!" Peter yelled. "Cricket, drop it!"

But still the dog dragged the calf towards the bluff, towards Peter. "What are you doing?" Peter said.

With the wind whipping about him, seemingly trying to push him over the edge of the low cliff, Peter watched as his dog slowly pulled the dugong closer and closer, making ruts in the sand, the sound of solid mass scraping along the beach harsh and teeth-scratching.

Cricket had trouble getting the beast up the low hill. At one point, she let go. Peter thought she had given up and would leave it there, her fun over. But she repositioned herself and then chomped back down on the tail, getting, presumably, an even firmer grip, and continued pulling the creature up the sandy slope.

She finally made it to the top, yanking with fierce tugs the final part of the dugong's journey. Once she was up on flat land, Cricket dragged the carcass over to Peter and dropped it at his feet.

"That's great, Cricket. Thanks."

The dead thing lay there, its black, beady eyes staring up at him. The plastic bag still tangled around its head and shoulders.

"What do you want me to do with it, huh?"

Cricket stood there, panting. The way her mouth was split, tongue hanging out, she looked like she was laughing. She looked happy with herself, proud of having pulled this creature, bigger than her, all the way from the beach, up to the top of the bluff.

Peter was deciding what to do with it, leave it or drag it back down to the beach, when Cricket leaned down, sniffed around the dugong's midsection, then opened her mouth and sunk her fangs into the animal. Peter watched, stunned, and sickened, as his beloved pet tore into the dugong. Like some ravenous wolf, Cricket bit down hard and started pulling at the dead creature. Flesh and fat and skin stretched before Cricket ripped the meat away, leaving a chunk missing from the dugong's belly.

Peter nearly upchucked over the sea cow, over Cricket. "Jesus," he said, swallowing the bile. "Cricket, what the fuck?"

Cricket chewed the piece she had torn off, swallowed, and then went back for more.

"Stop!" Peter shouted. But Cricket, snout mucky with blubber and blood, paid no attention. "Cricket, stop!" he cried again, and he even kicked at Cricket. He had never kicked Cricket, never even smacked her with a rolled-up newspaper when she was a puppy and made a mess inside the house. Still, she didn't stop. She chewed at the exposed flesh and blubber, slurping and munching, tucking in with a desperate hunger.

Peter looked at the spear gun in his hand. The fact the thought even crossed his mind disgusted him, angered him. He dropped the gun, reached down, and took Cricket by the scruff of her neck. Up close, the smell was pungent, vile. Bad enough the smell of rot; the stench of raw flesh, fat and blood made Peter's stomach churn like an especially big swell. But he didn't puke. He put all his effort into pulling Cricket away.

He half expected her to have a go at him, take a bite out of him for taking her away from her meal. But, with only a minimal amount of effort, Peter pulled the dog away from the baby dugong. "No! Bad girl!" Peter said, in as stern a voice as he could muster.

Cricket, face dirty with dugong muck, whined, as if realising her master was mad at her. When he let go, instead of powering forward and continuing her late-night feast, she sat and looked up at him, and then back at the dugong.

"I know you're hungry, but for crying out loud, did you have to do... that?"

Cricket didn't even have raw mince at home. Canned dog food was her staple diet, and when she got meat, it was always cooked.

Cricket stared at the calf, still with hunger in her eyes, but she remained obedient. He knew he couldn't leave the creature there. Cricket would most likely go back for seconds sometime during the night. But the thought of touching it filled him again with waves of hot nausea.

Peter thought of a solution. "Wait there," he told Cricket. He pointed to the dugong. "And leave it."

Cricket looked up at him with her big brown eyes. He hoped she understood.

Leaving his spear gun on the ground, he hurried back to the camp, found a thick, long stick in the pile of wood, stuck one end into the fire and when it was aflame, brought the firebrand back to the end of the path, where Cricket still sat, licking her lips.

"Move back," he said, and he nudged her out of the way. He touched the flaming end of the stick to the partially eaten belly of the dugong. Flesh and fat started hissing. Acrid smoke that smelled of cheap, fatty meat wafted into the air. He kept the flame against the increasingly blackened belly until flames started eating at the torn flesh and, shortly thereafter, the flames spread over the dead animal.

Cricket, whining, stepped back even farther.

"Sorry, girl, but you can't be eating that. It's not food. It's rotten."

Once the dugong was well and truly alight, Peter tossed the firebrand over the cliff. It tumbled through the air like a fiery spiral, landing on the sand and lighting up a small portion of the beach. Soon it dwindled, and then died, leaving the beach once again blanketed in darkness.

With the smell of burning dugong carcass thick, Peter said, "Come on, silly girl," then he collected the spear gun and started back towards the campsite.

Cricket, looking forlorn with tail drooping, turned and followed.

They had just arrived back when the wailing started. It rang out mournfully through the night. Peter covered his ears in an effort to block out the sound, or at least mute it, but it did neither. He hated that sound. It wasn't so bad the first time he'd heard it. Then it was just an odd, eerie sound that was only a little unnerving. But on each subsequent hearing, it grew more disquieting, more offensive, until now it hurt him, physically, like the sound was causing him pain. It was a horrible noise. To him, it sounded like someone in agony—a pained moaning. The last time he'd heard something so torturous was in the hospital, when his dad was gravely ill and dying. He'd moan in agony, even though he was being pumped full of morphine.

Finally, the sound stopped, leaving the campsite surrounded by an eerie silence and the faint smell of burning death.

———

Peter couldn't sleep. Even with the smell of burning dugong having waned, and even though the night was cool enough, and he was tired, his mind wouldn't let him rest. Nestled in his sleeping bag, he laid awake waiting, listening and wondering.

He wondered at every creak, every rustle. Every sigh of wind. Just nature, or something else? Something more malevolent? He felt twelve again, alone, listening to the strange sounds outside, wondering if they, along with the shadows, were friend or foe.

At one point he even thought he heard the sound of an engine close by, and tyres rolling over earth. But the sound faded, and nobody came into the campsite, so he figured it was just the sound of the bush, or his imagination.

He had left Cricket outside. She stunk of decayed flesh. Besides, she seemed happier out there. She barely gave him a look when he retreated into the tent to begin his fruitless task of trying to sleep. Better that way, he thought. She was safe. With all the smoke, with the dugong burning away nearby, it was doubtful any snakes would visit them tonight.

Just after midnight, eyes closed but mind fully awake, he heard the distinct sound of snapping, like a dead branch had become too brittle and had given up its fight to remain intact with its host. Soon, more sounds of wood breaking. This one closer. He heard the sound of jostling leaves and twigs snapping as the heavier piece of wood fell to the ground. Heard the thud as it met earth.

He heard the same thing over and over again. Each time, the sound was louder, and Peter started wondering if there were any branches overhanging the tent. He had erected the tent at the edge of the clearing, close to the bush. He hadn't taken much notice at the time, but now he feared that perhaps the branches of a massive gum did overhang the fragile tent, and the next crunching sound of wood breaking would be the one directly above his head. Before he could escape, the branch would come crashing down, crushing him.

Peter scurried out of his sleeping bag and, taking his spear gun and torch (he was still dressed, still had on his shoes, he didn't want to be caught barefoot), hurried out of the tent.

He turned and looked up. Sure enough, the end of a gum tree branch hung about twenty metres above the tent. He shivered. Looked like he'd be sleeping under the stars tonight— if he slept at all. Moments later, there came another sound of snapping. He stepped towards the sound. Cricket remained near the fire, her tail close to the pit, body angled so she was looking down the path leading to the dugong. Stopping at the edge of the clearing, Peter shone his light in the area he thought the latest sound had come from. Maybe the sound wasn't from falling branches, but from something else. He waved his light, hoping to catch sight of the branch toppling to the ground, or whatever it was making the noise. He heard the sound of cracking, what he assumed to be a branch making its final break, heard what sounded like leaves and twigs being struck as something big and heavy tumbled down. The sound was close, but as it continued to fall, he realised the sound wasn't just close, but right above him.

He jumped backwards just as a massive branch the length of an elephant's trunk and about twice as thick fell down in front of him, landing half a metre from where he stood, and shattered into pieces. Some of the splintered wood showered him, striking his face. He turned away, felt the last of the broken wood strike his back.

Bloody hell, that was close!

He felt his face. There were small nicks, but no nasty cuts. When he looked at his fingers, they were only faintly smudged with blood.

He kicked at one of the pieces of broken branch that had ended up in the clearing. Like the tree the spear had been stuck in, it, too, was rotten, breaking apart with just a kick. He aimed the light up at the tall gum tree from which the branch had fallen. It looked sickly; dry and withered.

I'll teach you to try to kill me. Peter collected the bigger bits of the dry, flaky wood and dumped it all into the fire. Like the other wood, the flames found it hard to catch hold. It ate up some of the splintered edges, but mostly it created more smoke. Unlike the previous nights, the weather was cool, so he needed healthy wood if he were to keep the fire going for as long as possible, especially if he planned on spending the night out here.

At the sound of flapping, Peter whirled around and aimed the spear gun at the sky. He saw only darkness. But the flapping persisted and as the sound passed overhead, Peter's finger close to squeezing the trigger, he heard something hit the ground near the tent; a soft thud, like something small and light had been dropped. The flapping faded, and then was gone. He walked over to the tent. In the meagre light of the campfire, he saw a shoe. Just the one, a black cotton lace up, the kind Marcia was wearing when she motored out of the campsite. He picked it up. What looked like rust was spattered on the white laces. He gazed skyward, baffled.

Another sound. Not the cracking of rotten wood or the flapping of unseen messengers, but a low growl. At least this time, he knew its source. Cricket, still facing the track, was now sitting, ears pricked. She made a low grumbling noise under her breath. Peter looked down the path but saw nothing.

"What is it? Huh? What is it, girl?"

Then Peter heard it. Beneath the wind, beneath the distant wash of the ocean, a scraping sound, similar to when Cricket pulled the baby dugong along the sand. But this was a heavier sound, its scraping long and cumbersome. It sounded close.

He raised the spear gun and aimed it at the narrow space between the vegetation. His arms quivered. He willed himself to keep a steady hand, but he couldn't stop from shaking.

Rawk!

Behind him, something streaked through the clearing. Startled, Peter whipped around, prepared to fire, but the bird, or whatever it was that had screeched, was gone. He hadn't even heard the flapping this time.

Another screech, possibly the same creature, this time from the front. A black shadow flew through the night. Peter heard its wings, felt the rush of air on his face. He depressed the trigger, but not all the way. The bird was gone before he got the chance to aim and fire.

The scraping noise continued to edge closer, but his attention was on the air, not the land. Cricket would have to be the gatekeeper for whatever was coming down the path (*you know what it is, Petey—something that should be dead but is somehow still moving*).

Christ, they were all around. He was surrounded by unseen phantoms.

Another screech. This one from behind. The flapping sounded closer. Peter ducked, felt the whoosh as the bird flapped by. But instead of flying away, the creature remained low and hovering. Peter took the opportunity. He aimed the spear gun towards the hovering bird. He could make out a dark shape against the grey surroundings, heard its wings madly flapping. The thing looked big, bigger than a seagull or sea eagle or crow. Just the shadows, he knew. Playing tricks. Just the phantoms trying to scare him.

He fired. The shaft shot through the air, towards the large shadow. He thought he had hit his mark, but the bird squawked with a less vicious-sounding screech and then took to the sky, the shadow flapping away, uninjured. He had missed, instead shooting the shaft into the bush.

With the bird gone, the world turned quiet. No more flapping or bird noise. The scratching noise down at the beach had also stopped. Even Cricket's growling had ceased. All he heard was a faint ringing in his ears, such was the suddenness and heaviness of the silence.

He stood there, as confused and unnerved as ever.

Peter lowered the empty gun.

He jumped at a loud cracking noise. In the silence, the noise sounded like a gunshot. Peter turned towards the creaking of splintering wood. He looked up. He knew which tree, which branch. Knew where the branch would fall. But he was powerless to do anything about it. The sharp cracking continued, until the branch, no less thick and deadly as the other one, broke off from the trunk and plunged down, down, down, until it fell on the tent, collapsing it. The branch lay on top of the flattened tent, the coup de grâce to this horrid night.

But you didn't get me, he thought.

"You didn't get me!" he cried.

Only the silence answered him.

6

———

PETER AWOKE to a dead fire and dead eyes staring at him.

The dead fire wasn't a problem. He expected it to die down, what with the bad wood unable to sustain a long, slow burn, which was why he had wrestled the sleeping bag from the clutches of the fallen tree branch to wrap himself up against the cold. Unlike the other branch that had fallen close to him, which had been rotten and brittle, the one that had flattened the tent had been solid and heavy. He shuddered to think what would have happened to him if he had been inside when the tree dropped its limb. So retrieving the bag from the squashed tent had been difficult. Once he had rescued his sleeping bag, he made himself comfortable by the fire, in one of the folding chairs, wrapping himself up in the sleeping bag. Sitting there in his cocoon, he hadn't expected to fall asleep, but evidently he had, as next time he opened his eyes, it was bright and no longer cool. The fire had died—he knew the fire was dead without needing to look by the lack of heat and smoke—and there were a pair of dead, black eyes looking at him.

Cricket's barking woke him. He started to open his eyes, but the light was too fiery. When he was able to open his eyes wider, the sunlight no longer burning his retinas, he saw a pair of black eyes staring back at him. Beady eyes. Dead eyes.

Peter jumped up, fully awake, the sleeping bag falling away like shedding old skin. He gaped at the giant dugong parked just a short distance away. The wretched beast was half-rotted, yet there it was, right before him, watching him. Clear drag marks extended from its tail, across the clearing, down the path, disappearing from view as the land gently curved.

"Impossible," Peter breathed. "How did you get up here?"

There was no way Cricket could have dragged this beast by herself.

"What do you want?"

The dugong remained still and mute. The decaying creature was covered in flies and smelled awful, and Peter wanted away from it. He wanted to destroy it so it couldn't ever continue its slow death crawl.

"I'm sorry, okay?" he said, backing away from the dugong. "I'm sorry about your baby. But it wasn't my fault. I didn't kill your baby!"

As he moved away from the dugong, he looked around for Cricket, who had disappeared. He could still hear her barking, but she wasn't in sight. "Cricket!" he called. "Come on, time to go!"

But Cricket didn't come. She was close, he could tell by the loudness of her barking, which was the type she did when she had found something. And whatever she had found was apparently more interesting than the dead dugong, more important than obeying orders.

"Christ, what now?" he muttered. Following the sound of barking, he left the clearing and ventured into the bush. He found Cricket a short way into the scrub. Standing there, tail down, as if on edge, though her barking wasn't one of fear or a warning; rather, it was to alert Peter she had found something.

And when he saw what she had found, his world crumbled.

More dead eyes. Only this time, they didn't belong to a dead sea cow. They belonged to his wife. Marcia sat up against a tree, body slumped. She was barefoot, the bandage on her right foot stained with dried blood and coming undone. Her clothes were torn, as if shredded by something sharp. Her face was scratched and streaked with blood. Her golden hair was mussed and matted with blood. A long metal shaft protruded from her throat.

Peter dropped to his knees. Tears blurred his vision. A whimper became a cry became a wail.

When, finally, his crying eased, he realised Cricket was no longer barking or making any noise. She just sat there, gazing at Marcia with curiosity.

Peter wiped his eyes and gazed at his dead wife. Whom he had killed.

It was an accident. I didn't know. I thought... oh God, what have I done?

"I'm sorry," he said, but the words sounded empty, pitiful.

Marcia, eyes fixed open with the onset of sudden death, stared at Peter hatefully.

He remained kneeling in front of his wife's skewered remains for an indeterminate amount of time, only breaking out of his stupor when a bird screeching startled him into action.

He had to get moving. There was no helping Marcia now. Somehow, she had been forced out of the car—by accident, by nature, by sheer frustration at finding herself going around in circles—and had taken to fleeing on foot. Somehow, she had ended up back at the camp. Stumbling through the dark, through the wild tangle of the bush, she had seen the faint light of the campfire or smelled the smoke. But before she had reached him, before she could make herself known, he had fired. At the bird, the shadow, whatever it was. But instead of hitting the bird, he had hit...

No, no use dwelling on it now. Nothing to be done except get the hell away from here. Get out of this place. Get to safety.

Then what? What he had done would be discovered. He'd

be charged with murder. Maybe they'd think he had killed Frank and his family, too. Could he blame it all on Frank? Say he had killed Marcia, then killed his own wife and daughter, before hanging himself?

Never mind that now, he told himself. *Get away first, deal with the rest later.*

He got back up. Before he left, he stepped up to Marcia. He remembered what his dad had looked like once the life had drained from his body. Like a wax dummy. Face almost relaxed. Despite having suffered through the past few years, dealing with the monstrous disease that had ultimately killed him, he had looked at peace. Not Marcia. She looked like a dead body that had died in shock and pain. There was no peace for her. Eyes locked open in a state of fear, mouth gaping and painted with dry blood that smudged her chin. Hands clenched. She wasn't simply pale, like how his dad had looked after death. Instead, her skin was a greyish blue. She looked ghoulish.

He also noticed a sickly blue fuzz on her skin. It was thin and patchy, but it spotted her arms, her neck. It looked like the same foul substance coating the doll on the beach and had been growing on Frank.

Staring at his dead wife, he contemplated taking the shaft. He loathed the thought of touching it, but he might need it. Also, it connected him to the crime. He reached forward, took hold of the base of the spear. He closed his eyes, not wanting to look at Marcia as he pulled. He tugged. Hesitantly at first. But he reminded himself she was dead and couldn't feel anything. So, he pulled harder. The spear wouldn't budge. He pulled until sweat squeezed out of his pores and his arms burned. But he couldn't rescue the shaft.

He let go of the spear. Let out his breath and wiped his wet palms on his shirt.

Forget it.

When he heard a rustling sound coming from deeper in the bush, he knew it was time to leave.

"Come on, Cricket," he said, and together they headed back into the clearing.

He gazed around the campsite, which appeared even smaller than just a few minutes ago. Saw nothing of great importance. He was heading for the track leading out of Moondah when he remembered his slingshot. It had been in the tent when the branch fell. He hurried over to the ruined tent and pushed himself inside. Like a snake, he slithered into the darkness. The branch was too heavy to shift. He could only raise it a little while he pawed at the area he remembered leaving the slingshot. He felt other items, clothing, thongs, toiletries, but not the Wham-O.

Must be in here somewhere.

But when he heard the horribly familiar sound of wood creaking, he crawled back out of the collapsed tent, sans slingshot.

Feeling tight in his chest at leaving the treasured item behind, he left the campsite. Cricket trotted behind him down the road. She didn't seem in any great hurry to leave.

"Keep up," Peter called over his shoulder as he jogged. "I won't wait for you if you lag behind."

But Cricket didn't quicken her pace, content to just trot along.

Peter didn't know the exact route out of this expansive bushland; it all looked different during the day. He moved in the direction he thought led to the highway, taking the wider of the two tracks whenever he came to a junction. He soon grew tired. He stopped jogging and took a breather. Hunched over, sucking in crisp air that smelled of sweet earth and, faintly, of smoke, he saw Cricket, too, had stopped. But she looked only mildly puffed. She ambled around, going off the road to sniff around the bushes, the ground.

When the air was back in his lungs, he straightened. Looked around, hoping for any sign of the highway—the sound of traffic, light glinting off chrome. He heard no traffic, but he did see something in the distance, through the trees. Only meagre streaks of sunlight managed to push through the thick tangle of bushland, but some of that light had struck something other than leaves; looked like metal. He hurried towards it down the curving road. As he rounded the bend, he saw it was indeed a car, but it wasn't parked by the side of the highway; it had been driven off the road, into a ditch. He jogged over, and when he got closer, he saw it was his car. The driver's side door hung open; the front end angled down. The front of the Nissan Patrol was crumpled, wrapped around the trunk of a gum tree. The windscreen was fractured. He jumped in and tried to start it, hoping it would still run. The engine simply clicked. Either the battery was drained, or the motor too damaged. He slapped the steering wheel.

He hopped out. Looking down at his ruined car, he wondered what had happened to cause Marcia to crash. Feathers were caught in the broken glass of the windscreen. Had the car been attacked by birds?

Dry, having brought nothing with him to drink, he wandered to the back of the truck and opened the doors. The cargo area was mostly empty, just Marcia's sleeping bag, her pillow. And the fridge. And, he noticed, the red jerrycan. He looked inside the fridge. Happily, found the last of the beer. The beer was warm, but he downed the bottle greedily. Once it was empty, he threw the bottle into the scrub.

Eying the petrol container, an idea started to scratch at his brain.

He didn't want to head back to the camp, but he had a couple of problems that needed getting rid of. Fire was the great eraser, and he had some things that needed erasing.

He took the container and started back down the road.

He whistled for Cricket. She came traipsing out of the scrub and reluctantly followed him back to the campsite. As he passed the tree with the arrow carved into it, a shiver washed through him, and he felt momentarily lightheaded. The feelings faded as he stepped into the clearing—which was no longer much of a clearing. In the short time Peter had been gone, the camp had been invaded by vines, much like at Frank's camp. They were everywhere, creeping over the tent, the camping chairs, the table, his surfboard. And the food was starting to mould, as if the stuff had been left there for weeks.

Cricket remained back, not wanting to cross into the campsite that was strangled with vines. Peter was hesitant, but he bit through his apprehension, at his common sense spinning out of control, and walked through the creepers, like wading through the ocean, towards the massive beast.

The petrol sloshed in the can, still close to full, but it wasn't a big container and though he wanted to douse the entire camp with petrol—if he had his way he'd burn the whole forest down —he needed to conserve the fuel for his intended targets. If there was any left after he had completed his task, then he'd scorch the vines. The mummy dugong had been caught in the vine web. Hopefully, Peter thought, that by burning the dugong and the creepers that covered it, the rest of them would also catch alight, the vines acting as a kind of connective tissue to the rest of the bush. He splashed the dugong with petrol. The creature was so large, he used half the container before the animal was fully wet. Then, moving back, he took out his matchbook, struck a flame, and flicked the match down.

The dugong immediately caught on fire. The creepers were eaten up in an instant and soon the giant animal was swallowed up by flames. The heat was intense, as was the smell. Only this time, the smell didn't bother Peter. The stench of roasting dugong was welcomed.

You won't be following me any longer, Peter thought, smiling triumphantly down at the burning sea cow.

He left the dugong and headed into the bush to Marcia. Creepers had started invading her body, too, as if reclaiming her body to the earth. The blue-green mould was now rampant, growing all over her skin.

She was dead; he knew that, yet he hesitated in pouring the petrol over her. It seemed a cruel act. A selfish act. Which it was. By burning her corpse, he hoped all trace of her would be lost; all evidence she was ever here, that he had killed her.

With tears staining his face, Peter dumped the remaining petrol over his wife. The dried blood became wet and trickled down her face. The smell of petrol mixed with the smell of death, the smell of the mould, created a rancid potpourri. When the container was empty, Peter tossed it away. He pulled out his box of matches. "Goodbye, Mars," he said, and then lit her up.

As he left the campsite—hopefully for the final time—he turned and looked at the destruction. The dugong burned fiercely, the flames dancing off the blackened carcass. Acrid smoke rose towards the sky—a sky that only a short time ago had been clear and silky blue but was starting to become overcast with dark grey clouds.

You can try, but you're not putting out this fire.

The flames were starting to spread, torching the grass and the vines surrounding the dugong. A short distance behind the clearing, orange flames could be seen through the trees, the bushes. They were already rising up the gum tree and had leaped onto nearby bushes. Soon, the two fires would meet. In time, the fires would become one, and then one inferno would spread its fiery wings across this accursed land.

Even if the heavens did open up and pour down, hopefully, by then, it would be too late. Hopefully, too much damage would have already been wrought; too much of this place destroyed.

Even now, Peter could hear the shrieks of the trees, the bushes, the vines, as they burned. The terrified screeching of birds, the frightful cries of the forest critters as they fled, attempting to escape. They had tried to get him, but he had outsmarted them, outlasted them. This place wanted to consume him, to possess his soul, just like it had done to others in the past. But they wouldn't get him. No, he was Peter; he was the true King of this land, hear him roar.

With the sounds of Mother Nature burning in agony, Peter headed back down the road, towards freedom.

———

This time when he arrived at the ditched Patrol he kept going. He moved slower than before, but with no less intensity towards his goal: getting out of this wilderness and back to civilisation. It had been a mistake coming here; he realised that now. He thought it would solve his problems. Three days in simple, pristine nature, and whammo! All his problems gone, all the anger, resentment and shit between him and Marcia evaporated like smoke in the wind. Go to where he had been happiest, camping with his dad as a boy, and he'd be happy again.

How silly of him. How naïve. Talk about jumping out of the pan and into the fire: except in this case, instead of fire, it had been scrubland, the beach, the ocean. It had been Mother Nature as the devil and Moondah as her cauldron.

But how was he to know? When he felt the calling to come back to Moondah, he hadn't realised the venomous intent behind it. Whatever the force was had tricked him, just like Marcia had tricked him. Everything and everyone he cared about, or he thought cared about him, had turned out to be traitorous.

Even Dad, in his own way, had turned on him. He had gone and got cancer and then left him when Peter was only a young man. He had tricked Peter into thinking this place was good, pure, when in fact it was the opposite.

Not his fault, Peter thought as he trudged along the road. This place got to him. That night he went missing for an hour; somehow, the bad spirits had gotten into him, whispered to him, had tricked him.

You're not going to get me. You got to Dad, you got to Marcia, Frank, but not me.

With fresh determination, Peter ploughed on ahead. The imposing gums and hefty bushes gave way to scrubby bush and tea trees. The tea trees became dense on both sides of the track until he was travelling through a tunnel of warped, spindly trees. He was reminded of the story of Jonah. He remembered a book he had as a child, a children's bible. In the book there had been a drawing of Jonah inside the whale. Maybe Jonah had been praying. Peter couldn't recall, but what he did recall was the illustration, the curled bones, probably the creature's ribcage, how it had looked, so large, so strange, so white. It had frightened young Peter. Made him scared to go into the water for a long time, afraid he, too, would be swallowed by a whale and have to live inside its body for the rest of his life, with nothing to look at except the giant, white, curled bones.

The way the tea trees curled, embracing at the top, all white and bony, it looked like one long ribcage, like he had been swallowed by a whale.

Coldness tickled his skin. Suddenly, he felt claustrophobic, and he wanted out of this horrible tunnel.

But it looked endless. He quickened his pace, hoping to reach the end of the tunnel sooner. He glanced back to see if Cricket was keeping up. She was lagging a good ten, fifteen metres behind. He no longer cared. Let her catch up with him. He wasn't about to slow down for a dog.

He hurried along; the trees growing ever more tightly packed, squeezing out daylight, squeezing out, or so he felt, air, making it harder to breathe. His chest felt locked in a vice that was being tightened. He slowed but didn't stop as he continued down the sandy track. Moving, he had to keep moving; the tunnel had to end soon, it had to...

When he saw fresh, deep greenery ahead, Peter almost cried. He powered through the last of the dreaded tunnel of tea trees, until finally he broke through and he was surrounded by wonderful gum trees and bushes of all kinds, giving him light and air and a renewed sense of hope.

Surely, the unpaved road would also come to an end soon. He had to be close to the highway.

He continued along, moving with determination but not running, mindful of the need to conserve energy—he had no food, no water—and like always, when he came upon a fork in the road, he took the wider track, the one that, in his mind, paved the way west, away from the ocean, and further inland.

When the forest of gums and bushes fell away, replaced by an open heath, populated by mostly low, scrubby bushes and bracken fern, his hope grew. Surely, now, just past this wasteland, was the highway. He considered leaving the road and moving across the heath. Maybe that way he'd reach salvation sooner. But he decided to keep on the track, at least for the time being. Safer that way. No way to know what was lurking in the scrubland. He didn't want to be crossing a field and see the highway in the distance, to be so close, only to be struck by a snake and die there amid the ferns.

The heath continued for a while, before the forest once again took hold. That was okay, Peter thought. Forest lined the highway at the turnoff, and he remembered mostly forest on the drive in to Moondah. He expected the forest to return. That only meant he was heading in the right direction. That he was close to the end.

Walking up the road, he could hear the soft patter as Cricket trotted some ways behind. At least, he presumed it was Cricket. Peter hadn't looked back to check up on her for a good ten minutes. But he'd heard the steady padding of what he took to be Cricket as he made his way towards the highway. When he heard the sound of something scraping across the sandy road, reminding him of the sound he'd heard back at camp, the coming of the dugong, he stopped, heart galloping into his throat. He looked back. Saw Cricket sitting on the road, scratching behind her ears.

Peter sighed with relief, though he couldn't muster a smile. "Hurry up, girl."

Cricket had fallen a ways behind. She continued to scratch, taking her sweet time. Eyes closed, she looked to be enjoying it.

Peter, tired of waiting, continued walking.

He heard the scratching sound for a bit longer before it stopped. He expected to hear the sound of Cricket running to catch up, but all he heard was silence.

He stopped again and this time when he turned and looked down the winding track, he saw no sign of Cricket.

"Cricket!" he called.

He waited.

When she didn't appear, he sighed. "Stupid dog."

He was about to walk back down the track to see what the dog was up to when he heard the scraping sound again. Surely not Cricket scratching again. Sounded more like a giant snake slithering along the road.

A bird screeched.

Then another.

He looked up. Saw black birds perched high in the trees.

He noticed the sky, what little he could see through the trees, was gloomy. No longer a brilliant blue, it looked to be solid grey, with even darker areas looming directly above.

He heard the heavy slithering sound again. Looked back down. Couldn't see anything, but suddenly an overwhelming feeling of dread enveloped him, like a cold blanket studded with thorns.

The sound came from down the road, in the direction of Cricket. The sound, too much like when Cricket had dragged the baby dugong up the beach, was drawing closer.

Peter shook his head.

Impossible, he thought. *Can't be.*

At the sound of a bird's terrible high-pitched screech, Peter took off, like a runner at the sound of a starting pistol. Forget

Cricket. She would have to catch up. He had to get away from here, keep moving towards the highway.

He bolted up the road. His lungs felt tight and full of fire. He was dry and his legs were wobbly, but he started feeling better, less anxious. The scraping sound grew faint, the birds no longer screeched.

He rounded a bend, a bend that looked oddly familiar. As did the surrounding vegetation.

He had been this way before; he was sure of it. Twice in the recent past—the first after he left the campsite and came upon his car. The second after he had torched the bodies and...

Sunlight no longer shone down through the branches and glinted off the chrome, but there sat his car, in the ditch, twenty metres away. Peter came to a halt and stood there, full of disbelief at what he was seeing. He rubbed his eyes. But the crashed Nissan Patrol was there, just as Marcia had left it.

"No," he whimpered, eyes stinging with sweat and tears. "No, no, no!"

It was too cruel to be true. Yet, there it sat, the evidence. Somehow, he had gone in a complete circle. Somewhere along the way, he had taken the wrong track, which led him not away from the camp and towards the highway, but back around to near where he had started.

These roads were impossible; they were a maze. With no signs pointing the way out, it was like walking around blind in a darkened room full of connecting hallways.

He was positive the highway was somewhere off to the left. If he made a beeline through the forest, he'd arrive at the main road. It seemed to him not only the best option, but the only option. It'd take him all day to work out the correct paths to take that eventually led to the highway—if he got there at all. He couldn't take going in a circle again. Couldn't take going through the tunnel of bones.

His mind made up, he left the road and headed into the forest.

Just as he did, he heard the sound of panting behind him. Turning, he saw Cricket.

"Come on, slow-coach, we're heading off road."

Cricket looked at Peter, and then behind her.

"Cricket, come on."

The dog faced Peter again. Lowered her head and started backing away.

Peter frowned. "Cricket? Girl?"

She turned around and galloped away, across the track and into the bush on the opposite side of the road.

"Cricket!" Peter called. But she was gone.

Peter felt heavy. Heavy and empty, like some piece of himself had been yanked out and replaced by a brick.

Abandoned. Again.

Fine, be that way. I don't need you. See how long you last out there by yourself.

Steeling himself, Peter turned away from the road, away from where Cricket had disappeared, and pushed on through the thick forest.

From above, the sky growled.

7

HE THRASHED THROUGH THE FOREST, flattening saplings, mowing down ferns, snapping weak branches, and crushing leaves. He didn't care what he broke or hurt or ruined. All he cared about was his own salvation. Making it out of this hellish wilderness. Reaching civilisation. Going back to his job, his life.

The air had turned icy, though his body, sheathed in sweat, was steaming. The world had palled, which only made the dense bushland look ashen, like the colour had been washed away. Still, he pushed on. Bushes scraped his arms; thin, sharp branches cut his face. The smell of the bush grew sweet and sickly, like a too-flowery perfume. The stench of eucalypt and earth and autumn flowers got into his head and made him nauseous.

Still, he ploughed on, certain the highway was only a short distance away. If he just continued in this direction, angled to the north-west, he'd hit asphalt. Soon, he'd hear the wonderful sound of trucks rumbling along the highway. Smell the glorious bouquet of petrol and diesel. Soon, he'd be surrounded by steel and concrete and too many people and no sand or ocean or lush foliage—just the parks that man had created to give the illusion of nature amid the choking cityscape. Just the odd plant contained in a pot, harmless. That sounded fine to him. To him, that sounded like paradise.

The forest started to thin out. The broad gums and lush bushes gave way to gnarly trees and clumps of weeds. The sky opened up, and it still looked severe: dark clouds heavy with rain hung over the land in a vast sea of dull steel. The ground started becoming softer, wetter. Trees became strangled with vines. Soon, he was sloshing through knee-deep water. He looked around for dry land. Saw some to his left. A large patch of earth with short, wispy grass. He started towards it, wading through the frigid, murky water.

Before he could reach land, he saw something moving through the water. He froze. The snake weaved its way through the brackish water, heading towards Peter.

With water on three sides, the snake blocked his way forward, the safety of dry land. Peter had no choice but to either wait and hope the snake moved past without attacking him or go back the way he had come and hope he'd find another way through the swamp.

He decided to stand his ground and wait.

A metre or so from reaching Peter, the snake stopped and rested on the water. It stared at him, its tongue striking out repeatedly. Then the snake moved towards the dry land and remained in the water near the far edge of the lake. Taking it as a sign it wasn't intending to attack him, not if he kept away from the dry land, Peter turned around and waded through the water, continuing on what he hoped was a north-westerly direction. The swamp was large and occasionally deep. A few times he dropped to his waist, which sucked the breath from him for a few moments, before the ground sloped up and he rose back to knee or ankle depth. Finally, after wading through frigid swamps for over twenty minutes, he reached dry land. By the time he reached the bank, Peter was worn out. Cold, wet, he dropped to the ground and drew in much-needed air.

Sprawled on the muddy bank, eyes closed, he heard more

rumblings in the sky. The chilly air, damp with wet earth and stagnant water, grew even colder. The world was gearing up for a storm. It wanted to punish him, undo his actions back at the campsite. Stop the fire from spreading while dousing him with its tears.

Let the heavens cry, he thought. *I don't care. A little rain won't stop me.*

The rumbling faded. As it did, another sound took its place. A creaking noise close by, like the sound of limbs breaking apart. No, that wasn't exactly right. Similar, but this was more repetitive, like... like something swinging by a rope.

Peter's eyes flicked open. He saw a shadow over him, swinging across his stomach like the pendulum in that Edgar Allan Poe story. He gazed up, frightened of what he would see. Fortunately, it wasn't Frank, neck broken, face blue and swollen. Just a vine hanging from a branch, swaying in the increasingly violent wind.

But the fright was enough to get him back on his feet. He looked in the direction he thought he needed to go. The wetlands extended as far as he could see; an expanse of swamps, grasslands, and trees that looked like crooked skeletons with vein-like creepers knotted around their bodies. An ugly, hostile place. But he had no choice but to forge on, confident he was growing ever closer to his destination.

With the coming of the storm, the world turned dull and choked with shadows. The vines that dangled from the branches looked like ropes, and the way some branches jutted crooked, foliage drooping, they resembled bodies hanging from the ends; some small, like a child, others with long, wavy hair cascading. Dozens of bodies hanging in the swampland, all swaying in the wind.

He sloshed through the water, sometimes using the half-sunken trees to help him along. Vines jumped down at him, scaring him into thinking they were snakes. They reached for him, tried to grab him. He didn't know their intentions—drag him under the water? Hold him prisoner until he wasted away? Whatever they wanted, they never managed to get hold of him.

More birds started appearing. They squawked their arrival and then sat in the trees to watch his slow progress. By the time the wetlands ended, and he moved into woody bushland, there must have been a thousand birds of all types. As he staggered along, the forest not as dense as the one earlier and thankfully not as wet as the marshes behind, the sound of screeching grew to near deafening proportions. Peter put his hands to his ears in an effort to drown out the noise, but he couldn't block out the cacophony.

Sometimes the birds swooped down. They never attacked him directly, but they got close enough for him to feel their weight and see their razor-like claws and beaks. They swooped down in waves, always staying in one area—to the left of him, or the right, sometimes directly in front, almost as if they were creating a barricade. Almost as if they were directing him, channelling him in a particular direction. A ridiculous notion, but he wondered: were they helping him head the right way, guiding him to his destination? Why would they want to do that? They were enemies, not friends. Why would they help him reach safety when they had spent so long scaring him, clawing at him?

Because they weren't friends. They were just swooping because they hated him, because they saw *him* as the enemy.

Still, he continued. Clothes wet, the wind pressing against his skin, but the chill he felt barely registered. His sole focus was on making it out, not his discomfort.

When he broke through the woodland into a meadow, layered with green grass and sprinkled with wildflower, the birds stopped swooping and also stopped their cacophony. As he crossed the pretty field, a solitary bird, black as coal, flew overhead. Something dropped and landed in the grass, and then the bird sailed away. Peter staggered over to see what the bird had dropped.

A shoe. Or the charred remains of one. Looked like a sneaker. Marcia's sneaker.

Peter picked it up. The shoe was still warm and smelled of burnt canvas and rubber. His face stung with the memory of what he had done.

"Just leave me alone!" he cried. "It was an accident!"

He tossed the charred sneaker hard into the bitter wind. The shoe sailed in an arch and landed in a clump of white flowers.

Just an accident, he repeated, silently, and then a tiny voice said: Was it?

Yes! he screamed.

But you were angry at her, at what she said... at what she did.

Didn't mean I wanted to kill her. I didn't... hate her.

He heard his wife's voice: *I hate you!*

Suddenly, she was standing before him. Spear sticking from her throat. Looking dead, but not burned. Blue face stained with his mark of anger. She spoke again:

I killed our unborn child... because I didn't want it growing up with you as its father.

As she spoke, blood dribbled from her neck, down her chest, and into the valley between her breasts.

Somewhere in the deep recesses of his mind, Peter knew this wasn't real. Marcia wasn't really standing before him, but at that moment, he thought it was real; the pain and anger he felt was certainly real.

"But you didn't ask me what I wanted! I had no say!"

Did you want to keep it? Marcia said with a gurgling voice. More blood ran from the wound.

"I don't... that's not the point!"

What is? she asked.

"You betrayed me... *us.* I could never forgive you for that."

I know, Marcia said with a smile. *So, you killed me.*

"No!"

You've thought about killing me for years.

"Of course not."

But you couldn't do it; were afraid you wouldn't get away with it. Instead, you pushed me away... cheated, screwed around...

"No! I did that because you were a cold, sexless bitch. You became boring. Sorry, but it's the truth. It's your fault I cheated."

Marcia shook her head.

Still don't take responsibility for your actions, do you? You're a liar and a cheat. And a coward, she added, as blood poured down her body like bloody rain.

An egg appeared in her hand, a large speckled egg. She raised the eagle egg to her lips. Opened her mouth wide.

"No..." Peter said.

She bit down. Teeth cracked through the shell. She kept going. Thick embryonic fluid squirted up into her face, dribbled down her arm.

Peter felt like throwing up.

"It's just an egg," Marcia said. She began to chew, crunching on shell and on whatever else she had taken, as red and yellow fluid sluiced down her chin and dripped down her arm. Once she had swallowed, she took another bite, going in deep.

"Stop," Peter said around the bile filling up his throat.

This time, when she pulled back, she had a small bit of something between her teeth. Looked like a baked bean wrapped in jelly. Or a tiny dugong calf.

Peter shook his head.

"And it was just an abortion." Marcia chomped down. Peter heard a squishing sound, blood and other fluids jettisoned as the tiny morsel popped, life fluids rained down along with the blood that continued to pump from where the shaft was lodged in Marcia's throat.

And then Marcia vanished, the sky exploded, and fat, heavy drops fell as rain came down for real.

Still feeling ill and confused, but with no time to process any of it, Peter took off across the meadow, towards the scraggly bushland ahead. Had to keep moving. Had to get out. Away from this hell.

The bushland offered some relief from the rain, but he wasn't immune completely. It poured down from above, off the canopy, like hundreds of miniature waterfalls. He trudged through the bush, thinking not of how thirsty he was, or how hungry, or how utterly spent he felt, just about escape. Escape from Mother Nature, who was clearly trying to kill him.

It occurred to him, as he cut through the rain, the scrub, that perhaps the birds hadn't been directing him towards the highway, but *away* from it. They knew he was close, and they didn't want him to reach the road because that meant an end to their hold over him. If he made it to the highway, he would have won. And they didn't want that. Instead, they had pushed him back into the wilderness. Like before, like Marcia last night, like when they'd first arrived, he would find himself going in circles and he would never leave this place.

A maddening pounding began in his head. If he came out of this patch of bushland to find himself in the same wetlands or meadow or in the tunnel of tea trees or, god forbid, back at the campsite, then he'd likely collapse to the ground and wait to die. That would be the end of him. Nature would have won. They could have his soul, for what it was worth.

That's not going to happen, he told himself—tried convincing himself.

But the longer he trekked through the bush with no visible end in sight, the more he feared it would come true. He was locked in this place forever. There was no escape. Death was the only escape.

He thought about something his dad had said to him, not long before he died. He'd asked Peter what he believed happened when we died. The question had knocked Peter back. Not just because of its seriousness, that it meant his dad had been thinking about it, which meant there was no chance of him recovering, that he would almost certainly soon die. No, because it also reminded him of the last night at Moondah Beach with his dad, the one after that strange, fearful night that may or may not have been a dream. They had been sitting around the campfire. Dinner had been eaten; marshmallows toasted. Dad had sat there smoking his pipe, gazing out at the sea (odd, how back then the camp seemed closer to the beach, so close you could see it clearly from the clearing; Peter remembered that now), Peter sipping at a mug of hot chocolate. It was late, later than usual. But it being the last night before heading home, Dad had allowed Peter to remain up long past his bedtime. It had been a brilliant night, the kind where the sky looked like it was made of black glass and the stars glimmered so brightly, they looked unreal. Dad had downed more than his usual number of beers. Not so he was drunk, just calm, happy. Staring out at the dark ocean, the moonlight rippling over the water, Dad had said, after a lengthy but comfortable silence, "What do you think happens when we die, Pete?"

Usually Dad called him Peter or, when in a more playful mood, Petey.

To his ears, Pete sounded old. Formal. Like a doctor or a lawyer. Doctor Pete.

"Um..." he'd begun, cupping his cocoa. He had never thought about it before; at least not in any real, serious way. The question had taken him by surprise. "I guess we go to heaven."

A safe, predictable answer.

"Is that what you really think?"

Peter had shrugged.

"So, you believe in the soul? And that the soul ascends up into the sky? To, what, be with loved ones?"

Dad didn't ask this with any measure of derision or meanness. He simply asked in his low-key way.

"Yeah," Peter had answered, plainly. And he did believe it; had no other viable alternative. He thought there was a heaven, and that his mum was waiting for him up there when he died. That's what he believed; that's what he hoped.

Dad had waited a while before answering. "I think... I think death is like the ocean at night. It swallows you up, like some black, watery blanket. You sink to the bottom, and then... nothing. But it's not horrible or painful or icy cold. No, it's calm, peaceful. Warm. I imagine death is a lot like floating through a vast black ocean."

Peter had mulled over that for a long time afterwards.

When, later, older, and less naïve, Dad had asked again, Peter remembered what his dad had said about death being like floating down to the bottom of a black ocean. He also remembered, somewhat embarrassingly, what he had said as a young teenage boy. Now a devout atheist, he no longer believed in heaven, the afterlife, any of it. "I think, when we die, we..."

Peter had looked down at his dad, then, at his sunken cheeks, grey skin, eyes like black marbles. Oxygen mask over his mouth and nose that made him sound even weaker and raspier than he already was. A pathetic, almost child-like hope in his dying eyes. A need to believe in something more than what Peter now believed in—that death was the end. That there was no soul, no life beyond this one. When we bought the farm, that was it, eternal nothingness. So, when he answered, he hadn't told the truth. He had smiled and said, "I think it's peaceful and calm and warm."

Dad had tried to smile, too. Instead, he started coughing. Once he was done, he said, "Like the ocean at night. You remembered."

"Of course, I remembered. And I think you were right."

"Floating through a vast ocean," he said. "It's not the end, just... a new beginning. Our energy continues, helping to give new life. It's a never-ending cycle."

"Something like that," Peter had said, taking his father by the hand and feeling how small and cold it was.

Bullshit, was how he truly felt, but of course, he would never say that to his dad.

Now, stumbling through the bush, the drenching rain cold and hard, fearing he would never find his way out, he thought again of the question posed by his father, and concluded that maybe Dad's answer was closest to the truth. Although he wasn't sure how calm and peaceful it would be, and presently he felt it would be icy cold, not warm. But maybe energy did continue, infusing the world and sparking new life. Maybe it was like sinking through an inky ocean. Peter wondered: what would be waiting at the bottom? Something good and kind? Or some shadowy figure; a phantom with claws, or maybe fangs, or something more human-like?

As he crashed through the vegetation, he heard a sound over the streaming rain. The sound was distant at first, but it grew louder, cutting through the downpour. Not thunder. The sound was more drawn out, like the low, mournful blare of a foghorn.

His spirits lifted. Not the sound of a ship sounding its horn. No, the ocean was too far away and besides, there were no ports nearby. It had to be a truck. One of those massive eighteen-wheelers. Which meant the highway had to be close.

With renewed energy, Peter started jogging at a faster pace. His legs felt like iron, his chest ready to collapse, but he fought through the pain and lethargy.

On and on he ran, dodging trees, skirting around scrub.

The horn sounded again. Yes, that one was even louder! He had to be near the highway. But the horn sounded different this time. Less like the blast of a truck's air horn and more like...

Peter shook his head.

No, he was hearing things. Just his mind playing tricks again.

The horn only reminded him of the wailing; that horrible, pained wailing that probably came from the adult dugong. But the dugong was dead. More than dead, he had burned the carcass, so by now, even with the onslaught of the rain, the dugong would be a shrivelled, blackened husk. A giant lump of animal coal.

But Christ, the more he listened, the more it sounded like the eerie wailing that had haunted him and Marcia all during the long weekend. She had thought it sounded like a baby crying. To him, it had always sounded like a soul in great pain and anguish.

He tried ignoring the doubt creeping in and continued his way through the bushland, towards the highway.

He was running on autopilot now. His mind filled only with the mantra of *one more step, one more step...*

His body moved because that's all it was told to do. The rain started to ease. Its job had been done. The clouds ran away to hide, revealing the blue sky and a brilliant sun.

Still Peter ran.

Through the scraggly bush, through small patches of clearing, back into the bush; rinse and repeat. If he had been in a more rational frame of mind, he would have known that, going by how loud the horn had been, he should have reached the highway by now. In a totally rational world, he knew how small the area of wilderness really was between the highway turnoff and the beach—about a tenth of the size of what he had covered.

But rationality had long since flown away. He wasn't thinking logically; he was just trying to survive.

It was in one of the grassy clearings, bordered by tea trees and shrubs, that he tripped. He might have thought he had simply tripped over his own feet, but he had felt something on the ground, even if he hadn't seen it. Sprawled there in the small clearing, the smell of damp soil and wet grass as offensive to him as rotting meat, he hardly had the energy to get up. He wanted to lie there and sleep. Close his eyes, rest his weary body, mind and soul, and when he woke, he'd find himself back in his tent, realise all this had been a terrible dream. Marcia would be outside by the fire, happily cooking lunch. Cricket running around chasing birds. And instead of staying for the rest of the long weekend, Peter would suggest they pack up and head home. It's what Marcia wanted from the start. He should have listened.

If he really cared about her, he wouldn't have come up here to begin with. He shouldn't have messed around with things he didn't understand. He and Marcia were broken. They should have fixed their relationship—if indeed it could be fixed—before trying to mend it with a weekend away in nature.

He saw it all so clearly now. Like with the parting of the clouds, the end of the rain, his eyes, his mind, had been opened along with the vast blue sky and radiant sun.

But it was too late. Marcia was dead. And he was a broken shell that he wasn't sure could ever be made whole.

Finally, somehow, he got the strength to push himself up. He turned around.

And screamed.

There, lying in the grass, was the baby dugong. Rotting, plastic bag wrapped around its head. Thousands of tiny black ants crawling over the carcass. Except for the head. The head was exposed and in a blanket of black, it looked glowing. The dugong looked more like a dead foetus than he remembered.

"How?" was all he managed to squeeze out.

Dropping his head in utter confusion and exhaustion, he saw the trail of ants making its way through the grass and onto the beast. He followed the trail across the clearing. It looked like someone had drawn a thin, black line in the grass. The trail led out of the clearing and into the bush, where he lost sight of it in the darkness. But in the darkness, he saw two glowing eyes. Staring right at him.

Peter sat there, unsure what manner of creature the eyes belonged to. They looked wild, like the eyes of a demon. The eyes drew closer, towards the edge of the forest. Soon, a shadow emerged. The creature crept forward, and Peter first saw a snout, chocolate brown, and then the eyes, the ears. All familiar to Peter, yet... subtly different.

He smiled, weakly. "Cricket. Hey there, girl. Where you been?"

Cricket padded closer into the clearing. Her head was down, her tail stiff. She looked wary, like she didn't recognise him.

"Cricket? It's me."

Cricket stopped. She glared at him with those wild eyes. She bared her teeth.

Fear shot through his body.

Cricket growled, deep and fearsome.

Peter slowly rose up.

"Steady, girl," he said, backing away.

Cricket matched his movements, while still displaying her razor-sharp fangs, drool dripping from her jaws.

"What's the matter?" he said. "Why are you acting like this?"

From down on the ground, the baby dugong opened its mouth. It let out a moan that sounded more human than animal.

Peter turned and started running.

Cricket barked and ran after him. Peter heard her powering through the grass, a sharp swishing sound like a knife being sharpened on a leather strap.

The sound of the dugong moaning, so much like his dad as the cancer slowly poisoned him and ate away at his body, his soul, followed him as he ran out of the clearing, back into the bush. He heard Cricket galloping, gaining on him; sensed her lithe yet muscular body drawing closer. Her panting sounded less from exertion and more from hunger. She had tasted raw flesh, and she wanted more. Yet he didn't look back, just concentrated on moving forward.

Soon he no longer heard Cricket running behind him, her panting, her eagerness for blood.

He slowed to a jog and when nothing pounced on him with teeth gnashing and hot breath washing over him, he stopped and turned around. There was no sign of Cricket. He flicked his gaze over the thin, gnarled trees and past the scraggly bushes and tufts of grass. Just wilderness. Just Mother Nature.

He stood there, sucking in air, relieved, but baffled.

He half expected Cricket to come leaping at him from behind a tree, but she didn't attack. She wasn't anywhere. It was like she never existed.

He realised, then, that the moaning had stopped.

The world had grown silent.

Like it was waiting with bated breath.

For what? Peter wondered.

And then he looked down. Saw not grass or sandy earth, but asphalt. Actual hard, man-made road.

He started laughing.

A sound that to anyone listening could have been mistaken for the screeching of a cockatoo, the warbling of a magpie. He had made it. That's why the bush and everything in it had stopped. Not because they had retreated, getting ready for their next move, their next attack. They had admitted defeat. They had no power over him anymore. He stood there, frozen in awe. He had won. He had broken free of the cursed place.

His laughter died at the sound of the wailing.

Same as before, it was mournful. The sound of pain and agony.

It took him a few moments to realise what he was actually hearing.

Not the wail of a doomed soul, but the wail of an air horn.

Shaken out of his daze, he turned around. Had time to see a giant beast made of metal, chrome and glass barrelling towards him. A man sitting in the cab. A big man, about sixty, a faintly familiar man: familiar hair combed back, familiar haunted eyes. Except now he wasn't sitting at a table at the back of a pub, a figure drinking alone. He was flailing about as birds, black as the night, flapped about his face, attacking him through the open driver's side window.

Peter took all of this in, but it was too late. The wailing first blasted his eardrums, and then the metal beast slammed into him.

He felt pain—unimaginable gobs of fiery pain—and heard his insides being cracked and squashed, but it was the sounds outside his head that his brain focused on in the moments before death.

As he was punched to the ground, as the grill caved in his face and the asphalt broke the back of his head, as the full weight of the nearly twenty-tonne truck rolled over his body with its tyres, crushing his internal organs, his bones, and as he was dragged along the rain-slicked road for half a kilometre before being discarded, leaving a streak of blood and mashed viscera like a gory painting, what his brain heard was: the hissing sound of the brakes being engaged, the squealing of the tyres as they skidded along the wet highway, the heavy chugging noise as the truck came to an eventual stop, the birds flapping away, their squawking sounding like laughter, the gasp of the driver as he saw what had happened.

And lastly, the sound of waves, the surf crashing, followed by the softer swishing as the water was drawn back in.

His last thought before he was swallowed by the darkness: *so close. The ocean sounds so close.*

Then, broken and twisted and crushed, the life drained out of him. And like a plant neglected and left to wither away, he died.

ABOUT THE AUTHOR

Brett McBean was born and raised in the suburbs of Melbourne, Australia. A child of the '80s, he grew up on a steady diet of He-Man cartoons, Steven Spielberg movies and audio tapes such as Summer Hits '88. And yet, somehow he managed to turn out normal (well, kinda…). He started playing the drums at age ten and after high school, studied music at Box Hill College, one of Victoria's most renowned music schools, where he earned an Advanced Diploma. Shortly after completing the music degree, he turned his attention towards writing, and he now prefers to pound the keyboard rather than the drums.

An avid movie, book and music fan, he also enjoys the occasional (*cough*) bit of chocolate and cooks a mean spaghetti Bolognese. He also has a keen interest in true crime, in particular the infamous Jack the Ripper murders of 1888, and most of his fiction deals with true-life horrors, often using real-life crimes as a basis for his stories.

His books have been published in Australia, the US, and Germany, and he's been nominated for the Aurealis, Ditmar, and Ned Kelly awards. He won the 2011 Australian Shadows Award for best collection (Tales of Sin and Madness). He is a member of the Australian Horror Writers Association, where he has been a member of the judging panel for the Australian Shadows Award (2008), the AHWA Flash & Short Story competition (2010) and a mentor in their mentor program. He still lives in the wilds of Melbourne with his wife, daughter and German shepherd.

9 781960 721273